THIS IS NOT
A LOVE SCENE

THIS IS NOT A LOVE SCENE

S.C. MEGALE

WEDNESDAY BOOKS
NEW YORK

THIS IS NOT A LOVE SCENE. Copyright © 2019 by S. C. Megale. All rights reserved. Printed in the United States of America. For information, address St. Martin's Press, 175 Fifth Avenue, New York, N.Y. 10010.

www.wednesdaybooks.com
www.stmartins.com

Designed by Anna Gorovoy

Library of Congress Cataloging-in-Publication Data

Names: Megale, S. C., author.
Title: This is not a love scene / S.C. Megale.
Description: First edition. | New York : Wednesday Books, 2019. | Summary: Eighteen-year-old Maeve, a future filmmaker who has muscular dystrophy, fears she will never find romance until a project for her Video II class introduces her to new possibilities.
Identifiers: LCCN 2019002941 | ISBN 9781250190499 (hardcover) | ISBN 9781250190505 (ebook)
Subjects: | CYAC: Dating (Social customs)—Fiction. | Muscular dystrophy—Fiction. | People with disabilities—Fiction. | Video recordings—Production and direction—Fiction. | High schools—Fiction. | Schools—Fiction.
Classification: LCC PZ7.1.M4677 Thi 2019 | DDC [Fic]—dc23
LC record available at https://lccn.loc.gov/2019002941

Our books may be purchased in bulk for promotional, educational, or business use. Please contact your local bookseller or the Macmillan Corporate and Premium Sales Department at 1-800-221-7945, extension 5442, or by email at MacmillanSpecialMarkets@macmillan.com.

First Edition: May 2019

10 9 8 7 6 5 4 3 2 1

TO WEREWOLF

THIS IS NOT
A LOVE SCENE

1

I liked being ridden, and offered the chance to pretty much every guy in Video II. I guess it made me feel as if I had something to contribute to the group.

So when Elliot jumped on the back of me and I felt his weight pull me down, I smiled. Pushed the wheelchair joystick. Increased acceleration. The smooth terrain of Jackson Memorial Mall was perfect for showing off.

"Kim Possible, I mean, I thought she was attractive—that doesn't mean I needed to start jacking." Elliot laughed behind me, full of life. He was eighteen, like me. Tall, black, he wore skinny jeans and the hoodie of a band I'd never heard of. We were debating which animated characters of our youth were worthy of sexual awakenings.

"Robin Hood could get it from Little Maeve," I said. "The Disney one, the fox." I don't know. He had a mischievous smile.

"*Disney?*" said Elliot. He shook the handlebar of my wheelchair near my ear.

"Kim Possible is Disney," I retorted.

"Disney *Channel,* completely different ball game."

"No way! Disney jack sesh!" I said.

"*Maeve,*" Mags, my best friend, reprimanded me from my right.

Air conditioners wafted along the scent of free-sample lotion and buttery pretzels. One of those pretzels was folded in a paper bag resting on my footplate. KC had dove in front of the register to buy it for me. I couldn't lift my arm high enough to swat away his credit card.

"Abuse of the disabled," I'd accused.

We cruised our way back towards the food court now, after a few loops of circling.

About halfway through Video II an hour ago, my classmates and I—Elliot, Mags, KC, and Nate—had decided to dip for the mall. Not that we'd been doing anything in class. Mags had been sitting on the floor at my wheels, reading *Bridge to Terabithia,* and I was swiping through last night's fun with Hot Tinder Guy. "Mags, look." I'd shoved my screen in her face. She looked up from her book and then away real fast. All she must have caught were the words *swallow* and *babe.*

"Oh my God, Maeve."

I grinned and returned to the screen. I knew it was messed up, but I was proud I'd successfully sexted a guy from Tinder. I mean . . . after eighteen years of experience trying otherwise, it seemed like it could *only* happen on Tinder. With the photos I'd chosen, the guy couldn't see the whole me.

"He's so hot," I'd said.

"He's not, though." Mags hadn't looked up from her book. She was petite with long, dyed-red hair, and I was mad jealous of her in Video I until I realized having to reject a guy every day, like she did, sucked almost as much as never getting that chance, like I didn't.

Despite my handicap, I looked all right, I guessed. Brown

hair and eyes, almost acceptable weight at just under a hundred pounds. I sat a little crooked, but whenever someone held a camera up, I made sure to lean against my scoliosis so you could barely tell. My skin was nice. I always wore the same blue, low-top Converse shoes. And I had other things going for me—humor and dreams and an attempt at positivity. My life's ambition was to be a famous director, and I had twelve scripts completed by the age of sixteen.

Mr. Billings, Seefeldt High School's premier film teacher, had to combine Video I and II this semester in order for the school not to cancel both electives due to low enrollment. There was this really valiant entreaty at the beginning of the year in which Billings convinced the principal we were worth holding the class on block days, and the principal conceded with the requisite that Billings film the football games for the coaches every Friday. Then *maybe* he'd consider having Billings film baseball in the spring so we could have Video III. Billings literally took one for the team. But we were usually left to our own devices while he taught the newbies to render shit onto their Mac desktops. This was the first time things got bad enough for us to ditch.

The mall crowd's chatter rose near the food court. We picked a table for three since KC and Nate had left for physics; it was just Elliot, Mags, and me. Elliot hopped off my wheelchair and took a seat to my right. I bulldozed aside a chair and it screeched on the tile as Mags sat on my left.

Flapping ears and a jingle of dog chains ripped through the air next to Mags, and I looked down.

Technically, I wasn't supposed to let Mags hold the leash of my service dog. His nonprofit company had strict rules. But the way she'd walked through the mall with her leash hand dangling down, blasé as shit (not to mention totally able-bodied) to match François' blasé-as-shit expression amused me. Only two years old, François wore a blue-and-gold vest and silver choke collar. His half retriever, half Labrador fur was almost white, and everyone pretty much had to resist the urge to scrunch all that extra skin over his large brown eyes. I mean, that and the fact that his name was François.

Normally those eyes were dull and disinterested. Now, he looked up at me and gently swayed. Food.

I mouthed *no* warmly, and he kept wagging.

"Fam, I don't know what we're doing," said Mags, gazing absently around the food court and twirling François' leash on her wrist.

Elliot draped across the sticky linoleum table. "I know." He covered his face. "We need these damn shirts."

"I mean, we're filming next week; that's still enough time for eBay." I lowered my left arm for François to slap with his tongue. My right was too stiff and weak to hang down that far.

"Do they *have* to be identical?" said Mags. "Can some of the actors just have, like, different uniforms?"

"Nah . . ." Elliot and I answered simultaneously. We were codirecting the group's final project for Video II. I was glad we were on the same page. Most times.

"Imma get a wrap." Elliot drew out his wallet and plucked a few bills. "You guys want anything?"

"No, thanks," said Mags.

He pointed at me. "Maeve?"

I smiled. "I'm good, thanks."

"Aight."

Elliot left me with just Mags, his cologne pushing the air.

They were comfortable with me—my classmates. I had that weird bubbling happiness in my chest that reminded me it's not normal for me to feel normal. Being born with a neuromuscular disease that cripples your strength and locks up your joints and confines you to a wheelchair made normal an unrealistic standard. I had a form of muscular dystrophy, which is a pretty big sucky umbrella of genetic diseases that erode muscles and get worse as time goes on until you basically shrivel up like plastic sheets in the microwave.

As a baby, I'd begun to lose milestones rather than gain them. Only weeks after my first steps, I started to fall over and eventually never get back up. A shake developed. Making sure I could breathe whenever I came down with something became critical. But the severity of the condition varies for no explicable reason—there are those with my disability who use standers and others who are already dead. What's really messed up is when I drag through Google images of others with my disease that're frailer and more twisted just so I can think: *Screw that, I'm not like you.*

Yet.

Sometimes I'm an asshole, but only in my head.

"How are you doing?" said Mags. Her pretty eyes watched me with a mix of sympathy and refreshing nonchalance. Pain wriggled in my stomach. We'd been texting, and she knew I was depressed.

You'd think my reason for depression was, like, hospital visits and wheelchair parts on back order, right? I don't grieve my disability; I grieve the shitty side effects of it. Sure, you make the best of being different. I've shaken a lot of hands and looked into a lot of tear-filled eyes of really rich people I somehow inspired to make a donation that won't solve any of my problems. But for the most part? The pain of having a condition is about rejection and desires to feel human in ways that can never possibly be filled.

"Maeve?"

"Yeah, sorry."

"You're fine. Have you heard from R?"

Ugh. I don't let my friends use his name anymore.

"No." I shifted.

"I'm sorry."

I cringed. It sounded so final when Mags apologized.

"I'm used to it," I said. "I wouldn't want me either."

"That's stupid," said Mags. "Don't say that."

"It's true."

"Nah, fam, it's stupid." She never let me get away with bullshit and I smiled.

François sniffed the air gingerly with pushed-back ears and mollified eyes. He sort of looked stoned all the time.

"François," I said. He looked at me. I'd meant to chastise him, but I actually chuckled instead.

"Oh my Gawd!" a middle-aged woman with long dark hair and Chanel sunglasses (in the mall?) squealed at our table and made us jump. She held a vegan wrap in her manicured nails—I could tell from the VEGAN! VEGAN! VEGAN! print spiraling the wrap paper. "What a precious *dog*!" she said, and flipped that *o* pretty hard in her New York accent.

"Yeah, you can pet him," said Mags, without asking my permission. "She's not one of those crazy strict handlers." She let go of the leash.

"Oh my *Gawd*." The woman crouched and kneaded François' ears in her hands.

With my previous service dog, Martin, now was the time when he'd look at me like: *Why? Who is this? How is this supposed to help you?*

But François was my European second love and we have an open relationship, so he started smacking his tongue out for her face.

I'd typically use this time to hardcore flirt with whatever guy knelt in front of me, but in general, I was a little less invested in François' female catches.

"Yes," the woman cooed. "Yes." She made kissy noises at François, and Mags and I watched. Our boredom grew into furrowed brows as it started to get a little weird.

"*Mwah!*" The woman ended strong and rose, facing me. "So cute!"

IF SHE WERE A GUY: "You're not bad either. Can you pet me now?"

BECAUSE SHE'S NOT: "Thanks."

"Listen," the woman said.

Uh-oh.

"Have you heard of . . ." *Insert charity organization for physical handicap I've never heard of.*

"Nope."

"Oh my Gawd, you're kidding. They're right here in Fredericksburg!"

"That's wonderful," I said.

"We've been trying to get a service dog team in to speak to our donors for months. The top investor is a *huge* dog lover."

"Aww. Well, I could give you his company info," I said. "Maybe they can hook you up with a trainer to come in and—"

"Oh, honey, no. The event is next week."

"Ah," I said. "What do you do for them?"

"I'm their CFO. Isn't that right, sweetie?" She cooed down at François. *No,* I thought, *François doesn't know your career life choices.*

But François wagged.

"Anyway," the woman said. "I'm Patricia. I think you would be *perfect* for inspiring these donors to help out the kids at the special needs camp."

"Oh . . ."

Mags looked away and suppressed a grin. She knew she couldn't save me. Anxiety already built in my throat.

"I'm flattered, but I don't know . . ." I said. But gee, I always had a hard time saying no to special camp kids. "When is it?"

"It's on the twenty-first; they'll *love* you. Oh my Gawd, you'll be a *hit*."

Thank God—an out.

"Damn. I'm filming with my class all day that day." I motioned to include Mags.

An anvil fell down the woman's face. The tiny muscles in her expression stiffened. "Sigh." She actually said *sigh*. Awkward silence stretched. "If you change your mind, let me know."

"I'm sorry," I said. "How about I come this summer and read to the kids? Teach them about service dogs?" Blergh. "Do you have a card or anything?"

The corner of her mouth flicked up a little at my offer. "That'd be sweet. I'm out of cards. Just Google the camp. I'm at the bottom of their web page."

"I will."

When she left, I only had time to draw in breath at Mags' comical look before Elliot plopped back down in his seat, wrap and fries on a pink tray.

"Who was that?"

"Some wheelchair charity person," said Mags. She stole a fry and Elliot unfolded his wrap.

"So what else do we need still for the shoot?" I said as Elliot took a huge bite. "I handled the props. Location is locked. Do the actors know their call times?"

"Mmm!" Elliot hummed around his mouthful. He swallowed. "Bad news. Cole can't make it."

"*What?*"

"I know," said Elliot.

"No," I said. "Give me his number. Right now. He's making it. Dammit." I rolled my eyes. Actors.

Elliot laughed. "Okay, I will."

"Who is this?" said Mags.

"Cole Stone," said Elliot.

"Like the creamery?"

"No," I said, "like the actor."

Elliot huffed with humor.

"Yo, what did you and Nate 2.0 talk about last night?" Mags asked Elliot. Elliot and Nate went to the new Marvel film together. We call him Nate 2.0 because there was a really creepy Nate in Video I that we don't talk about anymore.

"I don't know." Elliot laughed. "He's wild."

"Sometimes," I said. Nate's humor was hit or miss with me.

"Why sometimes?" said Mags. I noticed she was starting to get defensive and inquisitive and highly interested in Nate.

"I dunno," I said. "I think he's really funny, but sometimes I think he doesn't like me." I wasn't sure I really believed that. I wanted to see what they'd say.

"That's stupid," said Mags.

"Mmm . . ." said Elliot. We looked at him as he wiped a napkin over his mouth. "He can be insensitive."

"How?" said Mags.

"He just says things to be funny sometimes and it's not funny."

"Like what?" said Mags.

Elliot rolled his shoulders uncomfortably.

"He said something about me, didn't he?" I said. "What'd he say?"

"I dunno."

"Come on."

Elliot sighed. "He said something like . . . *Maeve will be a virgin forever.*"

Mags fell silent. I did too.

Elliot made a sad, shrugging face. "He's just immature."

No. He was kind of right, though.

"Don't listen to him."

The humor and ease and acceptance I basked in extinguished. My teeth ground together and I nodded, staring across from them at the Chinese buffet.

One thing I've learned from getting endless feedback on my scripts is that criticism doesn't hurt unless you kind of agree with it.

"Well . . . that sucks," said Mags, genuinely.

Elliot rubbed my hand and some of that love flowed back into my blood. "Love you, co-director," he said.

"Love you, co-director," I mumbled back. Elliot smiled.

I ticked alight my phone on the table.

"My dad's probably waiting outside," I said. "I better head out."

"I'll walk you out," said Elliot.

"I'll walk *you* out," I said.

"Eyyyy . . ." Elliot grinned.

I tapped my joystick and my wheelchair gave its mechanical clicking sound before moving. I froze. François always leapt up from the floor at that sound. I looked down beneath the table and choked.

François was gone.

2

Once, I took François to Disneyland.

It wasn't my fault.

I couldn't just leave him in the hotel. He'd ridden in the boat for It's a Small World and because LITERALLY EVERY COSTUMED CHARACTER ANYWHERE makes a beeline for me, weird balloon-faced characters tried to pet him all day. When we got back to the room, François jumped onto the bed without my permission and lay down facing the wall. He didn't look over when I poked his fur. It was the equivalent of slamming the door and calling his mom to ask if he could live with her while he thought over our relationship.

It was possible now that he may have actually left me and filed for divorce. But something about the hammering of my heart and the leap of heat in my blood told me that wasn't so.

"The hell!" Elliot rose from his seat and scanned the food court, but I'd already done so in a millisecond. No dog. No white blur. I swept my cell phone into my hand and slammed a quick-dial tab.

Dad picked up. "Hey, Trout."

"Dad, come inside. Someone took François."

"*What?*"

I hung up and launched from the table in search of a mall cop. Mags was stooping to look under every seat, and Elliot jogged to keep up with me.

I crashed aside a set of plastic chairs and headed for a

circular information desk. The counter towered over my head by about four inches, but I started talking anyway.

"A dog—have you seen—?"

"Someone took her dog." Elliot was panting; he leaned against the counter. The clerk, stricken, looked at him instead of me because he was eye level.

"FRANÇOIS!" Elliot and I both turned to Mags' voice.

At a turquoise cinnamon-bun stand, François trotted towards a tall woman. I could hear the jingle of his tags from here. The leash trailed along the floor, and his ears perked at the smell of the bun.

I raced to him.

"François!" I scolded. He jolted and looked over, eyes fixed on me with adoration. But I dipped my whole torso over my armrest and swung his leash into my hand. Vertigo swooped through my head. It took a moment to straighten— I grunted with the weight of drawing myself back up. Then I looked at the woman he'd been approaching.

Sunglasses. Vegan wrap. It was Patricia. Wheelchair Charity Woman. Mags and Elliot stared at her, hands on their knees.

Flipping up her shades with one hand, Patricia turned and hooted with surprise down at François.

"Little François!"

François wagged. I resisted the urge to correct him.

"Why was my dog with you?" I challenged.

"I'm sorry?" said Patricia.

"My dog—why was he with you?"

Patricia giggled uncomfortably. "I guess he followed the smell of food."

"The smell of food is everywhere."

Her mouth hung open, and she darted a glance at Elliot

and Mags. For a moment, I thought she may have actually been alarmed and confused.

"What's going on?" A new voice. Dad veered up behind the woman, a hard note to his tone. Winded. He'd sprinted here.

Awkward looks were passed, a tense pause, Dad waiting to be told whose face to get into, and finally I let it go. Begrudgingly. "It's okay," I said. "Have a good day."

Patricia gave a sarcastic hum like *thanks* and left with her wrap.

Dad looked at me and raised an eyebrow.

Clang! The metal ramp collapsed onto the blue-painted asphalt, and I stared at it.

Neither Dad nor I are moms, and we both hate soccer, but we've only ever driven soccer-mom vans.

"What was that about?" Dad stood next to the van ramp and squinted in the setting sun.

Dad was in his fifties, but I could count on one hand the grey flecks in his brown hair. He was tall, strong, and rough skinned. He wore black-rimmed transitional glasses and a silver Bluetooth in his ear, steel-colored eyes alight. Maybe it's weird, but I always thought he was exceptionally handsome, and that made me proud. I enjoyed watching his expression grow horrified when I told him the old-lady neighbors agreed with me.

I shook my head and led François up the ramp, following after. "I'll tell you as we drive."

"Hmm."

Dad collected the ramp from the ground and folded it up. I heard him grunt as he rolled closed the van door and in the rearview mirror saw him rub his shoulder as he walked around.

There are all sorts of slings and machines and robots that drill into the ceiling able to transfer people like me from here to there. To and fro. Nothing makes me feel more dehumanized. So for eighteen years, Dad has carried me into beds, planes, bathrooms, next to a cow, up lighthouses, and one time into an ambulance—but that wasn't the best day.

He tells me his bad shoulder and knee and occasionally back are old lacrosse wounds from college.

I'm sick of watching his body tear apart for me.

On the way home, I told Dad about Patricia.

IF SHE WERE A GUY: "Sorry, Dad. It was a total misunderstanding."

BECAUSE SHE'S NOT: "Do you still know that lawyer in Alexandria?"

Dad glanced contemplatively at me in the mirror and kept both hands on the wheel.

"That was really weird," he confirmed. "I guess just be careful there next time. Ask Elliot to keep an eye out." There really wasn't much more to say. François panted in the back seat and filled the van with his breath.

I liked that Dad blasted radio. Our soccer-mom van had these little grooves in the floor meant for strapping me in with buckles, but I just tightened my hold on the handle behind the passenger seat. We never did that. In fact, Dad and I were totally rehearsed at nodding and pretending to take vigilant account of the safety steps when we traveled and rented a handicapped van. The renter by law had to go over the buckle procedures. The second the renter left, we'd rip them all off.

Dad turned up the volume now to a Pink Floyd song, and I poked in my iPod earbuds and looked out the window.

I loved highways. The camaraderie of cars merging onto freeways, cruising at sixty miles per hour alongside my window, all going the same direction, made me feel like part of the world.

That night, I lay in bed with François bunched into a ball at my feet. Ice tickled my toes. I dared not move or he would jump.

It was late, and Mom slept on a pullout bed next to me in case I needed to shift or turn. Other nights we'd use a baby monitor, or Mom or Dad would turn their ringers up loud and I'd call them. It just depended on if they felt like walking across the hall several times that night. Lately I've preferred the monitor option for privacy, though.

My phone splashed blue light all over the covers. I flicked through my email feed.

Mr. Billings sent out an impatient notice to all of us about getting our shit together for the shoot next week. Paraphrased. I still needed to track down matching uniforms for our actors without breaking budget. Honestly, I shouldn't be complaining. The Intro to Stage kids are slapping together a giant Venus flytrap right now. And then in the summer they're doing *The Little Mermaid*, which I'm kind of excited for—Prince Eric can get it from Little Maeve. I mean, or Big Maeve, I don't even know anymore. Actually, according to Cole's résumé, he played the guy who shouts *STELLAAAA!* in *Streetcar* for them a few years back. From what I remember of his volume, they made a good choice.

Then I opened another email I hadn't replied to—in a few more days, I'd be too ashamed of my lateness to even open it and look at the received date again.

Re: Still Alive?

Fred Kingfisher   Mon, Sep 10, 12:14 AM
to M. Leeson

Hey, kiddo. Been a while. Sure glad to hear from you,
but I know you've got a busy plate. Any more travels
coming up? Any guys I need to level my shotgun on?
—Fred

I pursed my lips in a sad smile.

I met Fred when Mom dropped me off at an outdoor
market while she hosted a "power lunch" nearby. Mom
uses words like *power* and *fierce* and *aggressive* a lot because
she's a total type-A, don't-need-no-man businesswoman
who also happens to wear flannel pajamas.

Anyway, I was at this lone book stand reading a TO-
TALLY INNOCENT DEFINITELY NOT EROTIC
how-to book when a grey-haired, scruffy-bearded man appeared out of nowhere and started comparing my wheelchair to an electric-propelled Tesla. I'd leapt and stuffed
the book back onto the shelf. Not noticing (I think . . .),
he insisted I come with him to the Tesla exhibit a few booths
down.

Don't try this at home, children, but I followed the
strange man, and we ended up spending the rest of the day
together, getting ice cream and playing with remote-control
drones in the electronics booth. He asked if he could kiss
me on the cheek before parting, and I, of course, said, "Just
the cheek? Shame . . ." and he laughed a big gut laugh.

We've emailed for half a year now. My responses have
been getting slower. Thing is, Fred is not the only old man
I've befriended who looks forward to my emails and gets

kinda sad when I don't reply quickly. Fred is not even the second or third. Fred is just the newest.

I backed out of the email.

No, Fred, I thought, *I wouldn't waste my money on any shotgun bullets.* I'd almost told him about R in my last email, but deleted it at the last minute. I worried that might make him sad too. Silly. I'm sure he would have been thrilled for me. But nothing to be thrilled about now that R shot me down a week ago.

At that moment, François heaved a great sigh at my feet and rolled onto his back. Paws folded. Perfect timing.

I won't grace R with the honor of a full description. Because he was the grandson of another OMF (Old Man Friend) whom I adored, it made his rejection that much more heartbreaking. To put it simply, he was handsome and foreign, and the thing I hated most about him was the fact that he wasn't a jerk at all. He was kind. His *rejection* was kind. He even continued to handwrite letters asking how my life was going. R's problem with me was the same as every other young, red-blooded guy in the universe. It was the same as *my* problem with me.

Just . . . not attracted. Just . . . not able to go there. Situation normal.

There was a lot more wrong with the universe than my love life. I tried to remember that. At least I wasn't the only one who forgot.

My phone buzzed.

ELLIOT

> Sup. Here's Cole's number.

A contact file with a ten-digit 800-number buzzed in a moment later, and I clicked on it.

ELLIOT

NO WAIT NOT THAT NUMBER

I smirked and decided to lie.

MAEVE

Too late

ELLIOT

OMG WHAT DID YOU SEND?

MAEVE

Who even is this?

ELLIOT

NO ONE STOP TEXTING IT
THAT'S NOT COLE STONE

MAEVE

. . . Which Cole is it then?

ELLIOT

It's a Cole that charges $4.50 a
minute . . .

MAEVE

Fam.

ELLIOT

Here's the real number.

A second contact buzzed in. This one looked right.
I shot back a smiley emoticon to Elliot and opened a new

text to Cole. Even though it was past 1 a.m. and I'd never texted the guy in my life, I was sending this tonight.

MAEVE

> Cole! This is Maeve. One of the directors. I heard there was some conflict with your schedule regarding the shoot. Look, I really want you. I'm willing to work around you and maybe even squeeze your scenes into one day. Can we make it work?

I sent it. The auditions had been several weeks ago—I had a vague mental picture of Cole strolling into the open audition five minutes before it ended, and from the maybe ten minutes I spent with him before we cast him due to the mutual instinct my friends and I all had. He was young, ruggedly huge, and bearded. That's all. So I actually was a little nervous about the audacity of my text. Guess I'd hear in the morning.

Sighing, I inched my left hand close to my mouth and parted my lips. I bit my finger. Clenching it hard between my teeth, I used the strength of my head to pull my left arm over my chest so I could scratch my right ear. Then I pushed my fingers over the itch, closed my eyes, and tried to invite sleep.

My phone buzzed. I froze. Shifting took a moment, but I wiggled my shoulder against the mattress and clicked the phone alight with my thumb:

COLE STONE
Text Message

That was fast.

COLE STONE

Hey Maeve

I stared at the screen. Was that it? I never understood anymore because punctuation went out of style and I'm still trying to adjust.

Another text came in.

COLE STONE

You're up late . . .

I resisted rolling my eyes at Cole. Again. *Actors.*

Burning that oil, I replied. Ew. Stupid *and* cliché.

COLE STONE

No doubt haha

I waited a couple minutes. He didn't follow up. Damn, he was really going to make me work for this.

MAEVE

Not every day you get a director begging you to rearrange your schedule after midnight. It's all downhill from here.

COLE STONE

I know :P

MAEVE

So do I have to get on my
knees . . . ?

What was happening? Was I flirting? Oh God, five minutes, no reply. I actually opened Elliot's text thread to tell
him we definitely needed a new Cole Stone when the phone
buzzed and Cole's tab overlapped the top of my phone.

COLE STONE

IT'S NOT THAT KIND OF MOVIE,
IS IT?

MAEVE

Ha you need to come out of
your comfort zone.

COLE STONE

You couldn't afford my love scenes.

MAEVE

We can't afford you now.

I was smiling now, eyes glued, waiting for his reply to
come in.

COLE STONE

So hey I could probably manage
one day. What date and time?

Back to business. Something wilted in my chest. But I
gave him a date and time that, miraculously, worked.

COLE STONE

Alright cool. I'll be there.

I breathed a sigh of relief. We had our actor again. See, Elliot? All it took was one headstrong text. Confidence. Bam. I thanked Cole and gave the air a weak punch of victory. *Now* I could call it a night.

Mom rose to her knees and sleepily flopped me onto my side at my bidding. I nestled into the blankets as she flumped back onto her pillow. The phone glass was still cool in my hand as I closed my eyes and breathed deeply. Sank like bait in a pond.

A minute later, my phone buzzed again.

Like pinching up a card in poker, I tipped back my phone just enough to see the text. My bleary eyes squinted into the bright light.

COLE STONE

So . . . you really want me, huh? ;)

"Dad, can you get a napkin and clean all the Frosted Flakes out of my shirt pocket?"

I took one last bite and more milk slopped off my spoon and onto my front. I can't lift the spoon all the way to my mouth without tilting it, so that happens. The spoon clinked back into the bowl, and I looked over. Dad appeared at the breakfast table and stared at me. He sighed, hands on his sides.

"That sounds really gross."

"You have to," I said. It was wet and sticky in my pocket, where most of the cereal fell. If I'm being totally honest, I probably could have scooped them out of there with a little effort, but I didn't want to touch the soggy flakes clinging to the inside of my pocket any more than he did.

"How come I have to?" said Dad, but he pinched my shirt and started wiping.

"Because I'm physically incapable?" Maybe.

"So?"

"So that's kinda shoddy craftsmanship on your end."

"Student projects always are," said Dad.

"*Ew*," I said. "That sounds like you conceived me in college."

Dad smiled slowly.

"Oh my God," I said, and pulled away from the table before he was done scrubbing my shirt. He straightened, napkin in hand.

"Ready to go?" he said.

I dragged my school folder off the table and lifted it. "Yup."

Elliot high-fived me as I rolled up next to my Mac in the back row of Video II. I flopped my folder onto the desk and read the updates on the whiteboard. Dates. Nothing I didn't already know. The shoot in three days. The music video project after.

But I drummed the keyboard in front of me and clicked

a pen out of the leather satchel hanging off my chair. After last night, I was in a good mood.

KC sat to my right. I smiled warmly at him. He smiled back. He was short, small-framed but muscular, and had a braid in his brown hair. A Thor pendant at his neck. Plaid shirt. We spent Memorial Day at his fire pit at the end of last school year, and since we'd been friends since kindergarten, I dared him to carve our initials into his tree.

Because the Video II crop came from last year's Video I, our advanced group was kinda small. We had two students drop in the beginning of the quarter. One person took a desk on day one and twenty-five minutes in said: "I think I'm supposed to be in geometry." Never saw her again. The other was our cinematographer, One Take Blake. He was basically my work husband on set and then I became polygamous and work-married Elliot too. Blake dropped out because he started getting crazy-good gigs making local insurance commercials look like Oscar bait in usually—you guessed it—one take. I'm assuming they'll nominate Meryl Streep for supporting actress in his productions and just totally ignore the fact that she wasn't in them.

We also had our audio kid, Michael, who never showed up for class, but he'd mysteriously appear for every shoot, hidden in a nest of wires, with a five-foot boom pole and a supposed new encounter with the audio waves of the dead on his transistor radios.

It was a good class.

Soon the lights cut, and Mr. Billings put on a YouTube video demonstrating everything we should pack in our supply bag for a film set. The video's red progress bar was only, like, a third of the way through ten minutes later, so we all snuck out our phones in the back row.

I texted Mags, of course. She sat one row ahead of me.

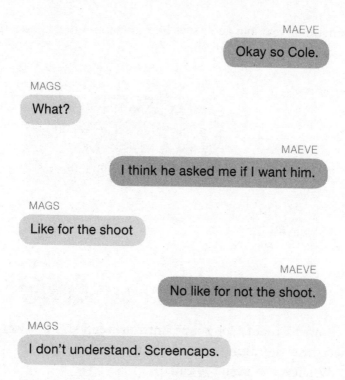

> **MAEVE**
> Okay so Cole.

> **MAGS**
> What?

> **MAEVE**
> I think he asked me if I want him.

> **MAGS**
> Like for the shoot

> **MAEVE**
> No like for not the shoot.

> **MAGS**
> I don't understand. Screencaps.

I provided a few selective screenshots and looked up at the boring YouTube video to save face while the grabs took a few extra seconds to go through.

> **MAGS**
> Omfg.

> **MAEVE**
> Right? It's not just me?

> **MAGS**
> Idk.

Ugh. Sometimes I wished Mags would just gush with me. It's not every day a huge, six-foot-one, bearded, twenty-

something-year-old actor says he wants me. I mean, asks if
I want him.

MAEVE

> I mean, I guess I did prompt it
> by telling him I'd get on my
> knees. But I'm kind of the
> perfect height for that as is.

MAGS

> Maeve . . .

MAEVE

> What? :)

It was kind of a long time until she replied. I was wor-
ried she was drafting a lengthy chastisement of my . . .
Whatever you want to call it.
My phone buzzed.

MAGS

> Just don't catch feelings.

My mouth twisted down. That was weird.

MAEVE

> Why not? I won't be
> unprofessional on set, obviously.

MAGS

> No no I know.

Okay, good. I looked back up at the YouTube video which, amazingly, was *a fourth* finished now. Did Mr. Billings rewind this shit or something?

My phone buzzed again.

MAGS

You just come on really strong.

I laid my head back on my wheelchair's headrest that I hated and let my phone relax in my lap.

You know when you're kind of aware of a flaw, but also kind of hope that maybe you're the only one aware?

Well. Ha-ha. *Well.*

A few years ago, I had this mega-dangerous seventeen-hour operation to correct scoliosis that was crushing my lungs. Because you kind of need lungs. It thinned me out and made me healthier but also misshaped me a little. I always used to think, *Nah, maybe that's just me.* Maybe I'm just super self-conscious. It wasn't, though. I've been posed questions about it and suddenly I like the questioner way less and I get much thirstier for whatever drink is in front of me.

Same goes for my "coming on strong" flaw.

I know I do. I flirt like I get laid every night and I give dirty comments to way too many older or married men, let alone young, single men, who get it from me like four times as bad.

Are people really that stupid, though? Do they really think I could survive playing hard to get?

If I don't come on hard, if I don't exterminate absolutely any and all doubt that I'm not asexual, doubt will exterminate me.

We all groaned as Mr. Billings struck on the lights unexpectedly. The seminar was apparently over.

"Your shoot is in *three days*. You've had a *lot* of time to prepare this so Elliot, Maeve, crack that whip. I want to see quality."

"Are we still doing that music video thing after?" said Mags.

Our project after the big shoot was to produce a music video for this local wannabe pop star. She was, like, fourteen, and the song literally was just . . .

"Yes," said Billings. "Did you all have a chance to review the song?"

"Yeah," Mags went on seriously, "the file you sent out said 'more clubby version'—is there a less clubby version we could hear?"

Elliot pushed out his seat next to me and rose, stretching. "Three days!" he said.

"I'm ready," I replied.

KC walked up beside me and looked down at François. François' ears pulled back and his eyes closed as he dropped his jaw in a yawn.

"You guys want to chill on the tracks for a little?" said Elliot.

I checked the time on my phone. Class had ended about twenty minutes early and was my last period, leaving me enough time to hang. Mom was my ride today, and she was less patient about waiting for me to come out than Dad was.

"Yeah, I got about twenty minutes," I said.

"Cool," said Elliot.

At the door, Elliot, KC, and I stopped to let Mags walk through. Nate joined her side and let his arm fall over her shoulders. He was wearing two different-colored long socks, and his hunter-green backpack sagged from his back. I tried not to let my insides sour, remembering what he'd said about me, as I waved goodbye to Mags. She didn't see.

KC and Elliot snuck out after. I halted at the doorway as Mr. Billings came over.

"See you guys next week," Billings said to me, scratching François' ear. I went ahead and hugged Mr. Billings. Then sped to catch up with Elliot in the hall, who was glancing over his shoulder for me.

"*So.*" Elliot sighed as he sat on an outside bench next to the tracks where runners were practicing in PE. I parked next to him, KC following. The sun was bright but cool. Someone had stuck their empty Gatorade bottle into one of the holes of the wire fence in front of us. A little blue liquid pooled in the grooves inside the plastic.

"So." I grinned back. But as KC took a seat next to Elliot, I checked my phone quickly. No one texted. No Cole. I looked back up.

François gave a distressed rumble at my side.

"Uh-oh," I said. François' head was tilted towards my wheel. I'd accidentally run over his leash and tangled it in my spokes; he was being tethered.

I tugged at the leash. François grumbled louder. *(Not helping!)*

"Could you—?" I implored Elliot, who was closer, but KC jumped up.

A second later KC was kneeling next to me and untangling François. His hands were gentle and loving. I tried to ward off embarrassment.

"Did KC tell you?" said Elliot. "He found the matching uniforms for the actors."

"No way!" I said. "That's awesome! How much do we owe you?"

KC rose, leash in hand. François shook a victory shake, and even though he was the whitest dog ever, I heard Martin

Luther King Jr.'s voice narrating it like a civil rights speech. *Free at last, free at last, thank God almighty, free at last!*

"Nothing," said KC, handing me the leash. "We had them in my attic."

"You had museum docent uniforms for three people in your attic." My words were skeptical.

KC rested both hands atop his head. "My family owns a lot of costumes."

"What?" I said.

"My family." He shook his head dismissively. "Don't worry about it."

"Well, I'm buying you dinner or something, then," I said with a finalized tone.

KC looked over at me.

"So, are Nate and Mags really happening now?" Elliot said, popping white earbuds into his ears. "I mean, damn." He scrolled through the music on his phone.

"He's a piece of shit," said KC, pulling his arms down. The language seemed a little strong for KC's quiet manner. And I wasn't sure Nate deserved that bad a verdict for saying something stupid. Maybe KC was jealous of Nate.

My phone buzzed, and I jolted for it. Hoping it was Cole.

MOM

Let's go.

My heart sank. "Hey, I gotta go. My ride's here."

"All right, hey!" said Elliot. "See you in *three days*!" He high-fived me again, and I laughed. Elliot's verve splashed all around him like a sprinkler.

"I'll walk you to your ride," said KC.

"You sure?"

"Yeah. No problem."

The gate into the track field screeched as he held it open for me and I rolled through. I bumped a little over the rough gravel, and the crunch was loud. Internally, I cringed at the noise I made.

KC loped next to me, hands in pockets.

"So, you really think Nate's a piece of shit, huh?" I said. "Why? Did he say anything more about me?"

"What did you hear?" KC asked.

"Uh." I tried to arrange my tone to sound the least depressing. "That I'll be a virgin forever."

KC scoffed. "Yeah. No. It was just that."

"It's all right," I said. Trying to shrug it off, be heroic. "It's just a comment."

"A messed-up one."

"People are dicks to each other all the time, KC," I said. "They say much worse things than that."

We neared that parking lot and my purple van, so he mumbled his words. "Which is why I hate everyone immediately upon meeting them."

So that was a little dark. I furrowed my brow. "You do?"

"Yeah. Until they prove me otherwise."

I stopped and turned to him. Only a few paces away from the car. He crossed his arms.

My smile was mischievous. "When did you decide that you didn't hate me?"

"Maeve?" Mom shouted from the van. "Ready?"

I groaned and bunched up François' leash in my hand. Smiled at KC. "Thanks again for the shirts. See you at the shoot." He smiled back, nodded. He waved once to my mom and then hung his head.

I turned and made for the van, François' collar jingling. Then I heard KC's soft voice. Almost like an afterthought.

"I never hated you."

The secretary pushed the clipboard towards me on the counter the next day. I tried swiping for it, but the weight of my flesh caused my arm to fall like a trapeze artist who missed his swing midair.

"Could you slide it a little closer?" I said. Three inches was all I needed.

"Oh, I'm *so* sorry!" The woman rose and shoved the whole clipboard in my lap.

IF SHE WERE A GUY: God, chivalry. Mmph.

BECAUSE SHE'S NOT: Overkill assistance. Offensive.

I clicked the pen and signed François and myself onto Riverside Assisted Living's visitors' list. François' nose was chugging along the carpet, probably vacuuming up the smells of too much soap and air freshener. I looked around as I moseyed to the waiting lounge. An ancient air conditioner hummed at the window, doing nothing to sway the heavy floral curtains. A lighthouse suncatcher, yellow when it once was clear, stained light onto the armchairs.

Those chairs held elderly residents. They slept, hung their heads, or stared at François. They maybe lived and sometimes existed.

I swallowed.

"Maeve?"

I turned to see a dark-skinned nurse in periwinkle scrubs smile at me. "Quinten's in the club."

The club was a collection of tables and one antique cathedral radio, a fake plant, and a bar that cruelly had alcohol bottles painted on the wall behind it but none of the real stuff. Nothing like that allowed here.

I reviewed the topics I planned to hit on and approached the round table where Quinten sat with three old women with short, curly pink hair.

I sighed and parked. "Hey, how many girls do I have to fight off you before you die?"

Quinten, riddled with arthritis and sitting in one of those scooter things that they maybe gave him at Walmart, raised his head and met my gaze with big, brown eyes. His moustache was grey to match his hair.

His shoulders started shaking with weak, breathy laughter, and I grinned back.

"All right." I whipped out a fresh deck of Bicycle playing cards. "We doing 21 or seven-card stud? You ladies in?"

The ladies giggled bashfully and waved their hands. One fixed her hair with her delicate fingers. I felt like Quinten should try to hit that.

They watched me shuffle.

I met Quinten at this little playhouse showing *The Producers* in Maryland. We were both boxed in the handicapped section. At intermission, I tried to joke with him about the unexpected raunchiness of the play, and he'd just slowly turned a baleful eye on me.

"Not easy being stuck in the box, is it?" I had said, suddenly soft and serious.

He didn't ask for it, but his lingering, contemplative gaze was just hopeless enough for me to write down my phone number and just hopeful enough for me to give it to him.

He called the next day like we were old friends. I've been coming to visit him ever since. Another OMF addition.

"All right, deuces wild." I dealt and included the old ladies anyway.

My phone buzzed as I studied my poker hand.

> MAGS
> did you tell anyone

I furrowed my brow and glanced to make sure the seniors were occupied with their hands before replying. The assisted-living home was a place I felt particularly judged for being glued to my phone.

> MAEVE
> What?

> MAGS
> why do kc and elliot know i'm into nate

Ooph. All lowercase and no punctuation. Mags was pissed. I asked Quinten about his children and threw in a bet of pennies that we pretended were twenties.

> MAEVE
> I have no idea. I didn't tell anyone

Right? I don't think I did.

> MAGS
> okay well

"So . . . how's school going?" Quinten wheezed.

I smiled at him. "Meh. Gotta keep the parents happy."
Quinten huffed with humor.

"But I'm filming a video on Sunday. I'm excited." I told
him about it until the nurse reappeared and administered
Quinten his pills. He blinked, silently resentful of the timing and probably even a little embarrassed to take them in
front of me. But he slowly took the paper cup. I used this
opportunity to write my longer reply to Mags.

MAEVE

> Why would I tell them? I'm not
> mad at Nate. I just think anyone
> who says that about someone
> literally disabled might be a
> little troubled.

I sent it and fired out another.

MAEVE

> I love you. If he makes you
> happy, I give zero shits how
> he treats me, I just care how
> he treats you.

Relief flooded through me when Mags replied.

MAGS

> No I know. Ly2.

Mags was only comfortable saying *I love you* in acro-
nyms. I stuffed my phone under my seat belt and refocused
on the card game after Quinten gulped down his last pill.

Elderly hands of every shade and varying levels of shak-

iness (though I probably topped them all) fell on François'
fur in passing. Residents thumped their medical equipment
slowly towards him like the *Night of the Living Walkers*. It
was great.

My phone buzzed. I really didn't know how much more
Nate discussion I had in me, but I flashed the screen on
anyway.

My heart clapped in my chest.

COLE STONE

Hey :)

*Oh my God, shut up, Maeve. He probably has a question
about the shoot or something.*
I replied way too fast.

MAEVE

Sup headliner

No punctuation. Seemed more casual.

COLE STONE

Headliner, huh? :P

Okay, I don't understand the tongue emoji. I don't understand if it means he's disgusted or is teasing me or wants
to star in a reality show about how many children we have
together.

MAEVE

The one and only. Call time's 9
AM :)

I figured that's why he was texting. Returning to my poker hand, I sighed and organized my cards. Almost a straight flush. "So, what's the craziest thing you ever did in Vegas?" I asked Quinten. Usually people ask nursing-home folks how the mushy food is or what evening activities were planned. I liked mining for the adult part of Quinten, the wild life that used to *be* and *want* things just like me.

Quinten released a long exhale. "I busted a one-armed prostitute in a coke deal on the nose of the Sphinx at that hotel one time."

"Oh, the Luxor is cool," I said, switching out two cards. Quinten was a former DEA agent.

"Mr. Mosby? You left your dentures in your room." The nurse set the glass of dentures in front of him. He stared at the teeth as they clinked around in the water.

I went on to save him embarrassment. "So how did that—"

I flinched and instinctively looped my arm around François' neck. Hugging him to my side.

That woman. That tall woman by the front desk. The secretary was pushing the clipboard to her too and letting her sign in.

I wasn't losing it. I was undeniably sure that it was the same woman from the mall who tried to take François. Patricia. Wheelchair Charity Woman. She slipped on her sunglasses and nodded at something the bubbly secretary was saying. Swept her head around the building like she was appraising the place. And then the secretary graciously escorted her down the opposite hallway, raising an arm as if giving her a tour.

What was she doing here? No, Wheelchair Charity Woman. You can't also be Old People Charity Woman. God, you can't have all the charities!

"Pssst. Quinten." I leaned forward. Quinten looked up. Eyebrows raised. "Who's that tall woman with the sunglasses who was just at the counter?"

Quinten peered in the direction I'd nodded towards. Musta caught sight of the back of her head.

He frowned and lifted his shoulders. "I think she was here last week too. Not sure why. Not a daughter or granddaughter or anything."

I shifted my jaw and considered how much I wanted to rope Quinten into my suspicion.

"I think she's up to something funny."

"Why?" said Quinten.

I glanced at the ladies next to us. They weren't paying any attention. Staring off into whatever. One had set her poker hand on the surface, so we could totally see her cards.

Briefly, I explained what had happened to me and François in the mall. Quinten's eyes sharpened and his brow lowered.

"Hmm."

"I dunno." I shrugged and let it go. "Just keep an eye out. Report back." I winked.

He liked that. Quinten smiled.

François' tongue snaked out of his mouth and lapped me to remind me I was still pinning him protectively to my side. I relaxed and consulted my poker hand again.

My phone buzzed.

Cole again? Really?

COLE STONE

Pfft. I know my call time. Making sure I stay in line huh? Lol

Hmm. I smirked and shot off a fast reply.

MAEVE

You didn't come cheaply.

When the phone buzzed in reply soon after, I had to resist. I'd been neglecting the card game a little.

I laid my elbow on the table and looked hard at Quinten. In my head, I tried to melt away the years. I dyed color into his hair and smoothed his wrinkles. I saw him smiling in the sun and reaching a hand out to a woman. I straightened him. And for a few moments, it wasn't hard to see. I wondered if I could teach someone like Cole to look at me that way too.

Quinten glanced up at my curious staring. He gave a half smile, as if not sure if he was in on the joke.

I set down my cards and rolled over to his side.

"Has it really . . . been an hour?" he said. Sadness gloomed over him.

"I know, buddy. Time flies. But I better wait for my ride outside." And I wanted to get out of there before Wheelchair Charity Woman returned and saw me. I heaved all my strength over the side of my chair to climb an arm across his scooter and kissed his jaw.

As soon as François and I were out the doors, I checked my phone.

COLE STONE

I come pretty cheaply :P

Okay, understanding what the tongue emoji means would totally determine the meaning of the word *come* in that sentence. I went with what I wanted it to mean.

MAEVE

Would you?

COLE STONE

> Probably.

Mmph. Check out that period.

His punctuation turned me on so much that I quickly cropped up a Facebook photo to refresh my memory.

As hot as I remembered. I loved that in a picture with four other people at Six Flags, he was the tallest. Broad, hair all over his arms. A silver necklace hanging onto his blue T-shirt. He was bearded but boyish looking, and his dark brown hair was mussed and fell sort of edgy to one side.

Fuck me . . .

No, really, that was an invitation.

MAEVE

> You know we just cast you because sex sells.

Risky. I concealed my phone as a senior rolled by in a wheelchair and gassed me with perfume.

COLE STONE

> So if I want to keep my role I should sleep with the director right lol

Wait.

So wait, we needed to make entirely 1000 percent sure that this guy had the right number and knew the director was *me*. Well, the female one anyway.

Should I literally text him like, *Hey, just making sure, you know this is Maeve, right?* because he said something sexual to me?

I stared at my phone and hesitated for so long that he probably got worried that *he* crossed a line. Which was the last thing I wanted him to think.

MAEVE

I might like that . . .

My eyes were *padlocked* to that screen, waiting for his reply.

COLE STONE

I know you would.

My mouth dropped. Ho-ly shit. My heart pounded just as Dad swung the purple van into the parking lot. Another text buzzed in.

COLE STONE

:P

5

My chair wobbled as Elliot and KC unloaded it. Buckets of gaffer tape, lenses, lights, and props had been hung on the handles, and our guy from audio even stuffed his entire duffel bag in the jungle gym of bars back there. I have no idea what the back end of me looks like. I keep figuring it must have the storage capacity of Mary Poppins' magical sack.

I yawned and turned as Elliot and KC hauled the materials across the floor to set up. It was Sunday, and the old glass windows were corroded while morning light in the hue you'd paint a nursery spilled in. The walls were red brick, and the ceilings, a heavy dark wood.

We were in the Spotsylvania County Museum. It had, like, half a cannonball behind glass and large black-and-white photos of country houses on the walls.

Four weeks ago, to ask for shooting permission, Elliot and I had sat in the office of the museum manager, a really old woman with black hair in a tight, terrifying bun.

"If I allow you to film, I'll have to shut down the entire museum," she'd snapped.

"Ma'am, there are literally no visitors," I said.

"Well, young lady, we close in thirty minutes, so of course not."

"Ma'am, we've been here since nine."

Elliot had put his hand on my arm. "We could offer free promotional photos," he said. She peered at him through her glasses.

"Fine," she said at last. Elliot and I sighed and rose. Well, he did. "But you have to promise not to film the cannonball."

"Ma'am, no."

Elliot had tugged me out of the room. I accidentally-on-purpose knocked the plastic trash can loudly as we left.

Now, we were here way earlier than nine—try *eight*, ooph—prepping the shoot, so I left François at home. Call time for everyone else, including actors, was in sixty minutes.

I checked my phone. Cole Stone's :P was still the first thing I saw on my feed.

"Is this where you want Camera One?" KC said, and I shoved my phone away. I joined him at the equipment to do my job—direct.

Mags was the next to arrive. She bombed into the room with hands in her hoodie's pockets and dark shadows under her eyes.

"Late night?" I said with sympathy. She worked at CVS as a pharmacist's assistant.

"Yeah," said Mags, not meeting my eyes. "I gave some guy his Sudafed and he rubbed my back really weirdly."

"Ew."

"Yeah." She stared off. I used to have zero compassion for the thousands of advances Mags got, since I'd be happy with just one. I like back rubs. But that slightly-concerned-yet-blasé accepting look in her eyes usually nudged the empathy out of me. I'd run them over for her.

I don't know why, but I didn't tell her about Cole's messages yesterday. I guess I just . . .

I didn't want to hear it. Her logical and quick *Fam. Pull back.* Or *Nah, he's prob just being coy.*

I wanted to hang onto my thrill. I wanted to play with him for a little. Alone.

Twenty minutes later—already fifteen minutes behind schedule—the scene was set. Mags' class-act buddy Nate, who I didn't even notice come in, operated boom for our audio guy, Michael, who crouched with the Zoom H4 recorder in his hand.

Our little comedy skit about three museum docents arguing over the true story behind an artifact was ready. One docent thinks the artifact is a piece of modern art, one thinks it's a fragment of an Egyptian canopic jar, and one—Cole's character—insists it's a hollowed-out mammoth fossil. In the end, a random museum guest walks up and throws away their soda in it. Kinda funny. Ten-page script, lots of dialogue, and one location. Easy. We'd planned on splitting filming into two days with more union-supported break times, but Elliot and I needed to run a tight ship to collapse it and keep my one-day promise to Cole. Later we'd snag some B-roll somehow to sell that it was in a huge, national museum. That'd be more interesting.

I was so focused adjusting Camera Two a centimeter to obey the rule of thirds, I hadn't noticed that our middle-aged actress had arrived and was smiling Hollywood-white teeth in conversation with Elliot. To my right, another actor, a hysterical five-foot-five Indian American college student, was cracking up with Mags. They wore the identical business-casual museum docent attire KC had scored. I checked the time on the camera screen: 9:07.

My throat went dry.

I rose from the camera and looked at the doorway.

Cole Stone walked in. Everything lost focus in my sight but him, the background telephoto. His almost-black beard was evenly trimmed, his head nearly grazed the top of the door frame. A lanyard was attached to his black work pants and jingled with his car keys. He looked around the room, size and aloofness out of place like an American tourist in Beijing, a wolf in a modern art gallery. His white shirt and black leather belt combo gave him a car-dealership salesman appearance, and his walk was more of a sloppy swagger, as if he never quite got used to his muscle and height.

Suddenly, I wanted to blend into the equipment. I probably sort of did already.

"Just in the nick of time, as usual," Elliot joked, coming over to Cole. Man, Elliot was really pulling my weight today with meet-and-greets. The two shook hands in a boyish, exaggerated way.

Cole cocked a smile and crossed his arms. Although he was standing, I noticed how he continued to rock side to side on his feet. Always moving.

Then his eyes fell on me. He continued to sway side to side.

I didn't have time for emotional vertigo or Kelly Clarkson's "A Moment Like This" to play in the background of my head. He looked away fast and just kept smiling like nothing was up.

Nothing was *up,* I reminded myself. What Mags hypothetically would have scolded to me was right. He was probably just being coy.

I had to get over this. I didn't even want to *move.* I didn't want to move because then the wheelchair motor would click and tires would turn and the floor would squeak and suddenly everyone would remember. Everyone would remember what I can never forget.

"All right, let's get shit done," I said. And moved. I homed in on the work and the other friends who were pretty used to me. In the four years we'd known each other, I'd only accidentally run over their feet, like, five times collectively. So their blanket of consistent acceptance made it easier to block it out and not look too hard at Cole.

Elliot and I waved our actors in place. I glanced at the highlighted scene on the script Elliot handed to me. KC was on Camera Two diagonal to us. Mags was slating (*"Take one."*). Audio called rolling.

I watched Cole. The two actors surrounding him seemed relaxed, into it. Cole was drumming his stocky fingers against the wall, mouthing his lines super-fast.

Then he stopped and kept his head hung. Everything was dead silent. No one moved. They awaited my word.

"Action."

Elliot and I held our breaths.

We took at least fifteen takes of the same scene. Once the actors were too rushed. Once KC accidentally hit the camera with his elbow. Finally we switched positions and moved onto the next two pages of script. I sped to Camera Two with KC to set up the frame.

Through the digital feed, I watched the actors. Although they'd just been arguing on screen, they talked with each other at the wall next to the cannon exhibit, loose. The middle-aged woman was graceful with her hands crossed in front of her. The other kid—majorly talented, by the way—was reenacting some ridiculous story with hand gestures and flinches. Cole listened to both of them. He resumed that sensual swaying, hands in his black pockets. Something about the way he did that entranced me. Something about him enjoying all the physical freedoms I can't.

Cole's résumé at the audition listed that he was a theater kid, not film. Made sense. He could project to the back row and his silhouette alone was cast-able. Last year, I hadn't paid much attention to the magenta *Beauty and the Beast* fliers plastered around school. Now I could shoot myself. Cole had played the male lead, the Beast.

I could so see it.

"That good?" said KC. He had been adjusting the framing by a hair for thirty seconds now, and I cleared my throat.

"Yeah, yeah. Right there."

KC screwed the tripod tight and locked the camera. It trained on a high-definition, clean shot of Cole.

"Hey," I said. "Take a still for me."

"What?" said KC.

"Take a still of that for me. For the portfolio." There
was no portfolio. Do films have portfolios?

KC gave me a weird sideways glance. Hesitantly, he
raised his hand to the camera and captured a still.

By the end of the day, every stomach growled in the silence after *Rolling!* It took a full five hours without break,
but we wrapped the film. Michael loudly clunked away the
audio kits. KC began shoving all the furniture back to the
way it was before shooting. Cole was damp with sweat from
the lights.

"Anyone want dailies?" I said. Dailies were the play-
backs of the best takes we'd gotten that day.

Elliot came up to my right and sat in a plastic chair,
focused on the camera's little digital screen. Mags pressed
the volume up as much as possible, and our actress and the
college student actor pulled up two chairs as well.

Just when I wondered where Cole was, weight pressed
onto the metal back of my chair. The handlebars creaked.
Behind me, *right behind me,* tired breath escaped.

I froze. Something swooped through me. A charge, a
feeling I usually lock my bedroom door for.

Cole Stone was leaning on my wheelchair and watching the screen of the camera. He didn't ask, didn't speak.
Just breathed heavily. Wiped a hand across his mouth
once, I think. I could smell his virile perspiration.

The dailies blurred into dirty paintbrush water on the
screen to me. All I could do was count the beats of my
pulse.

Eventually everyone was clapping and standing, and
I guess we finished the clips. Cole released the weight on
my chair and straightened. I didn't move.

"Hey, man, can I get you to sign a release?" Elliot said
to Cole behind me. "The paper's in my briefcase."

"Sure," said Cole. "Let me just hit the bathroom."

When Cole was out of the room, I thawed and got the release signatures from our other actors. Smiled. Shook hands. Talked with the actress for a few minutes about her three middle-school kids.

A lanyard jingled at the door across the room, and I looked over quick.

Cole was pumping Elliot's arm and turning for the exit hallway.

God. God. *God,* he was leaving. I hadn't said goodbye, I hadn't planned *anything.* For all I knew, I would never see him again.

I gave the actress an apologetic pat on the arm and before I could think one more word, raced for Cole.

Elliot turned his head as I streaked by and tried to take the bend of the door on two wheels.

I was in the brick hallway. Fire exit plan framed on the right. Cork bulletin board on the left.

Cole walked towards the exit as nonchalantly as he had leaned upon me. He cocked his head to toss hair from his eyes and flipped the jingling lanyard into his thick hand.

"Cole!" I said.

Cole stopped and spun around. He looked at me.

My mouth was dry. I fumbled for breath.

Talk to me.

His expression didn't change.

Let's move in together.

Definitely nothing.

Suddenly, everything deflated in me with a gust of breath.

"Great job today," I said.

Cole pursed his lips and nodded. He ran the lanyard through his hands.

I nodded too, and then he waved and was walking away again. *Away.*

And I watched him leave. Just like that. The sound of the exit door closing was like a bullet in my ears.

Then the hall was silent. So . . . so silent. For some reason, the corners of my eyes prickled.

A square of magenta drew my attention to the left.

Last year's old, faded flier for *Beauty and the Beast* was thumbtacked to the community bulletin board. Slowly, I ripped it down. I dropped my head to it and stared. Felt its cool, worn texture in my fingers.

I thought of the play and us, in real life. Cole and me. Beast and Beauty.

I wondered who would be cast as whom.

With a few pumps, the technician lifted my back left wheel off the ground. Wrenches and drills hung on the plywood wall and skeletons of pieced-apart wheelchairs surrounded me, covered in tarps. The air smelled of oil and fresh rubber.

"What have you been *doing* to this thing?" the technician said. He knelt and pulled out a mini flashlight from his jumpsuit pocket. Inspecting the wheel.

"Is there still blood on it?"

"Very funny," said the technician, without humor. He

grunted as he thumped to his knees. "You wore off every groove."

Sounds about right. I take my chair off-roading plenty, into woods and over gravelly fields. I must have ground that wheel down to the bone. Mom had noticed and drove me here right after school the next day.

"Gonna have to replace the whole thing." He reached over and grabbed a screwdriver from the plastic bucket François held in his mouth for us. François seemed to twitch up an eyebrow as he watched the technician.

I scrolled Instagram absently on my phone as the technician began the replacement.

Elliot posted a selfie from the Laser Tag Planet he worked at. He was throwing up a peace sign next to two super-serious ten-or-so-year-old boys aiming their plastic guns at his phone. I liked it.

My phone buzzed.

MAGS

What?

I forgot I'd texted her last night with just *Dude* after the shoot. I was gonna tell her about Cole leaning up on me, but she hadn't replied until now. I regretted sending the text. Some part of me still didn't want to tell her. The other part was dying to.

MAEVE

Nothing :) I just missed you.

MAGS

Nah what is it

MAEVE

Really lol

My chair shook as the technician yanked out something in the back. I jumped.

MAGS

You saw me like ten hours ago. What were you going to say seriously

Screw it.

MAEVE

Okay. Did you see what Cole did?

MAGS

Did he ask you out?

Ugh. Maybe this was why I always regretted starting these conversations with Mags. Here I am ready to gush about something probably platonic and totally vague and maybe .0001 percent sexual. She just cut to the chase of what a guy *should* do if he were really into me. And I always have to say no.

MAEVE

No

MAGS

He's kind of in another world.

I sighed and set the phone in my lap. Maybe that was a good place to stop replying.

"So once I'm done with this . . . you want me to make your headrest removable? Why?" said the technician, still tinkering back there. He might even find some leftover equipment from the audio duffel bag.

"Because headrests look extra handicapped," I said.

"But you need it."

"The aforementioned reason invalidates your argument."

Buzz.

> MAGS
>
> So what did he do?

I pursed my lips, grateful she at least followed up.

> MAEVE
>
> I know this is weird to make a big deal of but it kind of is. Did you see him lean up on my chair?

The drill roared out all other sounds as I waited for her reply.

> MAGS
>
> Yeah. So?

I stared at her question.

Cole leaned on me. So?

Many disabled people I knew were No Touch Nazis

when it came to anyone laying a *finger* on their medical equipment. Not me.

So how did I explain? How did I say that someone choosing to lean their weight on the metal that dehumanizes me humanizes it? That not asking my permission, just *doing it,* showed unquestioning acceptance? Maybe even intimacy?

I typed out a paragraph explaining this in the simplest and most poetic way I could. The cursor on the screen blinked as I reread my explanation three times.

I held the backspace button and watched it all swipe away.

Finally the technician rose and wiped his forehead with a soiled rag. I flipped on my joystick. The wheelchair illuminated to life.

Out in the lobby, Mom sat on the couch and typed on her iPad with a stylus, dressed in a business suit. Her edgy, sterling-silver earrings dangled. They looked like miniatures of the modern sculptures you'd find on the lawns of graphic design companies.

I'd heard her arguing before with the vendors in the office about insurance, about making sure I was serviced with only the best, highest-grade equipment. Mom taught me to fight, to not let anyone run me over. Easy enough. I glanced down at my new wheel.

I did the running over.

"How'd it go back there?"

I turned to the new voice. A man in his late thirties came out of the vendor office. He was in a power wheelchair just like mine.

Ralph, the office manager. Tattoos inked up his neck and his blond hair was long and scraggly. Even when it was hot out, he wore a running jacket. I wondered if it might be his way of giving his frame an extra boost of bulk to mask frailty. A tray was attached in front of his chair and held a laptop covered in Comic Con stickers that he could work on while he rolled around the office.

I'll be honest. Usually being around others with disabilities makes me uncomfortable. Those annual conventions where we all gather for *support* and *research* I don't touch with a 20,000-foot pole. That shit is just a giant-sized mirror I can't cringe hard enough away from.

But this guy was all right.

"It went fine," I said.

He smiled at me. "No more headrest, huh?"

"*Removable*," Mom corrected, rising from the couch. "We can put it back when needed. I don't like the idea of your head just falling back whenever." She studied me with concern.

"It looks better this way," I said. Ralph didn't have one either.

Mom rolled her eyes, but it was loving. A little. "It's not about what's attractive, Maeve. It's about what can support you."

Ralph just stared at me and tried hard not to smile. He was familiar with our mother/daughter push and pull.

"All right, let's get out of here," Mom said briskly, gathering her things and heading for the door.

"Don't forget the headrest." Ralph nodded to the wheelchair appendage I'd "accidentally" forgotten on the lobby coffee table; Mom was already out the door.

I grabbed it and stuffed it under my arm. Gave him two middle fingers before twirling for the door. He threw his head back and laughed, turning away as well.

It was late afternoon by the time we got home. Mom

stripped François of his work uniform, and he instantly romped for his squeaky toy and shook it with a puppyish growl. Stuffing flew everywhere. "I'll make you some tea, darling," Mom said, as she clopped into the kitchen with her high heels.

She handed me the hot mug a few minutes later along with a plate of cookies I couldn't really balance that well and then ran her fingers through my hair to tug loose a knot. I winced and smiled at once—such was Mom. The mug she chose for me was my favorite—the one with lilies. Mom never forgets the things that make me feel cared for.

I went to my room with some Western civ homework to knock out.

Spotify played in my earbuds while I labelled a map of the Central and Allied Powers in World War I. My first-floor bedroom was littered with so much crap, I could barely call it handicapped accessible. But at my little white desk with one lamp in the corner, I was safe to park.

Every now and then, I looked up from my homework. The faded *Beauty and the Beast* flier sat on my desk. I can't remember if I smiled or frowned.

I thought of Cole sitting at that long table on stage as the violins began "Beauty and the Beast." Some lucky sophomore in a beautiful yellow dress and perfect makeup with a graceful, normal figure took his hand then.

She led him onto the floor, and he stumbled in a way that was half acting and half who he was. He took her in his hands and drew in breath. The whole audience gazed at his beastly masculinity and perfectly trimmed beard and wetted hair and gold buttons that shined in the spotlight. Whatever low-budget ornaments they'd put on him to make him seem like a monster probably appeared natural.

And then he started to dance.

I can't imagine he didn't ask Belle out after that play. Everyone on that production probably thought they were adorable together. Fitting.

In that hall before he left me, I had only stared at him. I didn't say anything that was rising in my chest. But he didn't either. He was gone.

In the space of an hour, I'd finished my homework and gotten three texts that I'd worked hard to resist. Now, filing the map away in my folder and tugging out my earbuds, I could open them.

None were from Cole Stone.

MAGS

> But you're not going to see him again right? The film's done, so

I was sure Mags would just drop the Cole topic after I'd not replied. If I was done trying to discuss him before, I *definitely* was now. Yes, Mags. I won't see him again.

The next was from KC. I blinked in surprise. He was a rare texter.

KC

> Hey.

I shot something back fast.

MAEVE

> KC :)

Before I could even open the third text, KC replied.

KC

What're you up to?

MAEVE

Just finished some homework.
Fighting off the post-shoot
depression.

KC

Speaking of post-shoot, is Elliot
editing the footage?

MAEVE

I think so. Why?

For some reason, I was hooked to this conversation, eyes
lingering on the screen.

KC

Idk.

All right, interest faded. But another came in before I
could tap the back arrow.

KC

Thought maybe I could help him.
Also I have a question

Glued again.

MAEVE

Shoot.

KC

Have you heard of You Before Anyone?

I huffed in amusement.

MAEVE

The new movie about that Scottish dude in a wheelchair who falls in love with his careatekr?

I left the typo because I was excited to get the text out.

KC

I think so.

MAEVE

What about it?

My brow was lowered. Was he going to ask what my #OwnVoices opinion on it was, like if I thought it looked offensive? Had the film critic/blogger the class followed published a review? Maybe he wanted to know if he should read the book first.

KC

We should go see it

My heart softened.

MAEVE

Yeah? :)

KC

Yeah I'd like to see it with you

MAEVE

With me specifically?

I'm not sure what was I getting at.

KC

I mean yeah

I considered that for a minute.

MAEVE

Why?

There was a pause before he replied.

KC

It'd be cool to have your perspective and it looks good?

Oh. Okay, yeah. That makes sense. I didn't push it further because KC seemed to feel interrogated. Those unnecessary question marks always sounded a little passive-aggressive to me.

I told him I was in and he said he'd pick a showtime for Friday, four days from now.

Finally, I saw who the third text was from.

ELLIOT

%#@!!!DAMMIT.

I hammered out a reply.

MAEVE

WHAT?!

His wait time was an excruciating eight minutes.

ELLIOT

THAT !%#@DAMN CANNON BALL

MAEVE

Holy dicksauce did that lady complain about it being in the shot?

I was smiling now. Conversations with Elliot were always stress-free and amazing.

ELLIOT

No, but she's probably RIGHT

Hmm.

MAEVE

What do you mean?

There was a long-ish pause. He must have been writing an explanation.

Yup, the phone buzzed twice as it broke up his long message.

ELLIOT

I set up in the media lab at school and have been making sweet love to this damn film for three hours and I'm editing and all the sudden Nate 1.0 comes in (1/2)

(the creepy Nate from Video I, not Mags' asshole boy-friend, Nate 2.0)

ELLIOT

and he's breathing over my shoulder (remember how he did that?) and he goes "ha it's maeve." (2/2)

MAEVE

Oh my god what does he mean "it's maeve"

ELLIOT

You're in the damn shot. With the camera.

MAEVE

What?? How??

ELLIOT

THE DAMN CANNONBALL GLASS REFLECTED YOU.

MAEVE

NO.

ELLIOT

I KNOW.

I know it's bad, but I laughed. I leaned back in my chair and forgot my headrest had been removed. I jerked straight before my head could fall back. If it did, I wouldn't have had the strength the drag it back up.

MAEVE

So how many shots am I in?
Not the whole thing, right?

ELLIOT

No, but we'll have to do some
reshoots. I tried everything I could
to photoshop you out but it's
pretty obvious.

MAEVE

Okay, so . . . what parts do we
need to retake?

If I'd had any idea what Elliot would say next, my heart would have been pounding. Instead, when I read his reply, it just stopped.

ELLIOT

Pretty much everything with Cole.

7

The tickets spurted out of the machine behind the counter. A red-vested theater cashier ripped them out. He reached over for my cash before he'd give up the tickets.

I struggled to lift my shaking arm.

Out of nowhere, a male wrist shunted my hand aside and held out a credit card to the cashier. I jumped and looked over.

KC stepped closer and forced his credit card at the cashier. My wad of cash didn't stand a chance.

"*Hey*," I said, with playful anger. "Abuse of the disabled."

KC shook his head and smiled. He shoved his hands in the pockets of his plaid shirt and waited for the card to be swiped. Reluctantly, I folded my cash back into my wallet.

"Thank you. I was trying to surprise-buy *yours*, you know."

"I know." His skin was a little redder than I remembered, and his wispy brown hair neatly combed. The Thor amulet still rested at his chest. I ran my knuckles affectionately along his shirt sleeve. The flannel was fuzzy.

We wheeled towards Theater Five and looked around at the cinema. Popcorn makers rumbled like a rainstorm. The smell of oily "butter" made the air salty and thick. I left tire tracks on the freshly mopped tile—the yellow WET FLOOR signs were still out.

Down the hall, we passed my favorite part of the theater— the movie posters. All framed and illuminated with bulbs around the rim, I loved how they bared action and romance and thrill in one big augmented collage and the director's name was a little line of text at the bottom. It was like the directors were saying: *This. I am all of this.* Every little part of life, real and unreal. I wanted to be all of that and more.

KC was unusually quiet.

"Are you, like, nervous for this movie?" I joked and beamed at him.

"Nah," he said. A pause. "How did the editing turn out for Elliot?"

"Not good." I groaned. But it was fake. Not a single part of me was upset that we had to reshoot Cole. I'd been bouncing on giddiness as if a blow-up castle were in my stomach. "We gotta retake the scenes with Cole because I'm *explicitly* reflected in the glass."

"Hmm." KC blinked. "How'd we miss that?"

"Right?" I said.

We approached Theater Five, the banner *You Before Anyone* over the door. KC jogged forward on his light gait and pulled open the door for me. I dove inside the darkness.

The temperature dropped, AC blowing in nice and cool. I could hear KC's gentle pat on the carpet behind me as we ascended the ramp to the main theater level.

Previews splashed light on us. The theater was packed with silhouettes tossing back popcorn, rustling their hands in the bag, and slurping barrels of Coke.

I tensed up as I scanned the two handicapped accessible seats.

My heart twisted. I frowned. As usual, two able-bodied people were already sitting there. A normal couple on a date, I assumed, maybe nineteen or twenty. They were lounged back, dressed casually. He had his hand on her wrist. She was wearing long lashes.

God, I hated having to be the dick.

I acted quick before KC had time to get uncomfortable or ask if I should get a manager or even say, *Wanna go to another movie?*

I neared the couple and dropped my voice to a whisper. "Hey, I'm so sorry," I said to them.

"Oh!" the guy said. "Sorry." He rose quickly and the girl followed a beat after. I felt a little womanly hostility from her, like I'd interrupted a super-special moment. KC lingered in the background.

This happened a lot. I mean, can you blame them? These are nice seats. Private. How often do disabled people come and take the fun out of disabled spots?

I remember texting Mags about this once after Elliot and I went to see the new Star Wars.

MAEVE

So these guys were in my seat again.

MAGS

Ugh

MAEVE

Yeah. I felt really bad. They had to take, like, the first row.

MAGS

Why do you feel bad?

MAEVE

Because I'd be annoyed if I were them.

MAGS

That's stupid

MAEVE

No it's not. I told Elliot I'd be right back and I bought them both sodas.

MAGS

Maeve you don't need to buy people things because they were in the handicapped seats and you're handicapped so you made them move.

She tried to be as thorough as possible.

MAEVE

Well I did. But yeah maybe it was a little insensitive of them.

MAGS

It was.

If I were able-bodied, I can't say I wouldn't try the same thing. Get away with whatever you can. I still don't know where I . . . stand . . . on the issue.

KC nestled into the seat next to my open space. He didn't look over or say anything more.

It struck me how sweet this was. No one else saw the trailer for this movie and thought of me. He'd invited me out of nowhere.

Then the theater trembled as a preview for *Exploding Car Chase 3* came on, and I couldn't help but study KC's eyes reflecting the blue light of the screen. He was more youthful than I gave him credit for. His face kinder. His sideburns came down just a little farther than average, reminding me of a John Lennon vibe. I had a weird urge to reach out and lay a hand on him.

Something on the screen amused him because he huffed and crossed his arms before I could do it. I guessed I should have paid more sociable attention to what we were watching.

When I turned my head, I saw him.

I could never mistake that lope. That beard. The way he seemed to fill even a large auditorium. Green THE FOLLOWING PREVIEW . . . light backlit him and threw shadows on all the rough grooves of his face and hair. His rugged hand held an energy drink can.

Cole Stone was walking to his theater seat.

Alone?

"Cole!" someone whisper-hissed behind him. He spun and smiled as two kids joined him. One dude and another girl Cole's age. I squeezed my armrest.

Please don't walk over here.

Wait, why? What was I ashamed of?

Cole ambled to their row of seats ahead of me and sat. His tallness, even seated, made him the most protruding silhouette of the row. That girl with him didn't make contact, and he didn't do anything chivalrous like stand until she was seated. Were they together or not? What the hell was the situation? Siblings? Friends with *Amazing* Benefits?

I tuned back into the regular trailer-judgment-chatter

in the theater. The *Idiotic* or *We should go to that* and the relaxed laughter. When the screen sank to black and stayed there, the crowd hushed. Nothing but the sound of hands digging into popcorn.

Suddenly, with Cole now in the room, I coiled. I noticed that viewers in the rising seats on either side were glancing sideways at me. No doubt taking in the endearing irony of someone like me seeing a movie like this, representing *my people*. I shuddered.

I felt like a lobster in the tank. Rubber bands trapped my muscles. So I swallowed and tried to jiggle my foot on the footrest. Tried to shift. Tried to tell my body to move and make it listen. I wanted to feel like less of a lobster.

"You okay?" said KC. I turned to him; he was staring at me.

I flashed a smile. "Yes."

He lingered his gaze on me for a moment. I didn't think he believed me, but he turned back to the screen and the movie played.

I tried to get lost in the story, or at least the heathery colors of Scotland that reminded me of an enormous plaid quilt lain out over rolling hills. It seemed the film would be just as I anticipated from the trailer: the paralyzed rich man in a motorized wheelchair donned his dashing Scottish accent, and he and his American caretaker fell in love. They spun themselves into one awkward situation after the next, most of which I could relate to: getting wheels stuck in mud, having to address the uncomfortable "Who's gonna come into the loo with me?"

I should have been paying attention. Instead, I studied the back of Cole's head the whole time. How did he feel about this? When they portrayed the man limply being dressed, Cole didn't move. When the heavy wheelchair needed to be pushed up a steep hill, he scratched his forearm. When the man confessed his self-hate because of the disability, Cole didn't raise a hand to dry his eyes. He just watched.

Just. Watched.

Maybe he was dragged here by the other two, and the only thing on his mind was getting some eight-fifty nachos at the counter. Or worse, maybe he *was* thinking of me, with pity and that helpless feeling like you just can't wrap your mind around something.

My God, you deserve to be loved like everyone else. But it can't be from me.

I was used to men thinking, saying, or showing that on their faces.

A buzz in my lap made me jump, and I drew my phone out quickly. Heart hammering, for some reason thinking it could be Cole. The caller ID said QUINTEN. I silenced the phone and shoved it back beneath my seat belt. KC wasn't fazed.

For the remainder of the film, I leaned back and tried to rest.

Spoiler Alert: The disabled Scottish man decided life in a wheelchair was not worth living, so he performed medically assisted suicide to the heartbreak of his attendant-slash-lover.

When the brightening theater lights lifted everyone from their seats, tear-streamed faces shined. People gathered their things and sniffled, speaking in soft, awed voices. No one looked at me; almost as if they couldn't.

My arms were crossed. I stared hard at the rolling credits and even forgot Cole was there. My brow was low.

"Huh."

I looked over at the voice. KC was still too. His mouth was twisted in a contemplative pucker. "Well, that's not what I expected," he said. But he didn't sound too traumatized for my sake. I appreciated this.

"It was all right," I said. "The guy was kinda hot."

"Oh, yeah," said KC. "If I were gay, I'd be into him." His confidence assured me he wasn't.

KC rose and stretched. He scratched the back of his neck.

A line of people in the row ahead of me stood. Cole was with them, and my panic returned like tennis balls shelling me in a junior batting range.

"Hey," I said to KC, "I'm gonna go get some water."

I wanted to leave *fast*, before Cole could see me. Why was I so embarrassed? Maybe because of the hundreds of films I see a year, Cole had to catch me in *this* one. As if this is what I was all about.

"Yeah," said KC, "I'm kinda thirsty too. This place reeks of salt." He tossed his head for me to follow and headed for the exit on the opposite side Cole was walking up.

I made to move with KC, cursing the loud click of my wheelchair motor coming to life.

Too loud.

To my right, in the hallway leading to the exit, Cole stopped. My throat jammed. Heat flushed to my face and maybe some other places too.

For one moment, across the theater, Cole turned and his gaze locked with mine. He blinked, eyes a little confused, as if not sure it was me.

An instant later his buddies came up to him and patted his broad shoulder. They herded him on.

I took in breath and swiveled towards KC, who was tying his shoe. He popped back up.

"Let's roll," he said.

Outside the theater, I threw away the ticket stub and receipt.

I noticed KC slide his into his pocket.

Streetlights and headlights blurred out my window as Dad cruised me home. I held onto the cold metal ramp to my right as we merged onto a new highway. Staring at my phone and the missed call from Quinten. Maybe he had Wheelchair Charity Woman news. More likely he was lonely.

"So . . . did you like the movie?" Dad glanced into the rearview mirror.

"It was okay."

The highway hummed beneath the car wheels.

"Just okay?"

I sighed and clicked my phone to darkness. "Dad, if you were a burden on your family, would you want to die?"

Dad was silent as he held the wheel.

"Like, for your family," I emphasized. "Like, to free them."

"Maybe, if I felt I was really hurting quality of life for you and Mom."

My stomach knotted. "Yeah," I said.

"Why?"

"I don't know," I said. I didn't feel like admitting to myself that the movie might have bothered me.

"What made you think of that?"

I hesitated. "Maybe I could make the same argument. About myself."

Dad's brows pulled together. Concern clouded his face. I think he gripped the wheel harder because his knuckles whitened.

"Don't."

"What?" I said.

"You're not a burden."

I gazed out the window and tried to breathe against the weight in my chest.

"What would you do?" I said. A pause. "What would you do if I decided to commit assisted suicide, in a hospital bed and everything?"

Dad's answer was immediate. It even shook. "Then I'd be lying down with you."

"To comfort me?"

"No," said Dad. "Taking the same injection."

A bell jingled as Elliot pushed open the glass door and walked down the front steps of the parlor. He held two ice cream cones in his hands, and they dripped onto the red brick stairs. He lowered to take a seat.

Half a week had passed since the theater with KC. Right now I was supposed to be in physical therapy, but I might have lied to get out of it and hang outside in the sun in downtown Fredericksburg. Soon it'd be too cold. We'd invited KC to join us, but he said he "didn't feel like it," which was a little too honest. On Facebook, he didn't seem to be doing anything but posting a bunch of photos of ink-and-pen skulls he must have drawn. Like, three in a row, followed by a "Three Things You'll Abandon When You Realize Life is Shit" Reddit article. Trying not to be too judgy about how others use social media, I clicked on it out of curiosity. The three things were music, grades, and friends. I'd be more worried, but he also tagged me in one positive post about the movie last night. There was even a smiley face. Friends, apparently, were not abandoned.

I turned and sighed as Elliot sank his mouth into the cone and held out mine.

Bunch of kids our age laughed and hopped up the steps of the country-style, white-painted ice cream parlor. The boys had Lacoste shirts and khaki shorts. Probably the University of Mary Washington crowd. We didn't see many folks from the community college here, but that's probably where I'd end up going. Elliot, Mags, and almost everyone from our class were already getting together applications to the film program at UCLA and had been stapling together their reels. The deadline was November thirtieth. Elliot had been saving money since freshman year. It made my heart sink whenever they talked about it. Mom and Dad wanted me close to home, for my care and everything. Which meant no frat parties. No big games. No freedom. They would glance at each other sadly when I mentioned that during our talks at dinner.

They want everything for me, including college. I just wasn't sure what I wanted myself. *Living* and *staying alive* are sometimes an either-or for me.

Elliot shook the cone—I still hadn't taken it.

"Thanks," I said, grabbing it off him with my strong arm. "How much?"

"Nuh-uh," said Elliot, eyes closed, as if I were interrupting a special moment with his ice cream.

"Seriously," I said.

"Shh."

"Will you stop giving that cone a blowjob and tell me how much I owe you?"

"Mags bought yours."

Mags shoved the glass door open just then and flumped down the steps with her hands in her hoodie pockets. She flipped some of her long, artificially red hair away and sat on the step next to Elliot, drawing up her knees.

What the hell do people keep buying me shit for? Do they write it off on their taxes?

Still, I guess my heart sort of warmed at the way Mags paid it no mind and stared ahead at the crosswalk. Before I could thank-chastise her, she said, "I feel like I know those boys in there."

"The preppy ones?" I said.

"Yeah."

"How?"

"I don't know. I think one of them asked me out one time and wouldn't stop messaging me, so I blocked him."

"That's annoying," said Elliot. "Damn, this is good!" He grunted and crunched into the waffle part.

Mags gnawed her lip, and I watched her for a beat before another wave of young kids skipped up the steps. When they opened the door, laughter and music poured out.

For some reason, this little ice cream lounge became the hottest place in Fredericksburg overnight. Half the guys I knew made this their first date go-to, and Elliot once recommended it be our hangout for film planning before he remembered it had no handicapped accessible entrance.

In this day and age, it pissed me off that the extra buck

wasn't spent to even hammer a ramp into a sketchy back entrance for me. It wouldn't bother me so much if it didn't seem to pop up a middle finger at me with the swarms of kids going in and having a great time. Usually in a situation like this, I'd write a letter and toss in the Americans with Disabilities Act threat as if I totally knew what ADA policies were. Lately I've been using it a little generously.

Sorry, Maeve, we only serve Pepsi products.

The fuck do you mean you only serve Pepsi products? Do you want me to get the ADA involved?

I worried I'd just be making bitter noise now. I wanted Mags and Elliot to think I was blasé about it all.

I finally ran my tongue along the ice cream. It was thick and creamy. François chose that moment to sit nicely in front of me and stare.

"Wow," said Elliot. "I'm getting another."

"Go for it," said Mags, still gazing absently ahead.

Elliot pushed himself up and brushed off his black shirt. "Hey, Maeve. You text Cole yet for the reshoot?"

Mags jerked her eyes towards me. I swallowed.

"No," I said. "I'll do that."

"Cool. Be right back." He jogged up the steps.

"So . . . that's exciting," said Mags when the door closed behind Elliot. I felt heat rush to my cheeks.

"I'm kind of excited," I admitted. Of course I was. I'd be shooting Cole Stone.

"Yeah," said Mags. "You deserve to be excited."

Pause.

"I don't know. I really feel something with him."

"Like what?" said Mags.

Like he might be different.

"I don't know," I said.

"Yeah."

Despite what it seemed, Mags and I had just exchanged a lot of information. She knew I meant a lot more than *I don't know,* and I sure as hell knew she was processing bigger things than *Yeah.* Her reservation and too-understanding tone were indicators of her caution. Mags always tried to protect me from my own eagerness.

"How was your movie with KC?"

"It was good." I beamed. "I love KC."

"What'd you guys talk about?"

"Not much, we mainly watched the movie. But he was really cute for taking me."

"Hmm . . ." Mags picked at her shoelace. I let my hand drop so François could lap my melting cone with his tongue, his brown eyes popping wide.

"Do you want to have dinner with me and my dad Thursday?" said Mags, out of the blue. She pawed a hand over François' fluffy head. "He's in town from North Carolina."

Mags' dad was an awesome veterinarian and used to treat François for free before he divorced and moved to Charlotte. He gave Mags a cat named Zipper before he left. François is weirdly afraid of her, and KC is allergic, so we don't go over there too often.

"Oh my God," I said. "I'd love to, but I have this stupid appointment."

"What stupid appointment?"

"My annual physical with the specialist at Hopkins."

Mom had reminded me of this appointment once a week since she scheduled it three months ago. She'd had to practically threaten the secretaries with lawsuits and bad press releases to squeeze me in. This doctor was the only specialist on the East Coast primarily focusing on my disease, and once a year had to perform mad-professor measurements on me.

"No problem," said Mags, but she seemed disappointed.

The bell tinkled again, and Elliot came down with a milkshake this time. "They have a literal mechanical bull in there," he said.

"Ha." Mags snorted.

"It's lit." Elliot bit his straw.

I tried not to look up into the glass door.

"Hey," said Elliot. "You want me to carry you in there to see?"

A smile twisted my lips. I loved when men offered that. You know. It was one of the perks. Usually I'd be tempted to take it up.

But maybe I'd save that for Cole. Maybe he'd want to take me here.

"I'm putting the tissue box *right* next to the bed, Maeve," said Mom. "Look."

"Uh-huh," I said, scratching the dried tomato soup off my shirt from my place at the TV dinner tray in the living room. Dad took my bowl away, half of its contents spilled on my front.

"You're not looking," said Mom.

I groaned and pivoted to look through my first-floor bedroom door and watch her place the box of tissues on the shelf next to my bed. "I want you to see it in case Daddy asks where it is."

Mom is a more vital organ in my body than at least three arteries and a kidney. Nobody can keep me alive like her, and nobody would slaughter a longship full of Vikings to do so like her if she had to. I love her and would hide behind her leg as she mercilessly burned peasant strongholds. It was her strength (and a lot of PTA meetings) that got me off the short bus and onto a regular bus in elementary school, and her strength that made a lot of other dreams come true. But she had this habit of being *so* super-practical about providing for my needs that she sometimes forgot when they were kind of sensitive.

My disease affects *every* muscle in my body, and that includes the minuscule ones in my mouth and jaw that slacken even worse when I sleep. Slack, atrophied mouth during sleep means I pretty much need floaties to keep me from drowning in drool. It is one of the many side effects I am less than proud of.

"Thanks, Mom," I said.

"No problem. And don't forget—"

"Appointment Thursday, got it."

"Right."

I wheeled into my room and gave her a wry smile, prepared to close the door.

"And I bought you fresh sheets," she said. "With lilies on them." Mom remembered my favorite flower. My heart softened.

"Goodnight, honey," said Mom. She kissed me. Then she hurried out with one hand scrolling on her BlackBerry.

I closed the door, and it clicked.

That sound of confirmed privacy usually made me buzz with lust and tugged me towards some websites with a shitload of pop-ups. But I had a much better mission tonight.

I ambled to my desk and pulled out my phone.

Sent Cole a text.

MAEVE

Hey

There's the ambiguous *hey*. The tentative head poking into the door with no inflection or punctuation whatsoever. The "I want to talk to you but I'm not sure where we're at so your response will totally determine the mood of our conversation" *hey*.

Cole didn't reply right away, so I handled some other business. I replied to Fred, my OMF pen pal. It'd been embarrassingly long since I'd written back, and I knew that made him sad. I opened a new email thread—I think the last thing he'd asked was if I'd had any boy action and if he'd need to pull out his shotgun.

I'll be honest, I wrote, action is few and far between.

More like nonexistent.

But I'm into this one guy.

I told him a little bit about Cole.

I think I'm going to ask him out soon. So to answer your question, I'd load the shotgun but not cock it yet. How's the farm doing?

It was short, but I fired it off.

Replying to this OMF made me remember my other elderly friend. I scrolled to my voicemail and pulled up the new one, in bold, from Quinten.

My arm trembled lifting the cell phone up to my ear.

"Maeve . . . it's Quinten." His voice seemed so much frailer and squeakier on the phone. I had to really press the phone hard against my ear to hear him. "That woman came by again today. I asked the front desk about her. They gave me this website."

He read aloud a website address slowly, and I scrambled to copy it onto an old English Composition I packet on my desk.

"I don't have a computer, so no idea what it's about. Thought it might be sound evidence to report, though. Keep me posted. Over and out."

I huffed a laugh. I loved that Quinten still managed humor.

Just as I was about to type in the website address, my phone vibrated.

COLE STONE

Hey :)

Smiley face! Yes! We were good to go.

I shifted and pounded out a text, grinning. The English packet even whisked to the ground past my footplate accidentally.

MAEVE

Did I see you at the theater?

I wanted to get that elephant out of the way.

COLE STONE

Haha yeah! I thought that was you
:)

Nothing more. Good. I didn't really want to ask him about the movie's content or have him bring it up. I gave him enough time to elaborate if he wanted to, though, because I didn't want it to look like I was running from it. When he didn't, I changed the subject.

MAEVE

You were awesome on set

COLE STONE

Oh yeah?

MAEVE

Yeah.

Period. Take that, Cole.

COLE STONE

You weren't bad yourself.

MAEVE

I'm not sure I was as focused
as I'd like to have been . . .

COLE STONE

Is that right :P

I shook my head and smirked at that emoji.

MAEVE

Yeah, something might have
been distracting me.

COLE STONE

Hmmmm.

My fingers drummed on the desk. I took a while to think
of a response to that, but he beat me to it.

COLE STONE

:P

I drew in a shaky breath.

MAEVE

Hey

I sent it separately.

MAEVE

I have a question.

COLE STONE

Shoot.

I clamped my jaw. My muscles tightened as I stared at my phone and the blinking text cursor.

I could ask him about the reshoot. Right now. Or I could ask him something else.

Minutes passed. The longer I waited, the more I bet Cole expected the latter.

I started to type. This is a total shot in the dark, but would you want to . . .

I stared.

And stared.

And stared.

My eyes watered from not blinking.

I erased the whole thing.

MAEVE

We screwed up some shots and need to retake a couple of your scenes. Would that be okay?

COLE STONE

Oh. Yeah, that's fine.

Disappointment filtered through me like sour duck sauce. Heat prickled around my fingers, and I pursed my lips. Rapidly, I texted Elliot.

MAEVE

Cole's in.

I threw my phone onto the bed before anyone could reply again.

After a few minutes, Dad carried me into bed and turned off the lights. My cell phone flashed a tiny blue light as it charged next to my pillow.

It buzzed.

I figured an all-caps reply of happiness from Elliot. Instead . . .

COLE STONE

Was that all you wanted to ask?

I breathed in incense. The heady scent made my head lift. It was a couple days later, November first. A Catholic day of obligation—aka, church on a weekday. All around me the congregation stood at their pews and sang, heads hung over the hymnals in their hands. I let mine flop to the side in my lap and stared ahead as the altar boy held the cross high. The white-and-gold robed priest marched up behind him.

Stained glass and mosaics decorated the walls, and I was parked halfway in the center aisle because the only handicapped space available was in the first row. I felt like too much of a sinner for that.

When the priest neared me, my hand inched for my joystick and instinctively switched it off. I knew what would probably happen.

The priest's eye caught mine, and he swerved from the parade.

Without warning or permission, he folded me into his vestments and bowed his head over me. The cool, smooth fabric pressed against my face, and suddenly the sound of the hymn muffled away so that all I heard were his robes and breathing.

I closed my eyes and let him hold me. It lasted longer than I remember.

When he pulled away and murmured a blessing, I realized from the corner of my eye that I was being watched.

I turned my head.

Mom and Dad stood in the pew beside me. Mom held a hymnal and Dad had his wrists crossed in front of him—he never sang. They looked over and down at me. They were too used to this for their eyes to be watering, but for some reason, today, pause was in them. Dad's eyes were a little deeper.

I leaned forward and stuffed my hymnal back into the pew.

Later, Dad revved the van engine and Mom flipped down the car mirror to pick something from her eye. Midday sun poured through the windows and made me squint as we pulled out of the church parking lot.

I used to wonder if priests gave me extra attention just for my parents. Like this weird belated thank-you card for not having an abortion and taking care of me. I'm older now and think maybe it really is for me. Maybe they're looking for a way to apologize.

I guess I let them try.

"If we don't hit traffic," said Mom, consulting her GPS, "we should get to Hopkins a half hour early."

"Perfect," said Dad.

"Are you serious?" Mom's voice was granite. "We should be there at *least* an hour early." She had wanted to skip Mass.

"We'll be fine." Dad turned onto the exit for the highway.

I poked in my earbuds, and soon no words matched their moving lips. I smiled as music began, and I gazed out the window.

Mags texted me a low-angle, orangey selfie of her and her dad. She was beaming and resting her head on his shoulder. His expression was confused and speculating the lens, mouth parted, as if he didn't think the camera would work. My lips pursed and I shook with the movement of the van as we picked up speed on the highway.

MAEVE

Love you guys :)

Soon vehicles were charging by as we headed north to Baltimore.

Mom tapped her window, and I paused my music.

"Look at that enormous plane. Think it's going into National? Look, Maeve."

I tried to duck low enough to see into the sky, but because of the position of my wheelchair, couldn't. "Can't," I said.

Dad glanced at Mom and then straight at the road before him. I studied him to see if he would follow Mom's gaze.

"That's got to be a double-decker." Mom shook her head.

Dad still didn't look.

He didn't because I couldn't.

I pushed the colorful wooden beads down the metal wire in the waiting room. Grimy toys littered the fire engine–themed carpet in the corner. I was way too old for this junk, but I couldn't think of one good reason not to fiddle. Well, besides Mom squirting gallons of hand sanitizer on me every ten minutes.

Dad was asleep on the waiting room chair with its back against the floor-to-ceiling window overlooking the Baltimore concrete jungle. Mom read a magazine called *Hope* dedicated to families of my disease. I could spot the page she was on from here. It was the beginning of the ten-page spread featured in every issue with pictures of smiling kids: kids in Halloween costumes, kids on field trips to petting zoos, kids who all died from the disease. Well, the severe side effects of it. Respiratory or malnutrition complications.

I returned to the bead maze and twirled four of the beads through wire loops. They clacked to the bottom satisfyingly.

"Johns Hopkins Neurology," the secretary at the desk kept repeating when she answered and transferred calls. A man in his sixties paced the waiting room, pushing the wheelchair of what I assumed was his adult son whose head lolled. White plastic braces clamped the son's legs and only childish striped socks covered his feet.

I glanced down at my Converse.

"Maeve." The office door had clicked open and a nurse

waited there. Mom stood and Dad jerked awake. "Dr. Clayton will see you now."

I watched to make sure my wheel didn't graze the nurse's foot as I squeezed through the door and down the hall. The tile screeched below my chair as I rounded the bend. Magazine covers framed on the wall boasted the "Top 100 Doctors," and over one door read GINGER T. DUKE MEMORIAL LAB. Mom and Dad followed behind.

We reached a room I was familiar with; I stopped and looked through the doorway. The smell of rubber and antiseptic wafted from it. A Yale diploma hung in Old English font. A muscle-skeleton model guarded the corner, and cabinets lined the wall. Tissue paper lay over a tan bed.

All around were newspaper clippings tacked to the drywall of children with musular dystrophy doing various things. Graduating college, going to camp. One was a front-page spread filled with balloons, chronicling a $300,000 fundraiser.

I was trying to understand what this all made me feel. I can't promise I was feeling anything. I just didn't let it in.

The sound of a wheeled office chair rumbled and Dr. Clayton's dress shoes squeaked as he rolled himself into view.

With a salt-and-pepper circle beard and hair, he was in his fifties, sturdy and athletic. His brown eyes twinkled as they set on me and crinkled up when he smiled. He clicked his pen and tucked it into his white coat pocket.

"Dr. Clayton," I said.

"Maeve. Welcome to my house of madness."

"Have you harvested the abnormal brain?" I moved in. "I'm ready for the procedure."

Dr. Clayton groaned and stood. "The staple gun will have to do."

I inclined my chin and hummed disapprovingly.

Mom and Dad filed in. Their smiles at our immediate banter were lukewarm. Dad sighed a little shakily and leaned on the wall.

"Mom, Dad," said Dr. Clayton. He extended his hand, and they shook it firmly. He sobered and slid on a pair of glasses that looked a lot like Dad's. Clicking his tongue, he consulted a clipboard and licked his finger to turn the page over. "Maeve is due for—"

"Pretty much all my shit," I said.

Dr. Clayton's eyebrows rose and he gave me a mischievous smirk like, *Are you allowed to say that in front of them?*

Mom and Dad still weren't laughing. Their expressions were tight and nearly identical. This place and all its medical features made them think of some of the things I couldn't today.

"Pretty much," Dr. Clayton confirmed. "I'll conduct measurements and compare them to last year's, then we'll talk about management." He looked at my parents. "Good plan?"

"Good plan," Dad said.

Dr. Clayton turned to me and spread his arms. "May I?"

I liked when Dr. Clayton lifted me. He swooped his arms under me and vaulted me into the air in them. I could always feel the level of duress my weight put a man under; either their arms shook and sagged, or they were firm and buzzing with energy. Dr. Clayton was somewhere in the middle, but closer to the latter, and for his age, this surprised me. I guess he was experienced at carrying his patients.

I hit the tan bed with an *ooph* and the tissue crackled. Like a maniacal tailor, Dr. Clayton ripped out a tape measure and the experiments began.

He tugged and pulled things, opened and closed them. He measured the flexibility of my stiff joints. The pressure of my frozen foot muscles. With an unapologetic shove, he flopped me over to my side and called out numbers that Mom scratched down with a pencil. She had the professional intensity of a nurse practitioner.

This is what Dr. Clayton did: He gathered my data, tallied up spreadsheets, and presented the information to the labs and research councils to figure out strategies for my best life in the long run with my brand of muscular dystrophy.

My head spun by the time I landed back in my chair.

Dr. Clayton flapped papers out of a folder and compared the measurements. Mom's and Dad's gazes were hooked on him in silence.

"She's plateauing, for the most part," he declared. He flipped a page to its back. "Some areas are tighter by a degree and a half, but that's normal rigor effects from the chair."

"Is there anything we should be doing?" said Mom. It was amazing to see her aggression and ferocity diminished in the specialist's presence.

"What do you mean?" Dr. Clayton retook his seat in the office chair.

"To prevent the decline of her muscles and mobility," Mom asserted. "More physical therapy?"

My heart clenched at the idea.

Dr. Clayton's lips pursed. He looked at me when he answered. "I don't want more therapy for Maeve. I want more life for her."

There was a silent pause. Dad kicked my rear wheel lovingly with his foot.

"I was reading in *Hope*," said Mom, "about a steroid

called Alvatraxon being introduced to improve muscle capacity. It's being hailed as a breakthrough treatment. How do I get Maeve on the trial? Can you recommend any—?"

"It's not effective." Dr. Clayton shook his head. "It's good press, but no more than a steroid you or I could take."

"Won't it help her? Even a little?" Some of Mom's insistence was returning. "She's lost the ability to raise her elbows."

Dr. Clayton studied me again, sort of like I wasn't there. "It would give her a boost, and she'd crash after. The effects prove short-term, but are almost counterproductive in the long run."

The juice ain't worth the squeeze. I glanced at Mom. Her determined expression was wavering. Dad put his arm around her shoulders.

"There's no treatment," said Dr. Clayton. "But I don't blame you for exploring everything." We had heard this before; his tone was a gentle reminder. Still I noted how *cure* wasn't even on the table. "You'd be my first call. This is my favorite patient, you know." He grinned.

"You say that to all your patients," I said.

"No." Dr. Clayton smiled. "I really don't."

Silence stretched. Dr. Clayton looked at everyone. We felt the pressure of our time being up; more patients outside waited to be seen. Just as Dad inhaled a breath to say the parting words, I spoke up.

"Mom, Dad," I said. "Could I have a few minutes alone with Dr. Clayton?"

Mom and Dad looked at each other. With slightly confused expressions, they nodded and slowly, wordlessly, slunk out of the room.

It seemed to take forever for the door to close.

Dr. Clayton turned and looked at me.

"If you don't ask the questions that I hope you do," he said, "I have some for you."

"What?" I blushed.

Dr. Clayton huffed and crossed his leg over the other. "What did you want to ask?"

I swallowed. The ticking of the wall clock seemed like dynamite in my ears all of the sudden.

Dr. Clayton cleared his throat playfully.

"All right," I said. "I just have some questions 'cause . . ." I sighed. "There's this guy."

Dr. Clayton's face broke into a wide grin. He raised his hand up to me for a high-five and his voice was hushed. "*Yes!*"

I laughed and high-fived him. What was going on?

"Yeah." I chuckled, feeling like my blood was bursting with confetti.

"That's what I hoped you'd say," Dr. Clayton replied. "What are you wondering about?"

"Well." I reddened deeper. "You know. I heard you rattle off about my stiffness and plateauing and everything, I just want to know, like . . . *How?* And *Can I?*"

"Of course you can," said Dr. Clayton. "Masturbation isn't a problem; that won't be either."

"What do I need to say so he won't hurt me?" I said.

And when I said *he,* did I speak in generalities? Or did that *he* have a name, a face? I imagined Cole's enormous height and muscle pushing over me. I should be terrified, but a swoop of excitement went through me instead. I want to be crushed.

"You need to let him know you can, and you want to," said Dr. Clayton. "It's understandable that he'll be hesitant."

"Right," I said.

"And you need to tell him that *this*"—Dr. Clayton grabbed

my forearm and hovered his hand over mine to showcase how badly my fingers shook—"is not because of him."

"Right," I said.

"You're going to have trouble with some positions, but you'll figure out what's fun."

"Are you feeling like a creepy old doctor yet?" I said.

"A little." Dr. Clayton was blushing now too. "I'm just so happy for you."

Sadness draped over me. His pride in me was premature; I didn't *have* any guy. There just *was* this guy. I wasn't going to break that to Dr. Clayton now, though.

There was a pause, and Dr. Clayton laid his hand on my arm. "You know your parents know what we're talking about right now."

I blinked, and my brow pinched. "They do?"

"Of course," said Dr. Clayton. "They worry about it too."

Ew. That kinda killed the buzz for me, but I was curious. "I'm pretty sure they're not thinking about that."

Dr. Clayton's lips formed a hard line. "They want that for you like they want everything else for you."

I hushed thoughtfully.

"Now, what else?"

"During," I said.

"Yes?"

"I worry about my breathing."

"You're going to literally die, aren't you?" said Dr. Clayton.

"No." I laughed, swatting his hand off my arm. "Seriously. My lungs are weaker, my chest. I'm worried something could, I don't know, happen."

Dr. Clayton's face twisted in surprised confusion. "That's your worry?"

"Isn't lung failure the number-one killer of our disease?"

"Have you felt greater resistance lately?" said Dr. Clayton.

"I don't know," I said. "It's hard for me to tell."

Dr. Clayton rose and pulled a stethoscope from his drawer. He placed a cool hand on my chest and the instrument between my shoulder blades.

"Deep breath."

I obeyed. He moved the stethoscope around. Again. Again.

Dr. Clayton was very silent when he pulled the stethoscope from his ears and walked around to me.

"Your lungs sound weak," he concurred, lowering back in the chair. "More seriously than I hoped. Why didn't you say so earlier?"

"Weak is normal for me. And it felt like cheating on my pulmonologist."

Dr. Clayton doesn't specialize in lungs, but he watched me and his jaw muscles shifted. "That does concern me a little."

I nodded; my movements felt fast and jerky.

"I want you to do some breathing exercises once a day."

"Okay," I said.

"And I want your parents to consider a BiPAP mask for you at night."

"God, no," I moaned. BiPAP masks were loud oxygen masks worn over the face at night, like Uncool Darth Vader. They were for the Google Images result kids who I say *Screw you, I'm stronger* to, not me.

"I know," said Dr. Clayton, "but it'll expand your lungs and allow more oxygen to fill them. They're not expanding far now. One bad cold into pneumonia, and we could have a serious problem on our hands, Maeve."

"Okay," I repeated.

"Stay away from crowds, use that hand sanitizer. And don't stay out in the cold. All right?"

"All right," I said.

"Good." He stood, uncoiling the stethoscope from his neck. "And Maeve?"

"Yeah?" I said.

He tousled my hair with his knuckles. "He's lucky."

I slammed the door to my bedroom with my chair so hard that night, it made a dent in the wood two inches wide.

Tens of random messages sprang onto my phone screen, and I swiped them away fast like bugs smeared on a windshield.

Adrenaline ripped through me, thoughts that had been building with every mile since I left the doctor's. My eyes darted around the phone. My heart clogged my throat like a water balloon, and before I could lose the nerve, I was there, staring at the text message thread.

I'd never replied to the last one.

MAEVE

Hey

The reply *hey* came instantly.

MAEVE

Shot in the dark

COLE STONE

Okay . . .

The phone wobbled in my grasp. *Hard.*
Dr. Clayton was wrong about why my hands shook.

MAEVE

> Would you want to have dinner sometime?

10

MAEVE

> MAGSMAGSMAGSMAGSMAGS

MAGS

> What

MAEVE

> MAGS MAGS MAGS MAGS

MAGS

> Whaaaat!

MAEVE

> MAGSSSSSMAGS!

MAGS

> Omg stop

MAEVE

MAAAAAAAGGGGGGSSSSSS
GEOJFDCMDPSL

MAGS

WHAT'S HAPPENING

MAEVE

COLE. I ASKED COLE DAMN
SHIT FUCKING STONE OUT

MAGS

You did not!

MAEVE

I SWEAR TO GOD

MAGS

And???

MAEVE

AND WHAT DO YOU THINK?

MAGS

No way. Show me.

MAEVE

MAGS!

MAGS

Screencaps!

Forget butterflies in my *stomach*. I was loading butterflies into a *cannon* and blasting them through every corner
of my body, wings and severed antennae flying everywhere.
I sent Mags the screenshots.

MAEVE

Would you want to have dinner
sometime?

Good four-minute space between texts.

COLE STONE

Sure haha. Sounds like fun

MAEVE

Just to be clear, that was me
asking you out. Like, on a date.

Another terrifying gap, three minutes this time.

COLE STONE

I figured :)

I grinned with pride at the screenshots loading into
Mags' text thread. They were like certificates of authen-
ticity.

MAGS

Stfu.

MAEVE

I KNOW.

MAGS

Maeve!! Yay!

MAEVE

I'm so happy, Mags. I can't even tell you. I have never been this happy in my life.

I know it was intense, but I sent it. I expected Mags to reply with a sock of reality. *That's awesome, but remember it's just a date.* Or *Play it cool.* Or *Don't get too attached yet.*

MAGS

I know bud

I smiled at her on the screen. When I blinked, my eyes were warm and wet.

MAGS

How did the convo end?

MAEVE

I just said "Awesome :) I'll hit you up tomorrow to schedule something."

MAGS

A little businessy

MAEVE

I know but I was trying to be completely blasé

MAGS

I feel like that's not all you said.

I blushed. Dammit, Mags. She knew me.

MAEVE

I mean I might have taken it a little further

MAGS

How far

What the hell. I screenshotted the last slice of Cole's text thread and sent it to her.

COLE STONE

Cool :) I suspected maybe you felt something . . .

MAEVE

Oh yeah?

COLE STONE

Yeah.

MAEVE

How obvious was it?

COLE STONE

What in particular?

MAEVE

How much I wanted you lol

COLE STONE

A little obvious :P

Mag's reply came in.

MAGS

Oh Maeve . . .

MAEVE

What? Lol

I knew what. I just wanted to hear her say it.

MAGS

You're so into him.

MAEVE

I am. I don't even know what to say now. "I want to have sex with you"?

There was a lapse before Mags responded. I went to my bookshelf and slammed back in the print script of Alfred Hitchcock's *Psycho*. Usually that'd be a struggle; tonight, I had the energy to punch it hard. The cell phone buzzed in my lap.

MAGS

Not yet

I laughed, because Mags wasn't even being sarcastic.

MAGS

You should show Elliot too!

MAEVE

You think?? :) Should I show
KC?

There was an even longer lapse this time. The thrill and
novelty must be wearing off a little.

MAGS

Nah just Elliot

Hmm. My mouth sagged.

MAEVE

Is KC mad at me?

MAGS

Noo. I just think Elliot would be
more excited

I puckered contemplatively but let it go and was smiling again soon enough, sending Elliot no prelude, just
screenshots of Cole accepting my date.

By that time, I'd taken enough deep breaths and screamed
out my excitement to Mags sufficiently that I thought I
could call Dad in to carry me to bed without him asking me
what's up.

"Be there in a minute." Dad's muffled voice called
through the closed door.

I rolled to my desk where my petite laptop perched—I'd
bought it because its 1.8 pounds were just about manageable.

As Dad's tired, thumping steps approached my room, I snapped the laptop closed. Just in case. I never remember what shit I have up on there. But I didn't think I'd need it now anyway. I laughed once more, to no one. To me.

God. This was *happiness*. Happiness that could really exist for me.

I glanced at my phone.

ELLIOT

Eyyyyyyyy!!!

Dad knocked and opened the bedroom door. I loved that he knocked.

He lifted me into his arms and set me on the mattress.

Thump!

Someone dropped a pile of books at the table to my right the next day after school, and François lifted his head off his paws. A new stuffed giraffe toy was in his mouth—I'd treated him, for doing absolutely nothing, in the pet supply store a few buildings down. Now it was my turn: the specialty bookshop.

Late afternoon sun poured through the store's front windows; a brick courtyard with a splash fountain—the kind with just holes in the ground that little kids run around in—was outside. The fountain shot up like a geyser and misted down at that moment, raking sparkles through the air. It was totally erotic.

"It's okay, François," I cooed. François looked over at me with raised eyebrows, if dogs even had eyebrows. His mouth was lopsided with the stuffed giraffe filling it. I couldn't help but shake my head. God, he was cute.

The smell of old paper and loose cloth covers almost neutralized in my nose by now, I'd been waiting here so long. Pages flapping and books shuffling off the shelf and creaking open gave the ambiance a nice hush. This shopping center was only a few miles away from the community college campus, so you'd think it'd be affordable for, like, broke college kids. Instead it stocked weird antique tomes asking $800 and rows and rows of intense fantasy role-playing games. A gaming club was in the corner now, members drawing a tape measure over an intricate board and rattling sixteen-sided dice in a plastic tube.

But this store also stocked the things *I* needed. Film and theater scripts.

I'd studied the greats in here: Hitchcock, Spielberg, Tarantino, Fincher, Nolan, Francis Lawrence . . . I wasn't a Shyamalan fan. I know they didn't always write their scripts, but I'd read them and remember how they shot it and try to picture how they'd riled their actors up to deliver that line or this emotion.

One of the clerks had been looking in the back now for fifteen minutes for a special script I'd requested.

The truth was, I had a plan to produce this script. To direct it.

To cast Cole in it.

I sighed and pulled out my phone. It was on silent in here, so that meant I had to check it three times as often for messages.

There continued to be nothing.

In another hour, I'd text Cole to iron out the details of our date. I hadn't wanted to seem overeager by texting before now. But this silence—from *everyone*—was a little unnerving.

Then I remembered I had unfinished business. May as

well, to kill time. I pulled out the website Quinten had given me for Wheelchair Charity Woman.

It took a few spins of the arrows on my phone to load the web page, and I rubbed my temple with the tips of my fingers, unable to apply much more pressure.

Finally, some pictures loaded on the screen, then the website name, then the tabs.

In elegant, cutesy font, the web page title spread across my phone: *Caring Hands Camp.*

I groaned so roughly the gamers glanced over at me. I already knew what shit I was in for with that title. My thumb flicked the screen to scroll down.

There were blocks of writing authored by Wheelchair Charity Woman herself, starting with a brief biography of her career in social work and nonprofits on Long Island. It said she started the camp for a "darling" girl with muscular dystrophy named Ginger T. Whatever, and I clicked on the link to her photo but the link was broken. Then the content segued into the camp here in Fredericksburg, held four times a year, dedicated to special needs kids. My bitterness twisted and writhed into *maybe* empathy as I read about the adapted activities available: horseback riding, boating on the Rappahannock, even a prom night. On Wednesdays they had something called a *petting party* that honestly sounded right up my alley until I clicked on it and saw photos of wheelchair users in a circle petting rabbits on their laps.

But they looked happy. More high-resolution photos popped up of smiling handicapped children and laughing counselors outdoors.

Fine.

I sighed.

But why was Wheelchair Charity Woman at the retirement home too? Why did she maybe commit a felony by maybe stealing François?

A text window slid down the top of my phone like the map a teacher rolls down over the blackboard.

KC

Hey

I smiled at KC but x-ed it out. I'd have to respond to that after the investigation.

All over the camp's site were buttons to donate. There was even one of those thermometer-looking fundraiser bars on the side of the screen, showing the financial goal of the camp, which was $65,000. Right now, it was filled in with blue to about $17,000.

A highlighted line of text was beneath the chart, clickable. It read: *Why should you donate?*

I clicked it. A new page loaded.

We keep camper registration and boarding fees low enough for all campers to attend, but the freedom, happiness, and experiences Caring Hands Camp provides aren't possible without your generous donation.

Why is Caring Hands Camp so important to our campers? Imagine the constant struggles our campers face in the outside world: rejection, exclusion, and misunderstanding. Caring Hands Camp provides a refuge from that reality, if only for a few weeks out of the year.

I rolled my eyes and slumped my chin into my hand, scrolling down more.

The page's accompanying image loaded onto my screen. Then I choked. My eyes popped wide.

I recognized that building, those steps. The ice cream sign in the window.

And guess who sat stranded at the bottom of those stairs, looking forlornly up into the ice cream parlor, framed as the epitome of rejection, exclusion, and misunderstanding?

Me.

I flipped out a cuss word so loud the gamers in the corner jumped and the dice skipped off the edge and across the floor.

She must have stalked me there! She's fucking after me!

François was next to me in the photo, and Mags. Elliot hadn't walked out yet with his second milkshake.

My mouth dangled open and I tried to shake my head but I'm not sure if I did.

What the hell does she think she's doing? What's so special about me, besides the obvious? I can't have my picture plastered on this pathetic Caring Whatever Magical Wheelchair Place. Who the hell do I call about protesting it? The ADA SWAT team? The only emergency number I had in my phone was Elliot's phone sex number, and that was by accident.

"Maeve?"

I looked up, still numb. The young clerk with round black gauges in his ears and a white nametag had returned. Kinda hipster, but it worked for me. Although he raised an eyebrow at my outcry, he didn't reprimand me.

Instead, he pushed a heavy script across the table at me.

"Is this what you were looking for?"

I clicked off my phone screen and looked down at the script. Then I swallowed, because it was.

Beauty and the Beast.

11

I gripped the cap of the perfume bottle later that night and tried to twist. My hand wouldn't lock on it; the slick plastic cap kept sliding through my palm. I grunted and tried again. The muscles in my wrist, fingers, and arms shook as I pressed against it in a stalemate. Finally, I puffed a curse and relaxed.

I lifted the perfume and glared at it.

Buzz!

COLE STONE

Hey what's the address again

My heart hammered. I shot him the address and nothing more. Trying to be cool.

COLE STONE

Ok

Was that *okay* okay? Like, he didn't spell it out entirely. Did that mean he's dreading this?

I set the perfume on the desk in my room and texted Mags.

MAEVE

I'm freaking out

Outside my bedroom door, I could hear Mom on the phone trying to get the insurance to pay for that BiPAP mask Dr. Clayton recommended. I'd been holed up in here for two hours now, getting ready. Cole and I were meeting tonight for dinner at one of those restaurants attached to the mall. He was driving almost forty minutes from work for this. For me.

And I couldn't open a damn perfume bottle for him.

MAGS

Don't! Just have fun!

MAEVE

I think I'm gonna throw up lol

MAGS

Why?

MAEVE

I don't know

MAGS

Maeve this is normal. Like, people date

Another text came in.

MAGS

You got this!

I grabbed the bottle and slammed it against the edge of the desk. The cap loosened.

MAEVE

I'm not normal people

The cap finally popped off with my last jerk. Now I had to squeeze the damn thing. It was like practice for a later hand job, if I got lucky.

MAGS

You're a person so you're normal?
Like I don't understand

I groaned.

MAEVE

Obviously some things are not
normal. And look at Cole. He's
like a 6 foot tower of sex.

MAGS

And you're a 4 foot tower of sex

MAEVE

I'm the size of a mailbox.

MAGS

Mailbox of sex.

I was smiling at least. I squeezed and shook the perfume bottle hard enough that some sweet-smelling liquid squirted out and trickled down my wrist. I tried not to imagine an accompanying masculine grunt in my head. The tips of my trembling fingers spread the perfume around me.

I glanced at the clock on my laptop, next to the *Beauty and the Beast* script on the desk. Mom or Dad agreed to drive me in ten minutes to meet "a friend," even though our reservation wasn't for another two hours. I wanted to be early.

Taking a deep breath, I tried to normalize my voice and expression as I exited my room.

Mom hung up the landline on the insurance company.

"Ready?" she said. "I'm taking you. Daddy's going to finish the lawn before it gets dark."

I remembered not to frown. Truthfully, I was sort of hoping for Dad to drive me, just in case Cole happened to intersect with us in the parking lot. Dad is usually a little less inquisitive about these things. But I was leaving early enough that I didn't intend for Cole to ever know I didn't get there alone.

"Yep," I said. "Ready."

"Are you taking François?"

Good question. I liked the cute cuddly advantage of a dog with me. But . . .

"I think I'll leave him home today."

François, curled in his dog bed by the window, lifted his head at me and perked his ears.

Really? he seemed to say. *Will you be all right?*

Yeah. My heart warmed. *I'll be with Cole.*

François rested his head back on his paws, but his eyes continued to stare up at me.

He didn't seem sure.

I waited outside the restaurant doorway, the indoor mall entrance, gazing at my phone because I'd look stupid and ridiculous just sitting there. Mom and I had made great time, so I had more than an hour to kill before Cole arrived.

That was about how I liked it. He didn't need to witness me rolling across the parking lot like some Walmart scooter heading in to buy more microwave burritos. I looked a lot more chill, a lot less in-your-face, already settled inside the building and waiting for him.

Mom had left, but not before piling a jacket over the back handles of my chair, because it was chilly. Normally, I'd fight it, but it got her to leave quicker.

I flicked through my Facebook newsfeed, and then my Google calendar. I had next Tuesday after school blocked off for a confrontation with Wheelchair Charity Woman . . .

Technically, I couldn't tell my parents about the whole Caring Hands Camp photo thing. They thought I was, you know, *studying* when it was taken in front of the ice cream parlor I ditched physical therapy for. But I'd popped open the camp's "Calendar" tab and saw Patricia was speaking at an Investors Club in Quinten's nursing home next Tuesday.

I'd be there. I'd get to the bottom of things and have Quinten threaten his former federal agent weight on her.

Should be good.

"Excuse me, miss?"

I looked up. A man in his thirties with neatly combed valedictorian hair and the just-came-out-last-week smartphone in his hand stopped beside me. He looked like the kind of guy my older sister would date, if I had an older sister. But I'd probably hit it too.

"Hey." I smiled.

He smiled back. "Do you need help?"

For some reason, everyone thinks I need help when I'm just sitting somewhere doing nothing.

"No, I'm fine," I assured. "Just waiting for a date."

Really, Maeve?

He laughed, not in an unkind way. "Nice. Well, you look great."

"I don't know about that." I smirked.

He just waved—"Good luck!"—and sauntered off, head hooked back down to his phone again. Just like that, gone into the current of the world and never to meet me again.

Hmm.

Maybe I did look all right. Maybe.

Nerves stretched through my stomach, and I tried to return to my phone, but I'd sort of run out of things to do on it.

The ambient noise of mall chatter soothed me. Beside me was the hostess podium and a bar area for those waiting for tables. An aquarium threw turquoise light onto the floor. It was the sort of restaurant that looked fancy and quiet but where you could order reasonably priced pasta dishes. A few steps rose to the greater dining area, but I'd reserved us a table in the smaller nook on the first floor—more privacy.

I kept swallowing, kept trying to distract my thoughts. He should be here any minute.

Then I felt heavy steps behind me. Something felt different about those steps. I glanced up from my phone and straightened.

He walked around me, a great white shark rounding in out of nowhere. Hands in his pockets. Cole Stone cocked his head and cracked something and stood in front of me. My heart pulsed through my whole body. I shoved my phone away.

"Hey." My voice was level and smooth.

"Sup." His, loud and deep. He swayed side to side on his feet the way he does. Affection flooded into me.

Was he . . . nervous?

He still wore his Verizon nametag and red collared shirt, but a black nylon jacket was over it, unzipped. His beard was the perfect length—I liked more than scruff. The lanyard with his car keys dangled as always from his belt. Polished black shoes. He'd raced from work to get here, I knew.

Now what did we say?

"Did you have a rough ride?" I asked.

"Not bad." He pivoted and looked around at the mall crowd, still swaying. I grazed my eyes along his strong forearms and the hair covering them. It was amazing that one second I was alone, the next, *he was here.* My words tripped on happiness.

"Thanks for coming so far."

"I've done worse."

He suddenly made eye contact with me. Gripping, intense contact. Then his eyes were off again.

I laughed politely. "Wanna head in?"

"Sure."

Well, now was the time. I had to make my damn chair move. Had to hear the motor click. But when I did, when my wheels turned, Cole didn't even look over. Did he hear? He walked next to me without casting his gaze my way.

"I heard this was a pretty good place," I said.

"Is it?" said Cole. He still didn't look at me.

"They have good reviews."

"Do they?"

I glanced at him. He was still absorbed in the new atmosphere, looking around.

The young hostess peered over the podium at us. Her gaze lingered on Cole as she shuffled laminated menus.

Once we were behind the table, I felt better. We both were sitting now. We both were stationary. Cole never took off his jacket.

He leaned on his elbows on the table and shook his knee. He wasn't talking much. I was extra nice to the waiter, trying to make a good impression, and ordered a water. Cole ordered a sweet tea. The waiter left.

It was just us.

There was nothing else to do. And I couldn't help it. I grinned at him. He kept his gaze on me, and a small smile rested on his mouth.

"You look really happy," said Cole. His voice was amused.

"Sorry," I said. "I might be."

"Maybe," said Cole.

"Sort of."

He just kept watching me, half smiling. God, I'd die under that gaze. Or under other things. "I like your hair too," he said. Um, repeat? Was that *chair*, or did he just compliment my actual looks?

"Chair or hair?" I blushed.

"Hair. But your chair is cool. You could put rockets behind it." He stared and shook his leg. I relished the chance to study him up close now. The silver necklace hanging onto his shirt swung forward as he leaned on the table. I could finally decipher it. It was a pendant indented with a wolf's paw print.

"So, is the union going to be on our case?" I said, opening the menu.

"Union?" said Cole.

"You know, director dating her actor . . ."

"Nah." He said it a little too loudly and looked down at his menu.

The waiter thumped our glasses down. I took one look at mine, tall and coated with condensation, and knew I'd never be able to lift it. Usually I'd ask for one of those tiny plastic kids' cups to use, the ones decorated with, like, humanoid meatballs playing tennis with a random dolphin in a chef's hat. I couldn't do that now.

The waiter asked if we were ready to order and I realized this was all happening way too quickly. Cole held out his menu, knee still rocking fast beneath the table. "Brick-oven pizza," he said. "Thanks."

And I ordered something safe: grilled chicken whatever.

When we were alone again, I paused. Cleared my throat. "Maybe you'll get invited into SAG after our little Seefeldt High School student project," I said.

"I dunno, their membership fee is kinda high."

"Save up!"

"No!" said Cole. I was smiling now, because the more he bantered, the faster his knee rocked back and forth. "I already gave ten bucks to a homeless guy at a gas station tonight."

"Coooole," I said.

Cole shrugged. "He looked like he could use it."

I studied him with a trickle of warmth, but he was reading the back of an olive oil bottle.

"So how was work? What'd you do today?" I said. Dammit! Boring questions!

"Nothing," said Cole. "No one came in. I just watched YouTube videos."

"What do you like to watch?" I said. "Any, uh, things you can't find on YouTube?" There we go. That felt more like me.

"I watch magic tricks."

I laughed. "What?"

"Yeah, I'm trying to learn a bunch."

"Why?" This made me even happier.

He shrugged again. A pause. "Wanna see?"

"Fuck yes." I cleared the salt and parmesan from the table center, and he whipped out—!!!—a card deck from his pants pocket.

I homed in on his hands, his rough, male fingers. They held out a handful of cards. "Pick one."

My arm struggled to make it that far. He rose a little off his seat to meet my reach. I picked one—the four of diamonds—and put it back. Then he dealt several rows of cards.

Cole was super-focused on his tricks, like a mathematician counting cards in blackjack. He showed me three tricks, then asked if I wanted to see the first again. I, of course, said yes. Usually he could pick out the card I chose. I didn't tell him when he didn't.

"All right," I said, "I got one." I motioned for him to gather the deck and hand it over.

I only knew one. Dad taught me it a long time ago on a cruise for my grandparents' fiftieth anniversary. Naturally The Admiral (Mom's dad) wanted to spend it at sea. I remembered being annoyed I couldn't figure the trick out. A few years later, I'd looked it up and performed it on Dad—I hoped I could recall how it worked now.

Cole leveled his gaze on my hands as I conducted a similar introduction, inviting him to choose a card.

The trick's mechanics came back to me as I went along. I shuffled them around and laid out five cards on the table between us. Then I hovered my left, stronger hand over one.

"All right. I'm about to show you your card," I said. "Lay your hand on mine, and I'll say the magic word."

My hand shook in the air. Cole raised his eyes to me. Skepticism touched his expression—he knew I didn't need him to touch me. I looked back at him and blood rushed to my face.

Slowly, he reached out his hand.

"Brick-oven pizza?"

We jumped. The waiter was next to us, holding our plates on a black platter on his shoulder. He looked winded.

Cole leaned back. He cleared his throat, and the waiter set his meal in front of him, and then mine before me. I brushed Cole's cards aside, still facedown, so they wouldn't be stuck under our plates.

We caught eyes one more time and then lifted our silverware.

The restaurant got busier, later-evening dates of older, career couples passed our table. They wore a lot more expensive and sparkly things than a Verizon uniform and twenty-five-dollar perfume. Cole and I ate in more elongated silence. Our game was forgotten as we made small talk about our families and school. I told him about how I wanted to get a film degree at UCLA, but that I'd probably end up here at the community college. He said he'd probably end up at the community college too since he meandered without a plan for a year since his high school graduation. But after a pause, he added that he'd want his UCLA degree in theater if he were lucky enough to go.

When the bill came, he offered to pay. I insisted we split it. I left my water at the table, untouched. Cole hadn't noticed.

"So," said Cole, as we strolled out of the restaurant and into the mall entrance. The exit to the parking lot was to our left. "I'm excited to reshoot."

"Yeah?" I said. I looked up at him. God, I loved how far I had to tilt my head.

"Yeah." He gazed down at me. A long silence followed.

"Cole," I said.

"Yeah?"

Oh God. Why did I begin that sentence?

"Can I . . ." I swallowed. Too late to go back now. "Can I give you a hug?"

Oh God, why! My heart was practically fucking my throat. Heat swelled through my skin, but it was done. And I wanted it.

Cole hesitated. His eyes hung on me as he continued to look down. The beat was excruciating.

And then I heard the material of his black jacket shift. Cole lowered.

I shut my eyes when he enclosed me. Suddenly the sounds of the world around me sucked away. All I could hear was his breath leave him and his cool jacket ruffle. His prickly beard tickled my neck. He smelled male.

Cole drew back to his full height. Over in a flash. He took my breath with him.

I cleared my throat and recovered. "You gonna be okay riding home?" I said. Then I did something I wasn't even aware I was capable of doing. I nudged my wheelchair just softly enough to prod the side of his leg gently. An affectionate bump.

"I'll be fine," he boomed. Goose bumps shivered over my body at his voice. He zipped up his jacket. "How about you?"

"My ride will be here any minute," I said. "Then I'll head out."

Cole studied me. "Do you have a jacket?"

"Yeah, but I don't need it," I said.

"It's cold."

"Really," I said. "It's—"

He spotted my jacket hanging off my chair and tore it off the handles. Then he threw it over my shoulders.

"I had fun." He poked my temple with his finger and then swaggered off for the exit, striding in that careless, slightly duck-footed way I loved. His phone was already alight in his hand as he pushed open the exit door and walked towards the parking lot.

It was night outside, and cold air wafted in. I vibrated with giddiness and excitement and relief—I'd survived my first date—and watched him swing into his beat-up Lexus sedan in the parking lot and rev the engine. It had super-black windows and a random stripe of spray paint three shades darker grey than the body color, used to cover up some dents.

He drove off a little jerkily, wobbling as he took the right at the curb and disappeared from my view.

That's when the elation dissipated. That's when disappointment soaked through my blood.

It was over. Just as fast as he had showed up next to me, he was gone.

The jacket Cole had draped me with burdened me, and he didn't set it on too comfortably. But I cherished its warmth and closed my eyes next to a mall trash can near the exit doorway. Because I'd timed everything safely, I had a good forty minutes until Mom or Dad would arrive to pick me up.

Images and everything we'd said flashed through my mind as I waited, as I almost dozed.

I woke to the buzz of my phone.

COLE STONE

So what was my card?

12

Wet hair stuck to my shoulders and goose bumps covered me a few hours after seeing Cole. I lay on a rough towel on my bed and shivered. Dad had showered and dressed me in nightclothes. He'd lathered clean-smelling lotions onto me and hosed me off with the shower nozzle, shouting demands that I tell him where the bomb is.

We call it waterboarding.

Now, as I rested on my back, Dad said he'd be right in with a surprise. I hoped it had nothing to do with my date earlier. Like, a "Congratulations! We're So Relieved" card from my parents or something.

Speaking of, I didn't reply to Cole. I was trying to be cool and play the game. Make him wonder about his card. Mags would proud.

But Elliot's Facebook profile picture popped up on my screen and I tapped it.

ELLIOT

Hey I talked to Cole, he's good to shoot on Tuesday. And I left Museum Lady a voicemail.

MAEVE

What the actual hell would this class do without us

ELLIOT

Nothing

He followed it with a thumbs-up emoji. I smirked.

Then I jumped. Orchestral music blasted through my closed bedroom door. I looked over just as Dad opened it.

"The Imperial March" from Star Wars blared from his phone in one hand. In the other, he held up high a clear, gas mask–looking piece of equipment.

"Oh God," I said.

"Darth Maeve," said Dad. Mom cut by him with the

big boxy generator it was meant to hook up to and started fixing it to the outlet near my bed.

"Already?" I moaned. "Why didn't the insurance deny us?" I despaired.

"Because they're terrified of me," said Mom with pride. "I went and picked it up from the medical supplier after I dropped you off."

"Dammit," I mumbled.

Dad's hands lovingly closed in on my face with the mask. He pulled it over me. Its snug rim covered my mouth and nose, and I closed my eyes. The machine flicked on and began to buzz. Oxygen pushed in.

I could hear Mom rise and, I assume, survey the equipment with Dad. They were quiet.

More machine. More metal.

What if Cole saw me?

I didn't open my eyes. I kept them closed long enough for Mom and Dad to leave.

I think Dad's fingers almost touched my hair before he went.

The next day, I headed to the shopping center across the street from the mall. Earlier there, I'd picked up a new bandanna for François and bought myself some mysterious bohemian takeout—sauerkraut with social anxiety and sausages that couldn't quite get it up. Cars seemed to patiently and affectionately pause on the busy highway for me to wheel past.

Between a Chinese restaurant with granite dragons flanking the entrance and a family-owned dry cleaner's with dying lucky bamboo in the window, Laser Tag Planet's neon Mars logo glowed.

I'd told Elliot I'd come hang out with him at his job one of these days, and I wanted to stay out tonight anyway. Otherwise I'd be wishing I were back in that restaurant with Cole, watching my water imprint a ring of moisture on the table.

Since I had to wait for a random person walking by to open the door for me, I checked my phone to appear occupied and relaxed. That was when I remembered I'd received a text from KC just saying *Hey*. I'd never replied to it, so I shot one back now before I forgot again.

MAEVE

> KC!! :) I'm so sorry I missed this. How's it going?

I shoved my phone away fast as I spotted a stranger approaching with a dry-cleaning bag over her arm. I gestured towards the door, trying to get the request out rapidly and clearly before the woman assumed, like they sometimes do, that I'm begging.

She opened the door for me cheerfully, and I slipped in. No François toted along. I gave him the day off from school. The lasers would distress him.

The room inside was dark except for neon-green lights on the walls and screens playing a reel of overemphasized laser tag fun in the corners. Black couches for waiting by the front desk. A birthday party room to the right with a cheap table and wall decals of balloons and aliens. Some bored-looking adults held paper cups and talked.

"All right, bro, have fun!" said Elliot from behind the front desk. He ripped out a receipt and handed a ten-year-old boy the plastic laser gun. The boy bolted off through the double doors to the arena as his mother stuffed her wallet back into her enormous purse and headed for the birthday room.

I rolled up.

"Maeeeeeve!" said Elliot. He stepped around the desk and swung a huge hand at mine and clasped it. "You came!"

"Of course," I said. "I told you I want to chill with you at work."

"D'aw . . ." Elliot shook his shoulders bashfully. I cast my eyes around the room in the following pause and nodded.

"Cool place," I said.

"It's fun," said Elliot. "Lots of kids." He sighed. I knew he made pennies here, but his spirit glimmered like Waterford in everything he did. Then he jolted towards me. *"WAIT, HOW WAS YOUR DATE?!"*

I blushed and lowered my head, trying not to smile too big. "It was great."

"Awww! What'd you do?"

"Just . . . ate. Talked."

"Hey, that's how it starts." He crossed his arms.

I nodded. Maybe.

Actually, no. Not maybe. I can't get hopeful.

Elliot must have read something on my face, even in the dimness.

"What?" he said.

"I don't know," I replied. "I'm worried."

"About what?"

I rescanned the evidence in my head to make sure it really was there.

Cole was jittery. He didn't talk deeply. He hesitated when I asked to hug him.

And man, did he drive off fast.

But he also looked at me hard. He poked my temple. Don't these mean things too?

"I guess just because I'm the one who asked *him* out, you know?" I said. "He could have said yes to be polite. Like, gotten the dinner over with and did his good deed for the day."

"Son." Elliot gave me a face. "Take it from a guy. He wouldn't have said yes if he didn't want to."

"Maybe," I said.

"It's okay if he's figuring it out as he goes," said Elliot. "Sometimes it takes me a few dates to figure out where I'm at. He prolly spent all night thinking about you."

I nodded, half to get him to stop talking about this and half because I love Elliot. In no part because I agreed with him.

"Anyway." Elliot punched my arm. "Guess what?"

"What?"

"I'm off work!"

My mouth dropped. "What, no! Dammit!"

Elliot laughed. "You know what we should do?"

I gulped. He held up a finger at me and walked around to the desk again.

I stared as he returned with two laser guns in his hands.

Flashing red and green lights rotated around the arena like a disco ball, but everything else was black. Speakers snarled and rumbled out alien monster noises, and every now and then the shooting engines of a spaceship soared across the audio loop.

Bells rang everywhere. Kids clacked their triggers a million times and screamed and ran around.

Glitter clung to the fabric of my shirt from some of the weird obstacles and glimmered when I got "hit" with the laser. I lifted the plastic yellow gun in my hand and pulled the softer-than-cream trigger. A laser beamed out of my gun and struck one of the reflective target pads attached to a little girl's jacket as she dove for cover. I laughed.

Elliot ran across the center of the room, clicking his trigger over and over and laughing too. Three little kids, who must be regulars, jumped out of their cover and tackled him to the ground.

I rolled out of my own cover to his rescue. He reached out a hand and grabbed the handle of my wheelchair, pulling himself free. He hopped onto the back of me.

"Retreat!" he hollered. "Retreat!"

I charged off with him.

Back in cover, he stumbled off me and panted, wiping sweat from his cheek. "I need to get those bastards back." He shook his head. "Cover me."

I thumped him, and he ran off for revenge.

My arm was tiring from hoisting the gun around. My breath quickening. I needed to take a break.

At some point during my extraterrestrial adventure, I'd felt a vibration on my cell and assumed it was KC responding. So I tucked the gun onto my footplate and pulled out my phone.

My eyebrows rose.

COLE STONE

Hey

I replied immediately.

MAEVE

Hey :)

Safe.
He buzzed in alarmingly fast.

COLE STONE

I had a good time last night :)

MAEVE

You did? :)

There was a brief pause.

COLE STONE

You're over 18 right?

Oh shit. I suppressed my smile.

MAEVE

Yeah . . .

I sent a second text that I probably—no, definitely—would regret.

MAEVE

You asking for reasons I'd like?

A pause.

COLE STONE

Pretty sure.

My heart skipped. My head was tilted, gaze glued to the screen.

MAEVE

Oh yeah?

COLE STONE

Yeah

He was hot right now, wasn't he? Like, was that what was happening? I darted my eyes around to make sure no kids were nearby, and for some reason, something told me to strike while the iron burned.

MAEVE

You know I want you.

COLE STONE

Oh I know you do.

Behind me, the alien-monster audio loop screamed with hatching eggs and goo glopping from the yolk.

MAEVE

I'm not sure you know how badly.

COLE STONE

Show me how badly.

Why did my fingers know what to type so fast?

MAEVE

You first.

All the little pterodactyl alien babies in the audio loop hatched and squealed tinny little squeals and scrambled in every which direction while I waited, hooked to the screen.

A text came in from **COLE STONE**. But instead of the message preview, the screen just said: (No subject)

That meant the text was nothing but a photo.

My thumb shook over the message icon. Heat pulsed down my body and I fumbled my breath.

I pressed the button and opened the photo from Cole.

Blood shot through my veins like the laser beams from the gun. Every muscle tightened, and my lower body went weak.

The word breathed from my mouth.

"*Fuck.*"

13

I used the side of my chair to bang open the wide teal door of the handicapped bathroom stall. Kinda . . . winded. No one else was in the restroom, and brown paper towels lay wet at the sink countertops. It smelled like chlorine.

I'd headed here immediately after Cole's text, making sure my phone was on vibrate and telling Elliot I needed to check on something "medical."

I guess you could say that's what I was doing.

Shakily, I took one last glance at the picture Cole sent and the following few exchanges of me cussing my satisfaction at him (that escalated kinda fast) and him asking me how much I liked it anyway, then *where* I'd like it, and finally a few lines of him saying I made him *hot af*.

Our fun ended when he suddenly became more calm and monosyllabic in his reply texts. I can assume he'd wrapped up . . . whatever had started him off in that mood, and he said he thought he heard his mom get back from grocery shopping downstairs.

As crazed and pumped with adrenaline as I was, I still cringed when I caught myself in the mirror above the sinks. There was no way I was able to return any photos to Cole when I could barely look at me. Before I was eighteen— and, you know, sexting was legit illegal and I wasn't about that life—I had a good excuse not to engage. Now my only excuse was cold, all-encompassing fear. But even my reflection I could shove away and feel an ecstatic buzz. He said I was sexy. He said I made him hot—I mean, I saw the proof. But did he mean that? Was he really thinking of me?

I stopped next to the silver hand dryer, not quite ready to leave. I took a deep breath and pulled up Mags' text thread. That's when I started grinning again.

MAEVE

MAGS.

MAEVE

MAGS RIGHT NOW I NEED
YOU RIGHT NOW

MAGS

I'm eating rice

MAEVE

I GOT MY FIRST DICK PIC!!!!!
HUG ME!

MAGS

> What position

I laughed out loud at her blasé reaction. Not a single damn thing could bring me down right now.

MAEVE

> NO! HUG MEEEEE!!!

MAGS

> Nah what type

What *type*? How many fucking types of dick pics are there?

MAGS

> Bird's eye, standing up, lying down, holding it, straight on

Is there literally a National Audubon Society Field Guide to this?

MAEVE

> Standing up!

MAGS

> What angle

MAEVE

> HOW ARE YOU SO FUCKING EXPERIENCED OMG

MAGS

Nooo this is not experience this is like OKCupid gone wrong for me. But really what angle

MAEVE

Uh, bird's eye standing up

MAGS

Ah nice one

MAEVE

I just . . . talked dirty to him and told him how much I want it. I think I got him off. I legitimately think I got Cole Stone off. I was so worried he was just POLITE hanging out with me, you know? Like he was just pitying me or something. But after this, like . . .

MAGS

Did he get *you* off? Cuz that's what I care about. He seems kinda one-sided. Like he just kinda absorbs your attention

MAEVE

Yeah, obviously. I mean . . . are you okay? You seem a little flat about this

MAGS

I'm sorry! I don't mean to be. I'm
just looking out for you

Half of my mouth lifted.

MAEVE

I know.

There was a knock on the bathroom door.

"Maeve, you better not be dead in some stall." That was Elliot.

"I'm fine," I said. "Help me out."

He opened the door and scanned me. Everything seemed to be in order.

"Get over here," said Elliot.

I rolled over to him, and his large, warm hand fell on my shoulder as I passed. He muttered, "Giving me a damn heart attack."

The next day was Sunday, and that morning François trotted along the gravel dog park with a rubber Frisbee in his mouth. A parade of mutts all different shades of mud followed him, going after the toy. I sat with a few other disconnected owners at the bench. Stains and puddles darkened the gravel all around; whether water or slobber or projectile canine vomit, none of us could tell. But it smelled, and the wire fences were rusty.

François had the time of his life. He wriggled with a dorky swagger and his shoulders seemed high. The mutts tried to jump on him for the Frisbee.

His sweet little uniform hung off a hook on my wheelchair, along with his leash. I let him play off-duty now. The exercise was good for him, and the sociability. He was awkward with other dogs because of his isolated training to be my companion, and now it was like a kid's first time on the schoolyard blacktop.

"God." The middle-aged, corpulent woman next to me bristled in her tan coat. "It's getting too cold already."

The air was crisp, yeah. Late autumn in Virginia seemed to put a thick piece of glass in the sky. The sun was there, sure, and bright, but no heat penetrated.

"Which one is yours?" I said.

"The little Chihuahua-terrier mix." She pointed. I followed her finger to a feisty little triangle-eared dog swiping François' Frisbee from his mouth at just that moment. François didn't fight back—I didn't think he understood aggression. He instead rolled on his back immediately and spread his legs, tilting his head in a bashful way. Damn, did he learn this stuff from me?

"What a cutie," I said. Not trying to be one of those overprotective owners that would demand the mutt return the toy and apologize.

"Yeah. I'm gonna get out his sweater soon." The woman shuddered visibly and crossed her arms.

"So you do the whole dressing-them-up thing?" I said with more humor than accusation.

"Oh, I'll have to this winter." She pursed her chapped lips gleaming with skin-tone lip gloss. "Farmer's Almanac says it'll be the coldest winter in a decade."

"Damn," I said. "Are those things accurate?"

François leapt up and scurried away with flattened ears as a bigger, boxier dog nipped him.

"My husband is a master gardener," said the woman. "He swears by them."

"Hmm." I nodded.

Was it weird that every single time someone casually said the word *husband,* I felt envy? I looked at my phone. There was a message, but not from Cole. I guess he needed to process where we're at too.

KC

Hey yeah np. I got busy too.

I didn't want to keep playing text-tag with KC. I replied right away.

MAEVE

How're things? :)

"So, yours is the white-golden one?" the woman said. "He's licking the inside of that Doberman's ear now."

"Yeah," I replied without looking up from my screen. "He's a little slutty."

The woman's face pinched up.

KC

Not bad. I was wondering if you wanted to hang out again.

MAEVE

Absolutely :) What did you have in mind? And are you coming to the reshoot with Cole?

KC

Well I don't care what we do, I just wanted to hang with you

I noticed he ignored the reshoot question. If he was going to skip the reshoot, I'd lie for him to Mr. Billings. KC and I had been friends way long enough.

> **MAEVE**
> I got nothing going on tomorrow!

That would really be my only day to chill. The day after was my "appointment" to sabotage Wheelchair Charity Woman at Quinten's nursing home (I'd already left him a voicemail to prepare him for the mission) and the day after that was the reshoot.

> **KC**
> Ok. You wanna go ice skating?

> **MAEVE**
> Oh my god yes. Is that even a thing?

> **KC**
> Yeah my old summer school roommate manages the rink at Greenbriar, he'll let you on.

> **MAEVE**
> This'll be freaking amazing

> **KC**
> Okay cool. Like 7:30

> **MAEVE**
> Perfect :) See you then bud

He didn't reply again.

When François' eyes were a little pink and his mouth never closed to hide his tongue, I knew he was dehydrated and called him in. With weak, floppy hands, I redressed him in his uniform. Many think that at this gesture, François would transform into a machine of militaristic duty. He did settle down, but his eyes darted for the mutts and he pulled a little towards them as we made our way to the gate. I waved goodbye to the woman on the bench.

Cold wind rustled through the trees in the distance, and like crashing waves, I knew it was only moments before the chill would bowl over me like uprush. As François and I mounted the sidewalk that would take me home, my teeth began to chatter.

A tickle spread in my chest.

14

The puffy green jacket I wore was stuffed into every corner of my chair the next night. Although light rayon and warm down, it burdened me. I struggled to keep my posture erect. Mom wouldn't drop me off at Greenbriar Towne Center without the coat zipped and tucked.

The shopping center was laid out with high-end department stores, restaurants, and wreaths hanging from lampposts. Buttery storefront light spilled onto the brick sidewalks. At the pinnacle of the center was the huge, white ice rink—

spherical bright bulbs illuminating it beneath an awning. Skaters drifted around it counterclockwise.

It was just past 7:30 p.m., and already dark. I moved forward and jostled over the bumpy brick terrain. If were being totally honest, I didn't always mind the bumps—especially with Cole to think about lately—but tonight they only made sitting straight under my coat harder.

I parked next to a steel kiosk where sugar-glazed almonds emitted a dizzying aroma. The man tending it wore brown gloves and a paperboy hat. When he exhaled, his breath was just slightly visible. I was at the corner of Williams Sonoma, where KC told me to meet him. No matter how dumb I might look just waiting here, I forced myself not to check my phone. Cole had gone totally AWOL after last night's sexting. I needed to stop checking for him and let him just . . . take his space, or do whatever he needed to do to reboot us.

And anyway, this would be great. Nerves filled my stomach a little; I hadn't ice skated in, like—

"Hey."

I jumped. KC was there. Quiet, gentle as always. Only a half a foot taller than me. He wore a plaid scarf, and his face was pink from the cold. His Mjolnir amulet still dangled far enough down to be seen. I eyed it and decided I kind of like this pagan, primitive-male-power vibe going on with men lately. Cole had that wolf paw print talisman dangling on a masculine silver chain too.

"How's it going?" said KC. He held a stained, beat-up pair of off-white ice skates. Sniffled.

I think he might have been wearing cologne, but there were way too many delicious food smells from the roasted nuts and restaurants to tell.

"Hey, you." I punched his arm playfully, and regretted

it when it took me a huge inhale to pull my arm back. KC looked down at the pathetically soft punch for a dry beat.

"Sorry . . . that was embarrassing," I said. Awkwardly sincere.

He waved me off.

"What are those?" I pointed to the skates, which were clearly from his home. "Doesn't the rink make you rent them for safety reasons?"

"My buddy is about to let a three-hundred-pound motorized wheelchair on the ice," said KC. "So nah."

I laughed. "True. Do you skate?"

"No." He glanced off at a couple pushing a stroller.

I arched an eyebrow. "Why do you have skates, then? That's random."

KC's eyes stayed on the stroller until he just shook his head. "You wanna hop on?"

I continued to study him with a curved expression. But he tossed his head and led us towards the rink.

As we got closer, I suppressed a groan at the Christmas music playing from the rink speakers—*two weeks* before Thanksgiving. The scrape and clop of the skaters' blades on ice ground satisfyingly in my ears. Chill rose from the rink to our faces as we approached the glass doorway.

The employee sitting on a stool there—KC's friend—had an acne-ridden face and wispy beard. It reminded me in contrast how effortlessly thick and rugged Cole's was. The employee mock-saluted KC and opened the rink door with one hand for us, not even standing from his stool.

KC tugged on his skates and entered first. I reeled in an excited breath and rolled over the small lip and onto the ice.

Worried glances from moms and dads drew my way as they rotated around, but fuck them. They're just as dangerous. I deserve fun just as much.

I surged forward.

My wheels skidded and felt like they were spreading apart. The ice was jelly beneath them, and for a moment they spun in place. KC cruised backwards on his skates a few feet and watched me as if to make sure I was okay.

I cracked an enormous grin.

A smile twitched on KC's lips too. He continued to slide back as I eased forward.

After a few wordless moments grasping the hang of things, KC fell in line at my side. Everyone else gave us a huge berth, and when I watched our reflections floating along the glass sides, it was almost like we were alone.

"Have you ever done this before?" said KC sweetly.

I paused. The truth was, I'd skated in my chair on *real* ice. Like, pond ice. Ice where you die if you fall through. My grandpa (The Admiral) had stomped on the ice at the bank one winter and said *Good 'nuff* and I'd rolled on there like a panzer crossing the frozen Rhine. Because I wanted to flirt with death, I even did a loop around the spots Grandpa said were *not good 'nuff*.

Normally I'd boast this fact. I like the shocked looks of awe and admiration this live-hard reputation of mine evoked. But something about KC's tone made me think he wanted me to say no. That this was a first, extraordinary experience. Instead, I said, "Not like this," as breathlessly as I could.

KC smiled wider.

And damn! It was fun! I laughed and swerved. A few times I bumped into the glass sides, wobbling them. My wheels left tracks that I tried to follow, but I zagged and must have looked drunk. After a while, it felt as smooth as driving on the glaze slipping down a pound cake.

KC and I talked about Elliot and Mags, our show-and-tell memories from second grade, and then we talked about how pretty everything was. I was finally grateful for my encumbering coat; my fingertips were swelling from the cold.

When KC and I exhausted all the topics we shared interests in, he sobered and we seemed to slow.

"Do you need any props again for the reshoot?" His voice was a little flat.

"Oh," I said. "Yeah, we need all of it again. The uniform shirts, bucket, the museum docent badge. How did you find all that random shit anyway?" I smiled at him.

KC nodded but didn't answer the question. "I'll drop a bag off to Elliot tomorrow."

"You won't be there?"

"Nah."

A beat. I frowned. "Okay."

The lights were shutting off by the time we left, and the Zamboni was rattling and making its final lap. I bumped over that lip at the exit again and my wheels found rough, solid ground. It was weird, like a sailor experiencing land wobbles.

"See ya, man," said the employee. KC waved.

I could see my soccer-mom van already parked at the curb of the shopping center, fumes chugging out of it while it shook with the inside heater. That heat would feel nice.

KC walked me towards it while I lusted for its warmth.

"This winter is gonna be, like, *The Day After Tomorrow,*" I said.

"Wednesday?"

I laughed. "No, the movie."

"What movie?"

"You haven't seen the movie?" I mock-gasped.

"No . . ." He hung his skates by their laces over his neck and held a boot in either hand like a boxer would hold a towel in the locker room.

"Oh my God, where were you during the 2012 apocalypse scare? The Mayan calendar thing? It's the millennial generation's Y2K."

"Our world could use a good cleaning out," said KC gravely. "Maybe I'll build you a handicapped-accessible bunker."

"Well, it never happened, and people got, like, therapists for nothing. *Anyway*. The movie was good."

"We should see it sometime," said KC.

"Yeah," I said. "I could bring it to your house and watch it."

"That's not a good idea," said KC.

I looked over at him. "Oh?"

"My house is not a good place for people to be." He stared ahead and didn't say anything more.

I paused for a second. "That's kind of a weird way to think of your house."

He glanced over at me and then rolled his shoulders as if to wriggle some warmth back into his body.

"It's—remodeling. Noisy."

My brow stayed low. I *hmmed* and looked ahead too. I think he knew I didn't buy it, but I didn't pursue.

Before I got in the van, I hugged KC. He kept open his eyes and wrapped one arm around me gingerly. It was so different than Cole's unintentionally but unapologetically engulfing embrace. KC was careful and calculated. He was wiry and thin but familiar, and now I definitely could tell he wore a cologne far too sophisticated to match his personality.

When people hug me, or even when I request hugging them, the only role I can play is the ask. *I can ask*. They get to decide everything else: to oblige, the duration, and how tight.

Cole's hug was tighter. But KC's was longer.

That night, I fell asleep with the BiPAP mask strapped

over my mouth. I jolted awake to the sound of a ding on my phone, and for a second it felt like my heart slipped on ice again.

I pawed at the phone and squinted at it.

2:00 a.m. The text was from KC. Not Cole.

I closed my eyes without reading it, and the mask buzzed me back to sleep like the thrum of the Zamboni.

When I woke in the middle of the night again to a beeping, I groaned and reached for my phone. *Who the hell now?*

But there were no messages on the screen. That was when I realized it wasn't my phone.

It was the BiPAP machine's alarm, and Mom and Dad came bursting in.

15

Dad tore me out of the bed with the covers still on me and flung me into my chair. The wheelchair was cold and stiff compared to my warm bed; I swayed and blinked. That beeping noise shut off when the BiPAP mask was pulled off me.

What's wrong? I feel fine.

"Maeve," said Dad. He lifted my chin and looked into my eyes. I winced and shoved him off. Mom toppled over books and clothes hangers in my closet and emerged with an old albuterol machine I hadn't seen since elementary school. I used to suck on this vapor-steroid that cleared my lungs through that machine.

"Guys." My voice was groggy. "I'm fine."

"Are you breathing?" Mom demanded. She stared at me fiercely, in her slippers.

"I mean, obviously."

"Don't talk to Mom that way," said Dad. But they both seemed to relax at the sight of me lucid and not struggling.

"You guys just ripped me out of bed because the stupid BiPAP broke. I didn't stop breathing. I'm fine."

"How do you know?" said Mom. "The purpose of the BiPAP is to keep your lungs functional at night and detect when they aren't."

"Let's take a little albuterol just in case," said Dad. He waved for Mom to bring forth the machine.

"*No.*" I threw my arm down on my knee in objection. "*No more masks!* If my lungs gave up, I'd literally recognize the feeling of suffocation."

"In sleep?" said Mom. "No, Maeve. It doesn't work that way, all right?"

Yes, Mom, in sleep. I'm pretty sure I recognize the feeling of an orgasm in sleep when I dream of Cole and a dark room. I'm sure this would be no different.

"I'm calling the insurance company tomorrow for a new one," said Mom. "Then we'll see."

I huffed. I could hear myself having too much of an attitude—Mom and Dad only cared about me—but I just wanted to sleep. I hated this mask already. And I wanted everyone to not treat me like I might die. They might too.

I glanced at the red digital clock at my bed. It was 5:44 a.m. I had to get up at 7:00 to be at Quinten's by 8:00, and I groaned.

"I'll just stay up," I said defiantly. "Just leave me in my room."

Dad pursed his lips. He didn't approve of my behavior, I could see, but sometimes I just can't be gracious and demure. Sometimes I need to be mad. Mom shook her head and thumped the albuterol machine on the shelf and marched out of my room.

There was a pause with just Dad and me in the room.

"Do you want some tea?" said Dad tightly. I shook my head. He left.

I took a deep breath and watched out my window the navy-blue sky glow into dawn. It bloomed light over the bare branches of the trees like a heart surging blood back into dead veins.

With a click of my wheelchair motor, I went to my bedside and retrieved my phone. Turned it on and looked at the 2:00 a.m. text from KC.

KC

Maeve.

My brow pulled together. My thumb hesitated at the keys, and then I replied.

MAEVE

I'm here.

It circled for a moment and then sent. My mouth sagged in a confused frown.

François and I trotted up to the front door of Riverside Assisted Living. A garden statue of St. Francis stood in the mulch to the right, and some elderly ladies sat on the bench next to it. They didn't talk to each other, only looked around. In their hands were dried boughs of lavender that reeked. François' nose wriggled towards them.

Behind us, a field trip bus pulled in, the lavender farm's name decaled in purple over the side of the doors. Nurses led the residents towards the shuttle for their big day at the farm. I imagined the farm had a greenhouse, or these ladies on the bench still had their boughs from last year.

Inside, the smell of greasy breakfast made François give an enormous shake and wag his tail. Staff crossed the carpeted lobby from the cafeteria with food trays in their arms. I'd never been to the home this early; it seemed to be their busiest time of day.

I signed in and told the receptionist I was supposed to meet Quinten in the Breakfast Investors Club. The woman made a face.

"The BIC? That club is all women."

I shrugged. "I'll make sure they don't fight over him."

She stood and pointed me to the room down the hall where the club met. I nodded.

All right, time to go over some points. I was fifteen minutes late, on purpose. I told Quinten to be inside the meeting already. There was only one way I could confront Patricia without her running off, and I'd practiced my plan in the morning hours I had to kill thanks to the busted BiPAP. I went over a few of my planned lines and then headed for the BIC.

A cute, flowery sign with real lace trim hung over the door. MEETING IN SESSION—DO NOT DISTURB <3

I disturbed.

With all my strength, I twisted the doorknob with one arm and commanded François to push it open with his nose. He surged forward and wiggled with happiness to oblige. We burst through.

"Sorry I'm late," I boomed. Everyone jumped and turned to me—a semicircle of about a dozen old women with clipboards and horned glasses, their checkbooks handy next to their beige flats. Smack dab in the middle was my planted agent; Quinten looked over at me and smirked. His grey hair and moustache were combed neat as horse's hair. The Life Alert button necklace hanging to his chest made me flash to Cole's wolf print and KC's Mjolnir, and I had to file that amusing comparison away for later.

But most importantly—Wheelchair Charity Woman herself froze with her hand in midair. Her mouth was open, and she blinked at me. She wore a brown pantsuit and beside her was a presentation board of Caring Hands Camp. Photographs and rainbows and all sorts of shit. An 8×10 image of a bronze statue at the camp entrance of a girl named Ginger was tacked to the board too.

"Traffic was insane," I continued and moved in, right to the front, next to Patricia. The heavy door fell closed behind me automatically.

"Ex-excuse me?" said Patricia. She leaned down and hissed in her heavy New York accent. "What do you think you're doing?"

I ignored her and turned to the old ladies. "Morning ladies—gentleman." Quinten bowed and looked back at up at me. He grinned and his eyes sparkled. I noted how pink his skin was. He looked healthier than before. "My name is Maeve Leeson, and I'm a Caring Hands Camp alumna. Patricia asked me to come this morning to talk about the camp."

Just as Patricia gasped in a breath to refute me, the ladies cooed a collective *"Awww."*

"Precious."

"What a dear."

I looked over to Patricia, heart pounding. She glanced at everyone, heat rushing visibly into her skin.

"Right," said Patricia. "As I was saying, Caring Hands Camp welcomes campers with *all* sorts of disabilities. Maeve here has an intense social disorder." Patricia shot me a meaningful glare that said, *Get out or else, sweetie.*

"Oh yeah," I said, "intense. But you know what, Caring Hands Camp helped me with that tremendously. Stripper Saturdays really brought me out of my shell."

Patricia's eyes popped as the old ladies' expressions clouded with elderly disapproval. Murmuring spread, and I could hear Quinten's poorly suppressed cackling over the whispers.

"No, no," Patricia said. "Maeve is kidding."

"No, I'm not," I said. "I'm not shy about my sexuality anymore, Patricia. Fabrizio was so patient with me. You guys really only hire the best."

Patricia gasped to rebuke me again, but I placed a dramatic hand to my heart.

"I owe *so* much to Caring Hands Camp."

"Now that sounds *inappropriate,*" one of the old women said, and the others nodded seriously.

"What kind of camp is this again?" One adjusted her glasses and squinted at the presentation board of smiling, giggling disabled children.

"Y-you know what?" said Patricia. "Could you ladies wait here for a few minutes while I talk to my former camper outside? We'll be *right* back."

The muttering continued, but I said, "Great idea," and waved for Quinten to join us.

As soon as the door closed behind Quinten, Patricia, and me, she spun and pointed a finger in my face.

"Who do you think you are? *What* kind of person sabotages a camp for the disabled? Where are your parents?"

"Patricia, let me introduce you to former DEA agent Quinten James." I used his agent name.

"Pleased." Quinten smiled.

"*So?*" Patricia placed her hands on her hips. "What is going on?"

"You've been exploiting me on your website," I said, "outside of the ice cream parlor in downtown Fredericksburg. And I *know* you tried to steal François to flaunt in front of the donors. You're doing everything you can to manipulate more money into your 'camp.'" I made air quotes with my fingers.

"Do you have other interests?" Quinten said in a firm, croaky voice.

"Yeah, 'cause he knows people," I said.

François sneezed agreement.

Patricia laughed. "Oh my *Gawd,* this is bonkers. No. François was drawn to my food, and I have no other interests but the children!"

Bonkers. Jesus, this woman. "Take my photo down immediately," I demanded.

"I don't even know what you're talking about." She bristled and removed her Chanel sunglasses from atop her head.

I pulled the photo up on my phone—I had it bookmarked—and shoved the screen at her.

She scoffed. "I—I didn't even know that was you."

"Take it down," said Quinten. "Or I'll have an investigative team called in to review your company."

"Fine!" said Patricia. "I'll take the photo off my website. But I didn't take your damn dog."

"Right," I said. "You said a service dog on the campus would double your donations."

Patricia cocked her head indignantly and crossed her arms, but I thought she might have reddened.

"How much of those *donations* go to camper facilities, Ms. Weinhart?" said Quinten.

"I am *not* required to discuss assets with *either of you*. Now march back in there and tell the investors you were making it up!" She pointed to the door. "I cannot *believe* you would try to hurt the children."

The children. I huffed. "Look, I don't trust you. Don't really believe you either—I think you stalked me and are trying to rake in a suspicious amount of money using these disabled kids. But take my photo down, stay away from my dog, and never send me a brochure to your camp, and this'll be the end of it."

"And if you don't—investigative team," Quinten reminded.

"*I already said I would!* Now go apologize!" Her voice cracked with desperation.

I rolled over to the door, pushed it open with François' help, and poked my head in. The old ladies stopped murmuring and shaking their heads to look at me. "I was kidding about the strippers, by the way."

They stared at me and blinked.

"*Sort of,*" I whispered. Patricia didn't hear. I winked and pulled out, facing Patricia again. "There."

Muscles tense all over, she shook out a begrudging nod.

"I can't believe I mistook you so grievously before," huffed Patricia.

"Mistook me?" I made a face. "Mistook me for what?"

"For reminding me of someone I once knew and respected." She threw a crumpled tissue into her purse.

I reminded her of someone she once knew and respected? Um. All right.

Before she turned on her heel, I shrugged and said, "If you're really trying to help handicapped kids, thanks. Walk me out, Quinten."

Cool fresh air wafted over us outside the lobby and washed away the smell of mothballs and sour nursing-home soap. Quinten laughed next to me.

"That was the most fun I've had in years."

"You terrified her." I punched his wheelchair joystick playfully.

"Still got it," said Quinten. We parked by the St. Francis statue.

"Think that'll be the end of it?" I said.

Quinten took a deep breath and stared at the mulch. "Probably. It's possible she's embezzling money. But also possible she's not, and is just trying to stupidly cheat a little free sympathy from you for the camp."

His voice was still a little flimsy and breathless, but man, it'd been forever since I'd heard Quinten not wheeze through every third word.

"I'll let you know if she doesn't take the photo down," I said.

"Investigative team," Quinten repeated. I chuckled.

We grew silent. Then, slowly, Quinten reached for my hand.

I looked down at our clasped fingers. Instinctively, my thumb rubbed his dry skin. My throat bobbed with a swallow. I pulled my hand back a moment later to pretend I needed to scratch my jaw. His fingers curled away. Sadly.

"I better go wait for my ride at the stop sign," I lied.

"Okay," said Quinten. His head lowered.

I patted his back lovingly. "Thanks for today, Chief."

His mouth twitched.

"You still got it. I'll see you soon." I started to leave.

"Maeve," Quinten breathed. I noticed the wheeze return. I turned to him. He struggled to lift his head back up to meet my eyes. Then he lifted something in his hand. "Take this."

My brow furrowed and I approached him, taking the object—it was a little tape recorder.

"What's this?" I said.

"Transcript," said Quinten. I gaped at the recorder and a smile swelled over my face. I shook my head.

"For real?" I said.

Quinten wheezed. "What kind of an agent would I be without it?"

16

"What are you all jumpy about?" Elliot laughed. I blushed and stared at the bag of C-47s (clothespins) I'd just knocked off the table accidentally. They littered the floor. I was a hell of a lot more nervous about today than I was for yesterday's encounter with Patricia.

"Sorry," I said. Elliot swept them back into the bag with the side of his shoe.

"I'm gonna have to report you and Cole to the union."

"No," I said. "You really don't . . ."

It'd been three days, and he still hadn't texted. Mags

told me that guy time and girl time when it came to texting was an easy formula to remember: dog years. For every day a guy doesn't text, it feels like seven days to the girl. For every seven days a guy doesn't text, it feels like one day to him.

I don't know. I sort of call bullshit on that. Gay best friends in romcoms would say *he's just not that into you*. They're less biased than Mags.

Still, I dressed in my most womanly red blouse. I even applied a little lipstick. That was hard to do without being willing to look in a mirror.

"Well"—Elliot checked his watch—"he's a few minutes late."

"That's just him," I said. Affection in my voice. Elliot glanced at me.

We confirmed and double confirmed that the cameras didn't reflect in the glass of the cannonball exhibit like last time. With just a few short shots needed, no other crew was arriving. I think Mags and Nate were on a date, and I was worried about how to be supportive for Mags, how to be excited for her, when Nate was such a dick to me. She'd been so good with me and Cole.

The set was pretty simple—our equipment table wouldn't be in the shot. But it was after hours at the museum, the only time the museum lady would let us return, and already dark outside. A pitfall Elliot and I had to work with, to make sure the lighting was consistent with the other shots. The floor looked like a booby-trapped 007 vault with stingers—aka wires—everywhere to set up our key and fill lights. We'd gotten the lighting close enough for my satisfaction and could correct the rest in post—every filmmaker's famous last words.

Elliot ruffled out the plastic Giant food store bag KC

had dropped off to him and unloaded the props onto the table. That was when we heard the door open and shut.

Something swooped through my stomach. The jingle of keys on a lanyard neared from the museum lobby.

I snatched the empty bag and twirled it around my wrist, trying to appear occupied and helpful.

"Hey, man!" said Elliot. And I had to look over.

Cole strolled in. I could fill the space between his head and the doorframe with an apple. Per our request, he'd trimmed his dark beard to the exact length it was at the previous shoot. He scratched his strong jaw and moved with total blasé ease and carelessness. Not an ounce of nerves on him. He wore a plain, dark blue shirt and black pants, and my eyes trailed down his belt and to the lanyard I'd heard. Then I glanced over a few centimeters . . . I tried not to look below his belt too long.

It never seemed to be the case that men needed to pull their eyes away from me; I was always pulling away from them.

"Thanks for coming, man," said Elliot.

I donned my bravery and smiled at Cole. "Good to see you."

"Yeah," Cole boomed and didn't make eye contact with either of us. "No prob."

Elliot tossed him a bundle of clothes—his docent uniform. Cole caught it with both hands and looked down at the clothes.

"Cool," he said. "I'll go change."

I kept my eyes on his, waiting for . . . a nuance. A suggestive glance. Instead, he turned and headed for the bathroom.

"Gonna be okay?" said Elliot under his breath.

"Camera One is a little blurry," I said, and turned for the lens.

I set to work.

Cole waited by the glass of the cannonball once he was changed into the crisp white work shirt and black tie. He looked so handsome in a domestic, coming-home-after-work, providing-for-the-family type way. His hazel eyes rested, relaxed, on the tripod. I noticed he didn't rock side to side on his feet the way he normally did. His broad shoulders were slumped.

The lights were set. The script was in my hands. Elliot wore a headset to hear the audio take. I looked up and leveled my gaze on Cole. In the silence, he straightened, realizing it was almost time to shoot. His gaze met mine and locked there. But it wasn't deep and calculating. It was the way a dog looked at a tennis ball you held up high. Waiting for a cue.

"Action," I said.

The scene was a reactionary one: we needed Cole to give his lines and react to the other actors with only Elliot reading the opposite part back to him. The camera would be fixed only on Cole, so we could cut to him throughout, minus the reflection of the camera we'd fucked up last time.

Cole's body, while sedated moments before, surged to life. The movement I loved about him filled him. He rocked his weight to either foot, dropped his head, and smirked. It was pretty amazing.

"Yeah, well, you need to earn this cannonball, kid." Cole's voice was back-row-of-the-theater loud. It shook in my eardrums and erupted goose bumps on my skin. He cocked his head. "I've been polishing this glass longer than you've been scratching your—"

"Cut," said Elliot. I turned to him, confused. Cole didn't take it personally, whatever it was. He pushed a hand across his nose and loosened up, waiting for the criticism.

"We forgot his nametag," said Elliot.

"Ugh, stupid us. I got it," I said.

"Let me grab another headset for you while you do that," said Elliot. "One sec." He jogged for the lobby, where his backpack sagged next to the front door.

I snatched the fake nametag off the table and approached Cole.

"Just in case you forgot who you are," I said, and handed it to him.

"Ha. That'll be good," said Cole. He took it in one hand and read it with amusement. His other hand hung at his side. Right level with my eye. Elliot still wasn't back . . .

I swept my fingertips for his.

He lifted his arm and pinned the nametag to his shirt with both hands. My blood pounded with embarrassment. Did he see me?

Elliot returned, and I circled back to behind the camera.

"Here you go." Elliot snuggled the headset over me.

We called action again.

This time, Cole added a boyish squeak to his thunderous voice that was the most amazing mixture of youth and man. Honey mustard and bacon. Green apple and provolone.

"Yeah, well, you need to earn this cannonball, kid," said Cole. Elliot smiled because Cole was nailing it. "I've been polishing this glass longer than you've been scratching your—"

We all cringed as the key light flickered and popped. Something hissed at the outlet.

"Shit!" said Elliot. He jogged over to the stinger and tugged it out so we wouldn't all get electrocuted. Luckily no smoke trickled out of it to tickle the ancient smoke detectors above us. "Damn." Elliot lifted the cable and clicked his tongue.

Cole walked over to him. In the newly fallen dark, only the fill light illuminated Cole's back and toppled his long shadow like a redwood over me. His rough male hand took the cable and inspected it. "This a new cord?"

"Shit, I dunno," said Elliot. "I just rented it from Mr. Billings. What do you think, Verizon, it busted?"

"It could be a new cord and the outlet here is old as fuck."

Rmmph. His way of saying fuck.

"Yeah," said Elliot. "*Damn.*"

"We might get away with a simple floodlight," I said. "I could hold it. We're *not* rescheduling this, guys."

Elliot nodded. Cole still studied the cord.

"This is unbelievable," said Elliot. "All right, I'm going to Target. It's, like, across the street."

"You want me to come with you?" I said.

Cole chuckled at that, which alarmed me. "How?" He turned to me with amusement, not unkindly.

"You could carry me into Elliot's van obviously."

"I probably could."

"Aight I'll be back in like . . . ten minutes. Fifteen tops." Elliot muttered one more curse, patted his pocket to feel his wallet, and raced for the door.

"Thanks, Elliot," I said. Probably for the best. I'm known to accidentally steal things—tablecloths from restaurants, Sharpies from Office Depot. Once I put them on my lap, it's easy to forget they're there.

And then the door closed. Elliot was gone.

I gulped. Removed my headset.

There was a stretch of silence. I was reminded of how old and eerie this boring one-roomed museum could be. It was cold too. The ancient wood beams and brick were cavernous.

Cole tossed his head to flip hair from his eyes. He began to pace, looking around at the corners of museum. "So what's new?" he said. But didn't look at me. In fact, he kept talking before I could answer. "This is a weird museum."

"Yeah," I said. "Apparently that cannonball is haunted."

"Is that right?"

"No," I said. "I was kidding."

"Wouldn't surprise me." He shoved his hands in his black pants pockets and stopped walking. He swayed the way he does. Looked at me.

Our eyes connected, interrupted only by the flow of his movement.

"I missed you," I said.

Oh, Maeve . . . no. If I could have closed my eyes privately in regret, I would have.

"Nah, you didn't," said Cole.

"Maybe," I said.

"Nah," said Cole.

"Yeah, well. I still know your card."

"What was it?" He was immediate.

"Not telling. Stick around and find out." No. I was bribing him to like me?

"Hmm," said Cole. He watched me. I noticed the unusual, premature lines beneath his eyes. They couldn't be smile lines. I hadn't seen him grin but for the camera.

"Sorry for the delay, though," I said. "We promise to be fast."

"Do you?" said Cole.

"I mean you read Tolstoy in high school. So this'll be nothing."

"*Read* is a strong word," said Cole.

"At least it was only your medium close-ups we need."

"Is anyone else coming from the cast?" asked Cole.

"No." I scratched my knee. "It was just—just you."

"Just me, huh?" said Cole. His gaze harpooned right into me again.

Maybe I could have taken this deeper. But I already felt

like I screwed up; I already felt like I word-violated him. So when the awkward pause lingered, I just changed the subject to neutral territory.

"Your nametag is crooked."

He looked down, still swaying side to side. Pushed it with one hand. "Better?"

No. It did nothing.

"You might need to repin it."

He fiddled with it with both hands. "I don't know if I can."

"There's a trick to the clasp," I said, driving closer to him. "It twists before you can pop it."

He continued to struggle for a moment. I was close, but not about to try touching him again.

Cole grunted.

"You know what?" he said. He reached forward and grabbed the dark red metal bar of my wheelchair, then lowered to one knee. *Thumped* right in front of me. "Go for it."

My heart pounded. I flushed, and my muscles went slack. I smelled him: his damp-leaves, cold cotton, and indistinguishable man scent. And half of Cole's mouth smiled at me, his eyes power. He knew what he just did.

My hands shook as I reached for his nametag. Fingers brushing his shirt. I fixed it.

"Better?" he said. Low.

I didn't respond, because I was catching my breath.

His hand slid up my chair towards me another four inches. He was centimeters away. I dropped my fingers to where his should be on my wheelchair, but he pulled it back. Surely he saw me that time. Still he gazed at me.

The door opened in the lobby. And then my wheelchair shook with enormous strength as Cole pressed down on it to help him rise.

Elliot trotted in with the thick yellow floodlight.

Before Elliot came close enough to hear, and just as Cole glanced down at me one last time, I whispered, "Better."

Cole winked.

17

How the heck are ya?

Fred Kingfisher   Wed, Nov 7, 2:51 PM
to M. Leeson

Dear Maeve,

Sorry for the late email. And happy to hear you have some potential action in the forecast with a young man. How'd you meet him?

I've been hesitating to tell you I've gone on a few dates with an older woman from Christian Mingle. I like her a lot. The site makes it easier to attract some open-minded partners. If things don't work out, I recommend it.

Hope you're not getting your shotgun ready for me this time around.

Fred

I kept my thumb on the screen and scrolled the email up and down on my phone. I guess it seemed weird to me. Two things.

1. He hesitated to tell me he's seeing someone?
2. I need to find good *Christian* men.

God, you don't know how often I hear this. Come unto me, all ye sinners.

I closed the email because I wasn't ready to respond. Unfortunately for Fred, that usually means I'll forget for weeks. I sighed.

Departing from the digital world, I stowed my phone and returned my attention to the post office counter in front of me. I'd asked Mom to drop me off here and let me run some errands in the surrounding shopping center. François had joined me with a perky gait—errands for him mean service dog showtime. He should get little campaign medals every time he serves a tour helping me in a new place we visit.

François' eyebrow—a little whisker over his eye—flicked up now. Drool threaded down his mouth, making the blue pen he was holding very unattractive. I turned and took it from his jaw, wiping it on my shirt. Four unaddressed letters lay on the table in front of me, post office clerks scanning Priority Mail barcodes behind the counter across the floor. A few overachieving moms stood in line with gift-wrapped packages. Two-ish weeks before Thanksgiving.

My letters still had jack-o'-lantern stamps on them. I used the pen to fill in the inmate ID numbers of the four prisoners I was writing.

A couple of years ago, I volunteered with this anti-death-penalty coalition, and it rolled into me becoming pen pals with a few prisoners. They're always thrilled to receive my letters, and I don't sugarcoat the shit that goes on in my life. I send them pictures of me and François doing various activities. Unlike all the other female volunteers in the coalition, I don't have the problem of the prisoners wanting *more* from my friendship. I "inspire" them.

"All done?"

A young postwoman with long lashes stopped next to me and offered to take my letters.

IF SHE WERE A GUY: "Yes, sir. Can you overnight express me to your bed by any chance?"

BECAUSE SHE'S NOT: "I can do it myself, thanks."

She nodded and walked off. I can never tell how standoffish I sound. But it's her fault for not being a guy, right?

I dropped the letters in the regular-mail slot, and François perked up as I led him out the automatic door.

Cold wind ripped through us. It lifted François' floppy ears. He sniffed the air, almost smiling. I checked the time. Mom said she'd be at least another thirty minutes in the bank; the post office took a lot less time than I'd estimated. And it was too frigid to be waiting outside.

Next to us drifted the smell of spicy cinnamon. Hot cider. I groaned and faced the storefront.

It was an ancient home-decorating shop. Dried flowers in the window, little porcelain figures from Germany on a shelf. Ninety-year-old women were practically pitching tents waiting in line to get in.

François and I looked at each other. The wind blew.

The bell tinkled as I went inside with the next passing costumer.

1950s Christmas music played. A toy train circled the entire perimeter of the store on an upper ledge, stuffing nailed to the walls to imitate snow. I guess that was kind of cute. White-haired women, sipping hot cider from paper cups, pushed carts slowly through stands of artificial magnolia wreaths and stained-glass lamps.

I had to squish through a few tables to reach the free-cider dispenser. François crammed behind me. I filled a cup and drank; heat tore through my chest.

What was it about this place that was so comforting? There was barely a man depicted on the men's bathroom sign in here, let alone a live one. So why did I want to stay? Something nostalgic stirred inside.

I approached a table laden with china. Huge platter with a fat turkey painted on it. Gravy boats edged in gold. Crystalline candle holders.

My weak, shaky hand reached out to graze the edge of the gravy boat.

I realized I wanted this. I wanted . . . one day . . . this.

Yeah, I wanted to roll around with carousels of men and yank them dry and live like I'm not already wearing death's save-the-date. But . . .

I also wanted to cook Thanksgiving dinner for a man. I wanted to hold the door as he hauled in the Christmas tree. Pass out watermelon to neighbors as he snapped a lighter over fireworks on the Fourth of July. I wanted to hand him a beer as he watched the game and fold his camo sweatshirt he only wore on weekends.

Don't think of Cole. Don't think of Cole. Don't you dare plug him into your domestic fantasies.

Shit, he probably did all those things. His parents were probably the same way. Traditional, Southern Virginia home, a cross over the fireplace. His dad probably had a Republican congressman yard sign in his lawn and a gun to protect the family in his bedside drawer—the side where *he* slept.

Why did I want this? Why did I want what I *just can't* have? How would I open the oven? How would I make the bed for the in-laws? How would I do this?

MAGS

Oh my god why would you WANT to do that?

She replied seconds after I sent her a photo of the dinner set and expressed this in one line.

MAEVE

I dunno.

MAGS

You're more than that Maeve.

MAEVE

I'm not saying I'm not. I'm just saying it's part of what I desire.

MAGS

I'm never getting married oh my god.

MAEVE

Lol did the date not go so well with Nate 2.0?

MAGS

What? No, it was great. Why?

MAEVE

Oh, sorry.

I paced around the store now with my head hung to my phone.

MAGS

No it was amazing.

MAEVE

Tell me!!!

MAGS

I didn't think you'd want to hear

My mouth twisted.

MAEVE

He's not my favorite person but I'm happy for you. I mean, you don't really like Cole

MAGS

Yeah but you're not really dating Cole

Ouch. It was true, but Mags' characteristic bluntness hit hard.

MAEVE

I know. Just tell me :) I want to hear

So I let her gush, and she did. She almost made me like Nate. And I mean, I never hated the guy. I'd just never forget all the things he'd said over the years either.

MAGS

Anyway. How was seeing Cole yesterday?

I paused. Was it possible to explain the intimacy, the crazy sexuality of him simply *kneeling* in front of me and gazing at me while I fixed his nametag?

MAEVE

I literally will die if he doesn't consume me

Whoops, that was a little heavy, even for me. And for damn sure Mags didn't let it pass.

MAGS

Maeve whoa. Aren't you guys skipping a few steps?

MAEVE

I'm open to criticism.

MAGS

I just mean like you guys have sexted and you had one date where he showed you magic tricks the whole time

MAEVE

It was cute

MAGS

It was! But do you even know anything about him? What's his favorite color?

MAEVE

Probably blue. He always wears blue.

MAGS

Hmm. Well you should text him tonight.

MAEVE

Really? I thought, like, whoever texts first is disadvantaged

MAGS

Maeve, texting rules are bullshit. Just text him and talk to him. Like, actually talk to him. Try not to automatically flirt

MAEVE

That's hard for me.

MAGS

I know

Mom pulled in at the curb outside the store. She walked out and gave me a thumbs-up, I think as a gesture of approval for my choosing to wait somewhere warm. Lately she'd been doubling down on keeping me out of the cold and pumped with vitamins and doing lame breathing exercises.

François and I headed over there, his leash attached to my wheelchair so my non-joystick hand was free. I used the free one to send a one-handed text to Mags.

MAEVE

One other thing. Have you talked to KC lately?

MAGS

No. Why?

"Maeve, come on!" Mom reprimanded when I stopped in the cold to try to type out another fast line. I huffed and bowled onto the ramp and into the van, where I finished the text.

MAEVE

He sent me a text at 2 AM the other night with just my name and I replied and never heard back

Mom jumped in the front seat and blasted heat from the vents like volcanic geysers. François leapt onto the back seat. I jostled as we took off.

MAGS

I don't like that

MAEVE

Me either

MAGS

No like I have enough experience talking to depressed people that that concerns me

MAEVE

Me too. But we're Generation Z. We're all depressed

MAGS

That's not even an exaggeration.

I pursed my lips and looked out the window. I hoped KC would reply, and wondered if maybe I should focus on texting him tonight instead of Cole.

Another text from Mags came in.

MAGS

But if I have to be in this stupid world, you do too. Okay?

I read it twice.

MAGS

Promise?

A smile touched the corner of my mouth.

MAEVE

Deal.

"Dad, this is stupid."

"Maeve, I went to three Toys 'R' Us stores for this."

"Toys 'R' Us closed."

"Not the express ones," said Dad.

"That doesn't make it less stupid."

"I'm excited," said Dad. "Don't crush my excitement."

"Can we just admit Mom made you do this?"

Dad ignored me. "So excited."

I sighed, and Dad shook the bubble wand in front of me. "Colored bubble juice!" he declared. "Come on. See what's the biggest one you can blow."

That's what she said.

I leaned forward and blew into the bubble wand. The rubbery-looking, iridescent bubbles stretched from the wand and quivered into the air. Floating like spherical rainbows until they popped and sprinkled our faces. We both winced.

I practiced blowing the bubbles, exercise for my lungs, for about fifteen minutes and then said I was done. Dad didn't object and twisted on the bubble juice cap. "Let me know when you're ready to lie down," he said, and I retired to my room.

Door closed.

That click of the lock sent my lust buzzing.

I whipped out my phone. It was 10:46 p.m.

Bewitching hour.

MAEVE

So that nametag still crooked?

I waited with a taut stomach and frozen muscles for the few minutes it took for my phone to vibrate.

COLE STONE

I think you took care of it

Hmm. Hard to gauge his level of interest with that tone. But Mags' advice came back to me. *Try not to automatically flirt.*

MAEVE

How was your day?

Wow. That was weird.

COLE STONE

Not bad haha. Had another audition.

MAEVE

What! I'm so proud of you! For which production?

COLE STONE

For a TV commercial actually.

Although it wasn't *Beauty and the Beast* like I'd hoped, I grinned like mad.

MAEVE

Cole that's amazing :)

COLE STONE

I mean, I probably won't get it.

MAEVE

They'd be insane.

A pause.

COLE STONE

Thanks.

The smile faded as I stared at our text thread.

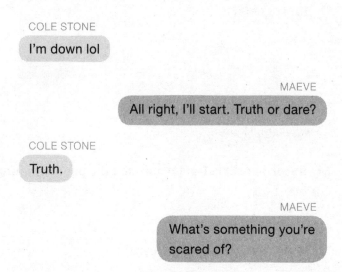

MAEVE

Wanna play a game?

COLE STONE

Lol what?

MAEVE

A game. How about truth or dare?

I rolled out my shoulders. I remembered playing truth or dare with my friends and KC in sixth grade. I remembered sitting in a circle and always picking dare because I was afraid of picking truth.

Tonight, I was afraid of dare.

COLE STONE

I'm down lol

MAEVE

All right, I'll start. Truth or dare?

COLE STONE

Truth.

MAEVE

What's something you're scared of?

I could think of a million.

Because it took over five minutes, I assumed Cole thought about his answer—or he was playing *Call of Duty* and responded whenever next he died.

COLE STONE
Probably being a disappointment

MAEVE
To who?

COLE STONE
I don't know haha

The *haha* made me question his level of sincerity in that answer.

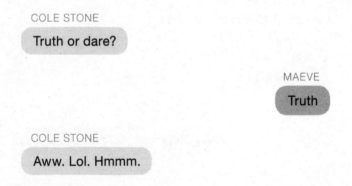

COLE STONE
Truth or dare?

MAEVE
Truth

COLE STONE
Aww. Lol. Hmmm.

My fingertips tickled as I drummed the phone, waiting for his question.

COLE STONE
Do you ever dream about me?

My brow furrowed. I was happy it at least wasn't a *What's your favorite food?* question. But it was sort of a . . .

self-centered one, albeit a playful one. I was so into him, though, I went with it.

> **MAEVE**
> Every damn night.

Ugh, I already failed Mags. But it wasn't a lie.

> **COLE STONE**
> I had a hunch :P

> **MAEVE**
> Truth or dare?

> **COLE STONE**
> Dare.

Oh man. The power. I could dare him to do anything for me. Anything. But Mags was right. I needed to learn about *him*. Where he comes from, where he wants to go.

> **MAEVE**
> I dare you to show me your parents :)

> **COLE STONE**
> Really? Lol.

> **MAEVE**
> Yeah :)

He sent over a photo. I opened it and wasn't disappointed. You know how when you love someone's parents, you love that person even more? Cole's dad was a big, burly, grey-bearded man with gentle eyes and a mellow smile. I could see so much of Cole in his face. His bearish arm was around his wife, who wore a red sweater and a necklace with fall leaves on it. They were posing in front of their house, and it seemed recent because it looked cold. No leaves on the trees, Cole's dad in a dull orange hunting jacket. I swear to God, a Republican congressman yard sign was hammered into the ground next to the front door.

MAEVE

I love them.

COLE STONE

Yeah they're alright :)

MAEVE

I love your dad's beard.

Could I not be creepy for literally a day or was that not possible?

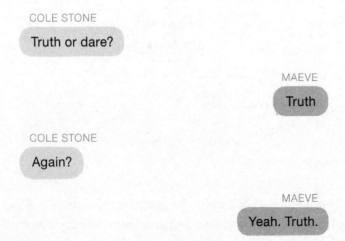

COLE STONE

Truth or dare?

MAEVE

Truth

COLE STONE

Again?

MAEVE

Yeah. Truth.

COLE STONE

Alright . . . what's the most you've ever done with a man?

Oh no. Would this scare him away? I already promised myself I would never lie to Cole. I guess it was true that I went on a failed date with the elusive and totally uninterested man codenamed R from my past.

MAEVE

Honestly, nothing but a few dates. Truth or dare?

I wanted to move on fast. But I did like the way Cole said *man*.

COLE STONE

Dare.

MAEVE

God, Cole! Lol

COLE STONE

Dare :P

MAEVE

Okay, I want to see home video of you in the Beauty and the Beast production

That really would be amazing. And that's *getting to know him*, right?

COLE STONE

> Uhhhh, okay . . . I have to find it in
> my old computer. I'll get it to you
> later.

He sent another text before I could respond.

COLE STONE

> Truth or dare?

MAEVE

> Truth.

I could almost hear the lustful growl in Cole's voice.

COLE STONE

> Pick dare

Nerves stole the rhythm of my heart.

MAEVE

> No lol. I'm nervous to . . .

COLE STONE

> Pick dare babe.

Halt the fucking factory. What did he just call me?

COLE STONE

> Have I ever made you
> uncomfortable?

MAEVE

Never.

Nervous, yes. Uncomfortable? God . . . I'd be safe in those arms.

COLE STONE

Pick dare.

So I did.

And his request came in. Exactly what I thought it'd be: a photo. Of exactly *where* I thought it'd be.

I froze. My stomach knotted and doubt and fear and *self-disgust* arrested me. I was a damaged, featureless, misshapen, flat-chested anomaly. I couldn't do this.

Could I?

I watched the time between his text and now stretch from five minutes to ten. My hand shook.

I opened the camera app.

18

By the time I struggled to undo the buttons of my shirt, flipped the camera into selfie mode, and aimed it at myself, several more minutes had passed. No angle made me look full and desirable.

Were there filters for this kind of shit? Could black-and-white retro make me look good? How about that one that turns me into an oil painting?

I fucking needed Annie Leibovitz to come in here and take my breast shots.

My gallery filled with grainy and unusable graphic photos and I wanted to keep trying but instead frustration built up and my eyes started to water and I think I was about to cry.

Buzz.

COLE STONE

Babe?

MAEVE

Idk. I'm scared.

Now would have been a great time for Cole to tell me he thinks I'm beautiful or that he wants me.

COLE STONE

Would another dick pic convince you?

My brain literally imploded trying to figure out if any of that meant that Cole did think those things. Maybe he was just being horny. But my chance to please him, to impress a man like *that,* was here and slipping fast.

I bit my lip until it bled and sent a few photos fast, so if he didn't like one, the next would pop in to distract him.

Immediately I closed out of the text thread and pulled up Mags'.

MAEVE

> I just sexted Cole photos of me
> and I'm worried he's going to
> hate them.

Thank God almighty, Mags was on her phone.

MAGS

> Omg he won't!

MAEVE

> What if he makes fun of me?

MAGS

> If he makes fun of you he's a
> terrible person and we hate him

Okay. Okay, I could work with that.

Something was wrong here, though. Instead of having fun, instead of being excited about this, I was scrutinizing and stressing. Cole was just over in his house, in his room, doing what I knew he was doing and probably not worrying about anything else in the world. I needed to be more like Cole.

When his reply came in, I was almost nauseous with nerves. For a full minute, I couldn't look.

COLE STONE

> I like it ;)

Relief flooded through me. I smiled.

He replied! I texted Mags, but she didn't respond. Must

have fallen asleep. After a few more exchanges with Cole, I would do the same.

Tonight was different. Tonight, I felt normal. Healthy. Not asexual. Tonight, I felt like a person.

So when I called Dad in to take me to bed, I made sure a few pillows covered the BiPAP machine on the floor.

KC

Who replied?

Uh-oh. That's why I didn't hear back from Mags—I'd accidentally texted KC that last message yesterday.

MAEVE

Oh damn, I'm sorry! I meant to send that to Mags.

It was morning, and I was outside in the backyard giving François a bath before my parents saw him covered in mud. I'd tossed his Frisbee right into a puddle of it, and François smelled like something died in there. He was shaking and streaming and miserable. The dog shampoo bottle was in the mud on the ground, and suds collected at his paws. Cold water pumped from the hose, and I wobbled to keep it steady while it gushed. Seriously, how much more of a euphemism could I make?

"No, no, no!" I shouted, as François poised his haunches like he was going to shake. He refrained, but bellowed out a sigh.

In my other hand, the phone vibrated—I was good at multitasking.

KC

Oh cool. Who were you talking about anyway?

I certainly couldn't tell him the whole truth.

We were—FLOOOOOOF!

Water exploded all over me as François shook his fur. I dropped the hose and François took off, tossing his head to clear his ears.

"François!" I scolded. He was long gone.

The hose soaked into the ground at my wheels, and I pushed my joystick to move. My wheels turned and burrowed into the mud. The heavy wheelchair sank.

I cursed, then called for Dad.

"Sorry," I said, when he walked down the backyard ramp moments later. He pressed a button on his Bluetooth and the little light shut off.

"Wow," said Dad. "You're pretty in there."

"Sorry," I repeated. Dad slogged over to twist off the hose. The spigot squeaked.

"All right, let's . . ." He stepped behind me and gripped two bars on either side of my wheelchair. With all his strength he heaved backwards, but the chair wouldn't budge. He puffed.

"Should I drive it back when you pull?"

Dad still panted. "Maybe on the count of three."

"Okay," I said.

We both looked up to a banging on the storm door above the backyard ramp. Mom was there, still in her white pajamas, hugging herself for warmth.

"Put your jacket on her!" Mom yelled at Dad through the door. "It's too cold!"

Dad actually grumbled. "I got it, Maura." He waved at her and returned to the chair.

"She's going to get sick!"

"Count of three," Dad repeated. His muscles braced.

"Ready," I said.

"One . . ."

"Two . . ."

"Action!" cried Mr. Billings.

The next day, Mags and I both tried to ignore the weirdness of Mr. Billings aiming a $30,000 RED Epic-W camera at a sixteen-year-old local pop star strutting out of a changing room in sparkly latex nonsense. She twirled and mouthed the lyrics to her song, which I would clip together in post because I was kinda useless on set if I wasn't directing.

Elliot stood right next to Mr. Billings, arms crossed, studying every twist of the lens. He would make a better Hollywood player than me one day. He looked at every script and location and piece of equipment with a seriousness like his life depended on it. In some ways maybe it did. He was the oldest in a family of eight in a little town house. Goofing off at Laser Tag Planet all day wouldn't get him where he wanted to go.

Mags leaned on my wheelchair the way Cole did and sucked on a lime-green smoothie. She definitely didn't hold the same sincerity on set.

"So, what did he reply?" said Mags.

"Cole?"

She slurped on her smoothie in confirmation.

"It was fine," I said, a little smile in my voice. But I'd

texted him good morning today before bathing François—
he hadn't replied.

"Cut," said Billings.

Mags crammed in closer to me as KC passed her with
a makeup bag. The little boutique clothing store Billings
secured for our location was super-tight everywhere but
next to the changing booth—racks and cardboard boxes
squeezing us in. KC scaled over a pile of accessory boxes
with lithe expertise and landed next to the pop star. He
seemed unperturbed around all the stuff, unlike Elliot,
who kept stumbling over shoe racks. This would not have
been a good set for large, clumsy Cole.

"I live-tweeted the new Star Wars movie last night on
Netflix and Peter Mayhew retweeted me," said Mags.

"What?!" I said.

"Yeah." She was deadpan.

"What did you tweet?"

"Something stupid. Like just how amazing it was."

Billings stood to coach the young pop star and actually
reenacted her strutting out of the changing room with totally enraptured, professional motivation. He really wanted
her to strut a certain way, and Mags and I were supposed
to be studying his directing techniques.

"Did you, like, take a screenshot and print it out and
frame it?" I said.

"Nah," said Mags. "It's just Peter Mayhew."

"Chewbacca is the shit," I argued.

Mags shrugged and stepped over to the refreshments
table a few paces away. She threw out her smoothie and
grabbed a juice box, then came back to me. I heard her
crinkling open the wrapper on the straw.

"You should get a Twitter, though."

"I feel like the last thing people want is a play-by-play of my life," I said.

"Are you kidding?" said Mags. She punched the straw into the juice box and handed it to me. I flushed with grateful warmth. It was awesome how she did what I needed without me asking. "You should write a whole book about your life."

"Sounds egotistical."

"Exactly."

In the corner, stuffed next to enormous, real-fur coats that Mags and I would probably protest under different circumstances, the pop star's parents stood. Her dad was this overweight, hairy Italian guy with a gold chain Miraculous Medal, and her mom was homely with bright orange lipstick. They were grinning and ecstatic the whole time. Nate 2.0—Mags' . . . boyfriend? I guess?—was standing next to them, holding the film clapper. He was charming them, making jokes I couldn't hear. Nate was smooth, always, and sometimes I liked him when his jokes weren't directed at my expense. Too bad they often were.

"I'm gonna go to the bathroom," said Mags, and left right in the middle of Billings calling action again.

I tried to pay attention to the production, but it was hard. Whoever's idea the style was—the music video company, maybe even her parents—I would have done everything differently. First, I'd have her not looking as if she were twenty-three. Then I'd suggest dressing her up and editing her as two characters: one setting the trends and one struggling to keep up with following them by hastily throwing on one outfit after the next and looking more and more helpless. It would show a lot more relatability and add a layer of depth to the lyrics, which were themselves superficial. Right now, she was just belting them out with no double message and as much flair as possible.

But Billings was into it, and his genuineness and earnestness made it a little better. I knew what it was like to be in the zone on your own set.

"So." I jumped. Someone squatted down next to me, and I looked over.

It was Nate. His curly brown hair gleamed in the excess fill light next to us, and I liked whatever Axe body spray he used, much to my chagrin. I recognized the old Nintendo 64 game logo on his orange shirt.

"Hey," I said.

"Hey," said Nate. His voice was high-pitched and always sardonic. "Mags been saying anything about me?"

I cleared my throat. Awkward paradox Nate and I were in. We both were aware of his unexplained antagonism towards me, but I was also Mags' best friend. If she was going to tell anyone a secret, it'd be me.

"Nothing much," I lied.

"Hmmmmm," said Nate. "Keep an eye out for me? Give you something to do."

See. That. It was comments like that. He assumed I had nothing going for me. I sighed.

"Maybe." A pause. "I like your shirt."

Nate clicked his tongue and gave me finger guns. He rose and wandered back over to the pop star's parents.

"Is he being a dick?" KC emerged from the clutter behind me a moment later and shoved his hands in his khaki pockets.

"No," I said. "He's all right." Maybe it was in my head.

KC stared steadily at Nate from across the room. I studied KC; I had to admit his plaid red shirt was handsome on him. I had to admit his sure way of maneuvering through the mess of this store—climbing over shit and slipping through cracks—was attractive. I thought I even saw some fluffy hair sprouting from his jaw. Was he trying to grow a beard?

"So, wait," I said. "You texted me late the other night. I was worried about you. What happened?"

"Huh?" said KC.

"When you just texted my name. It was, like, two a.m."

"Oh," said KC. He didn't go on.

"Were you—?" I started, but Mr. Billings called KC's name.

"Can you tape that wire down again?" said Billings. "Or get me a sandbag or something. Gotta pick up the pace, guys."

KC moved to Billings without answering my question. I chewed the inside of my cheek.

"But yeah, you should totally get a Twitter." I jolted again when Mags reappeared out of nowhere. Damn, with me being so stationary in these tight quarters, I felt like my friends just rotated around me in a carousel.

So Mags and I spent the next few takes creating a Twitter account for me. She chose a not-horrifying profile picture of me from my gallery—thank God I'd remembered to delete all my dirty ones. Then she chose the username before I could stop her: "Hotwheels215." That was the number of our Video II classroom. Then I filled in all the other info, including—what the hell—my real name under the username. Maybe some film people could network with me. Maybe I could pitch my scripts to agents in 140 characters or less.

"It's 280 now," said Mags.

"Oh, fuck that," I said. I followed Mags' account and sent out my first tweet: *Hi.*

We laughed.

While I was at it, I followed Elliot, One Take Blake (it looked like one of his commercials was up for a local award), our audio guy (his profile picture was a radio), creepy Nate from Video I (could be amusing), and KC. Sort of like his

Facebook, KC's Twitter had a bunch of depressing heavy metal song lyrics jammed into 280 depressing characters. The words *death, nothingness,* and *torment* appeared at least once in each excerpt.

"Look at you, already following me." Mags pulled me back to the present.

"This might be a good place to show off my disabled pickup lines," I said.

"Hit me with them," said Mags.

"All right, are you sitting down?" I said. "'Cause I am."

"Bad start."

"Here we go: Baby, this isn't the only joystick I know how to handle."

Mags choked with unexpected laughter . . . or disgust. "That's the worst."

"Yeah, I put the joy in joystick," I said.

"I hate all of these so much," said Mags.

"There's more. Ready? Baby, you don't need blue tags to park in this spot."

"How about, 'Let's see if you're handicapped accessible.'"

"Nice," I said. "I mean, I can always ask someone to be my 'physical therapist' and see how that works out."

"Porno material," said Mags.

Another hour passed, and everyone was starting to lag. There was just one last take to get right.

I got a boost of energy when my phone buzzed and I picked it up, hoping it was Cole. It was a Twitter notification.

Someone already was sending me tweets with the @ symbol. Usernames I totally didn't recognize.

Hey angel you inspire me

I raised an eyebrow. Okay . . .

There was another.

You're really brave and thanks for sticking
up for disabled people

What the hell?

More came in. Like, ten more. All real people, not spammers. All praising my crippled divinity. Why?

I clicked on my profile to see if these would show up on my Twitter page. Then my eyes bulged.

"Fuck," I breathed.

"What?" said Mags.

"My Twitter account. My followers."

"How many do you have now?" she said.

I looked up at her in shock, but I was actually worried. Why the hell was this happening?

"A thousand."

19

"Okay, wait. *What* is going on again?" Elliot held open the door to the camera shop for me later that afternoon, and I sighed and rolled in. Mags started to explain behind me.

I clicked on my phone and looked down at the article that pretty much accounted for everything: My photo, my damn photo in front of the inaccessible ice cream parlor, was published in the *Huffington Post*. And three guesses who was behind it.

Maeve Leeson of Spotsylvania County, VA, is calling for bold reforms to the antiquated (and not wheelchair-friendly) downtown Fredericksburg, according to her former camp counselor, Patricia Weinhart. Weinhart runs the city's only camp for disabled children, which offers accessible activities such as adaptive gardening, pottery, and even a creative alternative to soccer.

I imagined dozens of motorized wheelchairs driving around together on a field like bumper cars. Jesus, I'd rather be the ball.

Weinhart is very proud of her alumna-turned-activist. "Maeve is exemplifying everything we encourage here at Caring Hands Camp," says Weinhart. "Every disabled person sent to Caring Hands leaves with more confidence to face the world; every donation we receive goes to their future."

My blood boiled my bones hard enough you could paint them for Easter.

"So why don't you just tell your mom?" said Elliot as he walked in last, the glass door closing behind him. "Isn't she terrifying to people who get in your business?"

"Yeah," I said, "but I technically wasn't supposed to be out that day. I skipped physical therapy and told her I was taking a make-up test."

"How would she know?" said Elliot.

"'Cause she drove me there on a weird day. I guess I could lie more and say it's an old picture."

"I mean, I think at this point . . ." Elliot trailed off. "A thousand friggin' followers in sixty minutes?"

"Yeah, I deleted the account immediately. Fuck that."

Mags whistled. "Want me to take out this Weinhart chick?"

"Maybe," I said. I wondered if Cole would be protective of me too.

"I'll drive the getaway car," said Elliot. "What does she want with you, anyway? Why not exploit one of her real campers?"

"I don't know. At this point, it's probably revenge. We really pissed each other off at Quinten's." I didn't feel like explaining it further, but what more was there to do? I deleted the Twitter account, my Facebook was private; people would simply forget about this false news, right? I just needed to make sure Cole never saw it. It was pathetic.

We gravitated to our usual table in the camera shop. It was towards the back, near the register. All around, cardboard boxes were piled on grated shelves. Foam pellets littered the floor, which was black tile. It smelled of duct tape and Pine-Sol in here. All the walls were covered in either stage posters or Nikon ads. Elliot and I were more Canon lovers ourselves, and we engaged in debate with the storeowner often. The store sold more than cameras too: lights, audio, clappers, even theater products like props, curtains, and makeup.

We sat at the square workshop table where some lenses were out, a soft rag next to them. There was one chair left where KC usually sat, but he wasn't interested in coming with us today. He'd sketched skulls on his wrist with a black pen in the parking lot of the music video shoot and just lifted his shoulders. Elliot had thumped him on the back. And obviously Nate never came.

Elliot sighed. "I really don't want that music video on my reel."

"Dude," I said. Agreement.

"Whatever, nobody cares," said Mags. "Honestly nobody."

"Damn right," boomed a new voice. We turned to where the storeowner walked towards us, having come through the warehouse door behind the register. He was a big guy with dark skin and gold-rimmed glasses. Late thirties. His Afro made him look like he belonged in Earth, Wind & Fire, but he kept it short and well styled. It was a little theater punk.

"Sup, Roman," said Elliot.

"Mags, I don't mean to hop on your cynicism," said Roman.

"Go for it," said Mags. Roman huffed.

Legend had it that Roman was adopted by the couple who founded Shakespeare in the Park and performed as black baby Jesus twenty-six hours after he was born. Verifiable truth was that he spent the beginning of his career doing set design in New York City for the Radio City Rockettes. He knew all the latest equipment and trends, kept some contacts up there. But his real dream was to make it to Hollywood, like Elliot and me. He had a huge break once; Christopher Nolan was *this close* to hiring him to set design for the next Batman—finally getting him recognition in the big leagues—but somehow, for reasons Roman won't talk about, it all fell through. He ended up here. In this little shop. Hanging out with eighteen-year-olds.

The light in his eyes always seemed a little broken to me.

"Music video sucked?" said Roman. We all nodded. "Well, I got some good news for you. New Blackmagic in 4k came in."

"*Sweet!*" said Elliot.

Roman tossed his head towards the warehouse door. "You can go play around." Elliot wasted no time taking up that offer. He leapt up and headed for the warehouse.

"Do you still have those Bobbi Brown makeup packs?"

said Mags. Roman leaned his arms on the table and nodded slowly as if to say, *Naturally.*

"Acting section. Aisle F."

Mags went off, leaving just me.

"And what're you looking for?" Roman turned to me, smiled. A little.

"Nothing," I said. "Not this time."

"Hmm," said Roman. "Actually, I have something for you."

"Really?" I said. "Why?"

"Because you need it. Follow me into my office." He pushed himself off the table.

We passed Elliot rummaging in the new shipment box in the warehouse filled with reflectors, gels, and lenses. Roman shoved aside black boxes with his large foot so I could squeeze into the tiny room that was his office. I forged in and had about a centimeter to spare on my back wheel as he closed the door. His NYU college degree was framed on the wall, as well as a landscape-size photo of the Rockettes kicking in a line. There really weren't any family pictures on his cheap oak desk. Sticky notes with phone numbers covered his computer. Roman swung his weight around behind his desk and bent to retrieve something.

"Here," he said, box in hand. "It's a camcorder stabilizer. I ordered it for you to attach to your wheelchair. Figured you'd make the best dolly ever."

"Whoa!" I said, lighting up. "You mean this could hold the camera for me?"

"Yup," said Roman. "You can film alone now."

"No way." I beamed at the box and inspected the photo of the black metal stick that could be attached to anything to hold up the camera. "How much?"

"Nothing," said Roman. "It's a gift." He exhaled and

collapsed into his desk chair. A little sweat on his face. I thought I caught a sad note in his voice, though. I thanked him breathlessly, and he didn't look up to meet my eyes.

"Hey, Roman?" I said. "Can I ask you something?"

"Sure."

"How did it happen? How did everything . . . not work out?"

Roman was still. And then he threw his gaze over his shoulder to the Rockettes photo. "It doesn't really matter, does it?"

I was quiet.

"Right?" said Roman, looking back at me.

"Maybe," I said, unconvinced.

Roman sighed and looked down. Paused. Then he spoke. "It was my fault. They terminated me because they didn't want me anymore."

I blinked. For sure, I'd thought it was something beyond his control, some impersonal conflict.

"Nolan's people liked me at first. They had some improvements they wanted to see to my set designs. So I revised them. I just . . . could never get it perfect. I kept trying." He removed his glasses. "Finally, I explained to them why I couldn't get this one set to match their vision. I recommended we come back to it, move onto the next part of the set. They called the whole thing off; said they didn't trust me, couldn't work with me anymore. In one irrevocable email."

My heart hurt for him, and he didn't look at me.

"I couldn't face Manhattan after that. It was my fault, yeah, but the city broke my dreams, and I returned here. Never went back."

"It wasn't your fault," I said.

"Who's gonna believe that?" Roman scoffed.

"Me," I said. Silence. Roman pressed a curved look on me, but I didn't yield. He almost softened.

Before he could speak again, I jerked towards something caught in my sight: a framed white poster stuffed in the corner of the office next to the trash can. It had a rose on it.

"What poster is that?" I pointed to it. Roman glanced over. He swiveled around the office chair.

"In the corner?" He heaved himself to stand. "Something I never got around to hanging."

Roman grabbed the framed poster from the junk at his trash can and held it out in front of him in both hands. He gazed at it like an old basketball trophy.

"Production I did a long time ago," was all he said, and he turned it so I could see.

My heart thrusted against my throat.

The poster was Broadway's *Beauty and the Beast*.

Before dinner that night, Dad punched the tiny little beeper horn button on my joystick in passing.

"Family meeting in five," he said. "Living room couch."

I looked up from playing Temple Run 2 on my phone.

"All right, lay it on me," I said five minutes later as I wheeled into the living room. Mom and Dad sat together on the sofa.

"Are you guys pregnant?"

"No," said Mom.

"Getting a divorce?"

"No."

"Are books banned again?"

One time the hardcover book I was reading in bed fell forward on my face and I didn't have the strength to lift it off me. I'd laughed and yelled for Dad. He banned books for a while. But that wasn't it.

"Are we moving?"

"No . . ." said Dad. He placed a hand on Mom's knee, and they looked at each other and smiled. "But you kinda are."

"What?" I said.

"You're going to college," said Mom.

"I know," I said. "Go Grizzlies."

"Not the community college," said Mom.

A pause. Then slowly my mouth dropped. "Away to college?"

"Your mother and I have been saving to hire a personal aide to take care of you while you're in school," said Dad. "It'll take some planning, and we'll need to live with you for the first week or so to teach the nurse things, and we need you to call every night—"

"And you'll have to fly home with the aide to see Dr. Clayton once a semester," said Mom.

"There are a *lot* of nasty germs at universities," said Dad, "so that means you'll be—"

"No way." I actually laughed. "Are you serious? I can go away to college?" I could actually go to film school at UCLA with Elliot and Mags and maybe Cole?

"If you can keep your grades up and get yourself in, Mom and I will figure it out." Dad smiled at me. "We'll just miss the shit out of you."

I rammed into the couch to hug them and the whole sofa jostled about half a foot backwards.

"Whoa there," said Dad. He and Mom laughed.

"Thank you, guys," I said, and they both leaned forward to hug me.

"Thank us at your first Golden Globe," said Mom.

196 S. C. MEGALE

20

My phone buzzed once on the TV dinner tray and made François jump back from licking the fork on the edge of the table. It was later that night, and after I spent about two hours in my room working on my video reel for the UCLA application and had ALL CAPS CONVERSATIONS with Mags and Elliot to let them know about the big news, I was watching reruns of *The Bachelor* with Mom. She massaged my head with her hand in my hair and then sat down with a mug of Campbell's soup.

Juan Carlos really needed to send some of these girls home. He jetted them out to scuba with him in Bali and they basically flipped out switchblades to snip each other's oxygen when he wasn't looking. Spanish guitar music played in the background whenever the cameraman did some nice tilts on his biceps. I wondered what they'd zoom in to on me if I were the Bachelorette. Wheel spokes? Sexy polyester upholstery?

I picked up my phone.

COLE STONE

> Why did you delete your Twitter account?

My heart skipped. He saw my Twitter account? For whatever reason, it was otherworldly to picture Cole— all frustratingly masculine, six-foot-a-thousand of him— pulling up his phone and ending up on my Twitter account.

It was only live for a few hours before I committed infanticide and killed it. *Play it cool.*

> MAEVE
>
> You cyberstalking me now?

> COLE STONE
>
> Maybe :P

Well damn. I smirked.

> MAEVE
>
> It just wasn't for me

Juan Carlos lifted one of the girls onto his shoulders in the scuba training pool. She squealed, and they splashed around. The other women took that cue to remove clothing pronto.

> COLE STONE
>
> Oh. Haha. It looked like you deleted it right after I followed you. I was worried I scared you away or something

> MAEVE
>
> No I didn't even see you follow me

Shit. Playing disinterested now. New achievement unlocked.

> COLE STONE
>
> Well then :P

MAEVE

Uh huh lol

"Can I get you anything, honey?" Mom rose to take her mug into the kitchen.

"I got it," said Dad, taking the mug. "You rest." He added it to the pile of dishes in the sink. The faucet ran as he scrubbed.

COLE STONE

So what made it not for you

I pursed my lips. Did I have to tell him? I promised myself I'd never lie to him.

MAEVE

Okay, to be honest, I was getting some weird attention and didn't like being associated with the MD crowd on there.

COLE STONE

The what?

"Do you think these women get paid?" said Mom. They were now mini golfing on the Bali resort in dental-floss bikinis. Juan Carlos rolled up in a golf cart to whistles and bouncing curls.

"Millions," said Dad from the kitchen.

"Maybe I should sign up," said Mom. "Dad would understand."

Dad opened the refrigerator to stash the leftovers. "Take one for the team, baby."

MAEVE

Muscular dystrophy.

COLE STONE

What's that?

MAEVE

It's what I have.

There was a pause while I thought about this.

MAEVE

You didn't know that? :)

I really did smile down at my phone. I know it's weird.
But I loved that he had no damn clue.

Just as the final selection ceremony commenced, Dad
walked in drying his hands on a towel. Before Cole could
reply, I texted him again.

MAEVE

Hey, you know what I feel like
doing?

COLE STONE

Me? :P

MAEVE

Besides that.

COLE STONE

Hmmmmm . . .

MAEVE
But I mean if you're offering.

COLE STONE
What is it? Lol

MAEVE
Mini golf. I wanna mini golf.

COLE STONE
Do you?

MAEVE
Yeah.

COLE STONE
That's interesting . . .

MAEVE
Why?

Subconsciously, Dad bent to untie my shoes, eyes still on the TV. I stopped him just after he pulled loose the first lace. He looked at me, confused.

COLE STONE
Besides you, that's kinda what I want to do too.

So back when I was, like, eight, there was this enormous puddle on our block that formed without fail whenever it rained. Something about the way the pavement dipped and the gutters ran and the houses shielded the sun just right. Nothing blew the mind of Little Maeve more than plunging all four wheels into the water and reveling in the splash and ripples they'd make. I'd hang a U-turn and charge into it again and again. Then one day, the community noticed the fuss I was making and thought I was mad at the puddle or something (so I attacked it with my wheelchair? I don't know what they were thinking). They repaved and leveled the puddle and I grieved its loss until maybe last January.

Looking at the putt-putt course now, I felt a lance of that same annoyance. Where there used to be six, maybe seven holes of peeling green fabric and a few dollar store windmill birdhouses decorating the perimeter, there now were a full eighteen courses heated with Astroturf grass and mechanical alligators opening and closing their jaws. But worst of all . . .

"Hey, um, miss?" I rolled up to an employee.

"Hey." She turned to me, holding a clear bucket of those little pencils. Of course, she looked like one of the reality show women stepped through the screen and followed me here. "Can I help you?"

"You guys didn't have those bricks bordering the courses before. Are they removable?"

She turned to follow my pointing at the circle of single-file bricks outlining every hole.

"Oh. No, I'm sorry. They're glued down to keep the balls in." Okay but my new love life goal is to get the balls out, so. Not helping.

I guess her tone was genuine. She got the bigger meaning. How was I going to get my chair over every border?

Since Mom dropped me off here ten minutes ago, and I kinda had to beg her to spontaneously give me a lift before our show was even over, I couldn't change the meeting location now. Maybe Cole and I could just . . . watch people golf.

Shit, no, that's lame. Maybe I should text him and give him a heads-up so he can cancel if he wants, and then I could just sit here and pretend I met someone until it was believable to call Dad to come get me. I opened my messenger app to Cole's name and started to—

"Hi."

I jumped.

Cole was there. He stuffed his hands in his jean pockets and swayed side to side as he gazed around at the place, pivoting once to take it in. His hair and beard never seemed blacker than in the course lights. His shoes were frayed, soft-looking grey flats with black laces and white rubber soles. I immediately recognized his unique, masculine smell and wondered if maybe only I could detect it.

"Cole," I said. "Hey." I inched towards him and bumped the side of his leg with my wheelchair affectionately, the way I did in the mall. He didn't yet look down, even when I bumped him, as if it were normal to him. But his arm fell over me and engulfed me.

"This it?" he said. Finally his eyes met my gaze. They were a little sleepy, a little removed, but something about the way they didn't waver made me weak.

"Yep, this is it." I gestured to the course. "This is my childhood. Ruined."

"Uh-oh." He shoved his hands back in the pockets.

"They renovated it," I said. "I'm really sorry, but I don't think we can play."

"Why not?"

"They added bricks around the course."

"So?"

"So my chair can't get over them."

"It'll be fine," boomed Cole.

"What do you mean?"

"Come on."

He moved forward, and the lanyard on his belt jingled with his keys. At the club rack, he grabbed two balls and the longest putter they had. I grabbed the shortest. Then we approached the bricks.

"So . . ." Nerves and embarrassment shook my voice. "Are you thinking about—?"

I felt a tug on my wheelchair from behind. "I got you," said Cole. "Go."

I revved my joystick forward and Cole forced down the back of the heavy chair to pop a wheelie as I clattered over the bricks. He didn't even grunt.

My wheels surged over smooth turf and I grinned. Cole stepped over the brick and tilted his head to stretch his neck. He wasn't winded at all.

"We don't have to do the other holes," I said, but I was still smiling. "We'll just do this one."

"Nah," said Cole.

"You sure?" I wasn't about to question how many holes he could, uh . . .

He stared at me, and his mouth was cocked in the most perplexing smile. Demure. Relaxed. But not going anywhere.

I batted my club against the Astroturf. "All right, then. Hope you're scared."

Cole pretended the putter was a driver and swung it hard with his whole back. The club whipped through the air and stopped over his shoulder.

The way everything moved at his force, the way he shrugged to fill all of whatever space was around him, everything I can't do, can't be, he was. I wondered if I was anything he couldn't be.

He dropped the purple golf ball onto the grass and nodded at me. His dark, visceral eyes pinned me. Parallel parking, I cruised my chair into position and gripped the kiddie club tight with both hands.

It gave a satisfying *clop* when I hit the ball. Cole and I watched as the ball curved around a little hill and glided right into the hole.

We paused. Then we turned to each other with a long look.

All together we clambered over eighteen borders of brick. Cole always hit too hard; his ball skipped over the holes. Once, I hit mine backwards underneath the tunnel of my chair between the wheels. I turned to see it just graze the hole and roll past. Cole watched with his hands slung on either side of his club across his shoulders. For some reason, I thought of how KC would probably have nudged it in before I could see.

We did the whole damn course together.

"I like that you use the big club," I said. There was a little juice bar we sat at minutes later.

"Do you?" said Cole.

"Yeah," I said.

When he couldn't sway, he bobbed his foot. One rested on the prong of the bar stool; his other reached the floor. He wedged his credit card back in his wallet, having paid for our games despite my protest. I noticed a Best Buy gift card, a membership card to the local paintball arena, and his driver's license photo—it was less grim and more boyish than I thought it would be. He was smiling in black and white.

"So guess what?" I said.

"What?"

"My parents said I could apply to UCLA."

"Did they?"

"Yeah," I said, and wobbled the empty bar stool next to me with my good hand. "I'm stoked. Are you still going to apply for the theater program?"

"I might." His eyes sparkled at me, but the set of his mouth gave nothing more away. If I could lift my arm far enough to reach him, I'd try to graze his chest and feel the heat of his skin. I couldn't imagine what his muscle would feel like against the lack of mine.

I couldn't imagine the things I would do with him in a college dorm.

"Your shoelace is untied," he finally said. I looked down. Only one was—the one Dad had undone.

"Oh." I chuckled. "Yeah, I, uh . . . I can't tie a shoe-lace."

When he didn't comment, I got self-conscious and regurgitated more. "I can't reach my foot, but even if I could, I don't know how to tie a shoe because I never had to."

Cole nodded.

"And I don't trust everyone with my feet. Because they're brittle. From, like, disuse."

Oh my God, stop!

"I would trust you with my feet," I said.

I'll just see myself out. The silence was horrifying.

"There's a *SpongeBob* episode about that," said Cole at last.

"What?"

"He couldn't tie his shoelaces."

"I'm in amazing company." There. At least I was quick.

The holes were closing one by one with lights shutting off as a last party of fifth graders snaked their way to each one. They obnoxiously whacked their clubs against each other's like lightsabers and shouted.

"Do you like kids?" I said.

"Maybe," said Cole.

"Under certain circumstances?" Why did I always need to tug the conversation along?

"Sometimes."

He passed an investigating gaze to me. Foot still bobbing.

"What?" I said.

"Why are you asking?"

"Just curious. Being observant." A little color rose to my skin. Suddenly I wasn't sure that was the only reason I asked.

Cole studied me for another beat. Then his hand ran down my hair. I shuddered at his fingertips. Everything loosened and trembled. He withdrew it just as fast and took a drink of water. My glass sat next to his. Untouched. Too heavy.

"So," said Cole as he lowered his glass, not yet looking at me again. "What's our next production together?"

A loaded question. If it were up to me, we'd be playing with a green screen in some million-dollar LA or Atlanta studio; lights, cranes. And every camera rolling Cole Stone.

"I was thinking, like, a Michael Bay remake of *Love Actually*," I said. I could already see the American jet fighters streaking across the sky as a boring middle-aged couple giggled under the mistletoe.

"Sounds like a lot of stunts," he said. "Am I going to have to jump out of a helicopter?"

"Yeah, but I'll just bring my mattress for you to land on."

"That's one way to get me on it." He looked at me.

My throat caught. I looked at him too. God, what would

it be like to one day be carried to bed . . . and then joined in it?

"Cole," I said. Oh no. I was doing that thing again where I said his name and a reckless vomit of words followed. He didn't look over yet.

There's this hotel nearby . . .

Don't say it.

That's so cliché.

You guys can't afford these waters, how are you affording a hotel?!

"Do you want to sleep with me?" said Cole.

Excuse me? He played with the ice in the drink.

"What did you say?" My throat was dry.

"You heard me."

"Yeah," I blurted. "I do."

"One day?" he said.

"Yeah."

"What if you get pregnant?"

I told him we'd make sure to be safe and test ourselves for STIs if we decided to be active with each other, and that I was on birth control. With everything else involved in my care, adding monthly menstruation was kind of messy. Mom had started me on it years ago.

But I loved this. I loved that he didn't hesitate or question my ability to conceive. It was not even a thought for him. Most just look at me and are certain I'm not healthy enough to carry my own life let alone a second.

"Hmmmm . . ." said Cole. He leaned one strong arm on the bar. That smile started to creep back.

Throat still dry (other parts not so much), I swallowed. Then Cole moved.

I thought he was going to kiss me. I thought this was it.

Instead, he lifted my glass of water and held it out to me. Close enough for my mouth to meet it.

Did he remember from our last date that I couldn't pick it up? He watched me. I watched him. And I took a gulp. Water dripped down my lips.

"Maybe we should . . ." I began.

As soon as I did, the lights cut off at the bar.

They were kicking us out.

Dad had arrived a minute later because Mom had gotten worried and looked up the time the mini golf closed and was 100 percent certain my phone had died and I had been sold into slavery where they would use my chair to till fields until it broke and they sold it for parts.

Cole drove away as jerkily and fast as always. Dad never saw him come or go.

I lay in bed that night. Happy. But thinking.

The rules say I should have waited. Instead, I texted him.

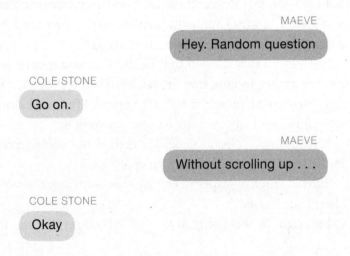

MAEVE

Hey. Random question

COLE STONE

Go on.

MAEVE

Without scrolling up . . .

COLE STONE

Okay

> **MAEVE**
> What disease do I have?

There was a good sixty-second wait.

> **COLE STONE**
> Idk the name

> **MAEVE**
> So you have no idea?

Another long pause, as if he worried he was in trouble.

> **COLE STONE**
> I'm sorry. Why?

I smiled.

> **MAEVE**
> Keep it that way.

21

Because I can't raise my arm over my head, Mrs. Chadwick in organic chem gave me this little orange flag to wave when I needed something. I flapped it around like I was landing a plane.

"Maeve?" she said.

"Can I go to the bathroom?"

"Yes," said Mrs. Chadwick. Then she nodded at Mags three rows behind me.

Mags' seat scraped, and she rose as I wound my way to the exit with François. A fresh waft of custodian's soap met us in the hallway, and we closed the door on Mrs. Chadwick's slow, droning lecture.

"You were early today," said Mags.

"I was falling asleep." I stuffed the flag into my footplate as we headed for the girls' bathroom.

It'd been three days since my last date with Cole, and he hadn't texted. My patience in general was thin. At least hallway monitors didn't dare ask us for a pass when they got a look at Mags escorting me with a dutiful stride.

Inside the bathroom, Mags hopped up on the counter next to the sinks. The mirror reflected her pretty red hair. I edged closer to her, and she reached down and crossed my foot over the other the way one would cross their legs in an armchair.

"You know," she said, "one of these days, if you really do have to go to the bathroom, I can do that for you."

I chuckled. "No way. Too weird."

"Seriously! I go to the gym. I'm strong enough."

"I know, it's just—"

"And if we're going to travel together one day, I want to help you do all the stuff. We don't want your parents there *all* the time."

I worried about when my parents wouldn't be there anymore more than she knew, but warmth tickled through me.

"Thanks." I blushed and imagined the idea of letting her do some of the things required with helping me use the toilet.

"It's not that big of a deal." It was as if Mags could read my mind.

Instead of me actually going to the bathroom and her actually "helping" me like every teacher in Seefeldt High School believed, we came here once a day during the pre-determined boringest class and hung out. That it takes us a half hour to "manage the bathroom" is entirely believable. It could theoretically take that long for someone as petite as Mags to get me dressed again.

I played with the foam dispenser and we talked about her dad's veterinary office while she petted François, and both of us said, "Sup," to the girls who walked in and out.

"Are you still getting another cat for Christmas?" I asked.

She wanted to name it Laces and eventually get a cat named Buttons so she can have an entire clothing-clasper collection of cats. I guess it's hard not to be indoctrinated with a love of animals while having a veterinarian dad, but Mags wanted to start a shelter for her thesis project in environmental science at UCLA if she got in. Film would only be her minor, which made sense to me.

We weren't always in the same library, let alone on the same page about men, but I told her a little about my date with Cole at the mini golf course. She still thought he was a jerk and that I should leave some of his texts on read receipts to take back the power, so her comments were minimal, but I got an "I'm glad he helped you over the bricks" as she rolled her eyes playfully and punched my arm.

I laughed and flapped François' ear.

"Have you ever tried eyeliner?" said Mags. "Not that you need it. It'd just look cool on you."

I wasn't much of a makeup person in general, but there were special occasions . . . "Lipstick is the only thing I can reach high enough to apply."

Mags held up a finger and jumped off the counter. "I have some in my backpack. Hold on." She pulled it off the floor and rummaged.

"Oh God." I laughed when she popped open this black stick the way one breaks open a nunchuck.

Mags smiled and approached me. "Try not to blink too much."

"Okay."

I tilted back my head. With gentle hands, she carved some shadow onto the sensitive skin around my eyes. Despite her request, I blinked a lot.

"There."

I looked down and into the mirror. Mags hung her arm around me and smiled into our reflection too. My eyes popped and accentuated my face. I looked older and more defined.

"I'm beautiful," I said with enthusiasm.

Mags shrugged. "You were before."

When the bell rang, we realized we'd stayed too long and left the bathroom to go our separate ways to separate classes. I moved my chair a little faster and with a little more confidence as additional students flashed around my periphery holding books as they crowded the hallway. I was pretty glad the Pokémon GO phase with everyone walking into me was over, and now they just filled my ears with dialogue and slang almost too fresh to even put in a script. It took me a while to figure out *alright bet*.

I made for music theory.

Bang!

A locker slammed right in front of me. I halted. Nate 2.0 was there. He munched on a random stick of celery and shoved his falling lunchbox back atop the locker with one hand.

"Hey, Maeve." His voice was as placating as ever.

"Hi." I tried to swerve around him.

"Hangin' out with Maaaaaagss?" He drew it out in as juvenile a way as possible.

"Yeah," I said. "You know we do that."

"Getting some more special attention?" He chewed. "Making sure everyone knows?"

Was that why he hated me? Because I got a little special treatment? Because I required a little more from the world?

"Playing the cards I was dealt, Nate," I said. "You know, in case I'm a virgin forever."

"Awww, Maeve. You know I didn't mean that."

"Didn't you, though?"

"Mags certainly doesn't think so." He winked. "But maybe you could tell her that next time you use your disability to sneak out of class. No one would dare stop you."

"What's going on?" KC stepped up just then. He looked from Nate to me and back again with a dark expression.

"Nothing!" Nate was chipper. He brushed his hands off. "Just getting back to class, KCeeeee." The same drawing out of KC's name.

The hallway was thinning out as students found their classes.

"You don't like me because I get attention," I said.

"Never said that." Nate clicked finger guns at me and started to walk past KC.

"No," KC said right to Nate's face before he could slip away. "You don't like her because she's powerful."

"THROW A MONKEY! THROW IT NOW!"

Some twelve-year-old boy from Michigan hollered in my headset after school that day. I stared dumbly at the screen at my *Call of Duty* character, white controller in my hands. Thumbs clacking against the two joysticks. With a button, I threw a stuffed monkey into a horde of glowing-eyed zombies to draw them off my teammate.

"Thanks!" said the boy, and he scrambled away on screen. I noticed that everyone on Xbox Live, without exception, was either a squeaky-voiced twelve-year-old boy or a creepy deep-voiced deadbeat-father type.

I pumped my shotgun and sprinted into the next room.

I'd been playing video games since maybe before I operated my first wheelchair. I loved the anonymity. I loved the deep camaraderie with guys all over the country. I loved the shooting and leading and jumping and all the things I couldn't do. Michigan Boy had never heard my voice (because I don't have a mic), but we'd been playing together for months, all different games, and he told other players with mics about me: "No, no! Keep him! He's good!"

He was right. I am good. In *Gears of War* I once sniped the head off the last surviving enemy player while he was *literally jumping off a balcony,* and Michigan Boy went "OHHHHHHHHH!!!" and the other players went "WHAT THE FUCK!" and it was pretty much the proudest day of my life.

They had no idea what I looked like. They just knew I was good.

Elliot's gamertag popped on screen to let me know he was online, but he was pretty hooked on *Fallout* and hadn't been playing live lately. His gamertag was Filmshooter89. Mine was Roadsmith1116. Much better than Hotwheels215, but similar concept. You know, I create roads anywhere I go. Something like that.

My phone buzzed. I unloaded the rest of my ammo on some zombies and then checked it.

COLE STONE
Text Message

I smiled and rested the controller on my knee.

COLE STONE

Hey :)

Ugh. So no mention of the three-day silence/ignoring my messages. Okay. But the last thing I wanted was to come off bitchy.

MAEVE

Sup :)

"Roadsmith, come on!" Michigan Boy shouted. I scrambled the controller into my grasp and ran away before the zombies could whack my screen entirely to red.

COLE STONE

Sorry, I've been a busy museum docent :P

MAEVE

Have you now?

That was cute at least. I struck a zombie with the butt of my shotgun.

COLE STONE

Yeah

MAEVE

I want to see you again.

COLE STONE

Hmmm

MAEVE

What?

My blood tightened. I hoped the rejection I anticipated wasn't about to hit.

COLE STONE

Anything you want to do specifically . . . ?

MAEVE

Talk? I do have some things I want to ask you

COLE STONE

Ask away.

MAEVE

No, in person.

I helped Michigan Boy back to his feet to escape the hellhound chasing him before I checked Cole's response.

COLE STONE

Fiiiiine :P

It dawned on me that maybe I was still "bribing" Cole to want to see me. Really didn't sit right in my gut.

MAEVE

> But don't come if that's the only reason you want to hang out - so you can find out what the questions are.

Bold. I made an explicit effort to play the zombie game hard while Cole chewed on that.

COLE STONE

> It won't be the only reason

While that statement would have been so much better with a period, I grinned. I'd take it.

I think I played my best game yet of zombies. Fifteen minutes later, Michigan Boy and I were on wave twenty-two.

Just as we were upgrading our weapons, more texts came in.

KC

> Remember when I texted you in the middle of the night?

I raised an eyebrow.

MAEVE

> Yeah. Are you okay, KC?

My mouth felt heavy. I didn't know how, or why, or how much, but I knew KC hurt. And that made me hurt too.

KC

> Yeah. I just wanted to tell you something.

MAEVE

> Do you want to call me?

I'd forfeit the game if he needed me.

KC

> I don't think so.

MAEVE

> What is it?

I barely even noticed what I was doing in the game anymore.

KC

> I like you, Maeve.

My controller vibrated nonstop as I took damage, but I focused on my phone in one hand.

MAEVE

> I like you too, KC. I'll always be here for you.

"Roadsmith! Throw a monkey! Throw a monkey!" My screen was being pummeled to red as the zombies bashed me.

KC

> No.

KC

> Maeve.

"KC," I whispered aloud in reply. His last message buzzed in.

KC

I have feelings for you.

My mouth fell, and the zombies overpowered me.

22

One time I read that people with Parkinson's have really clean teeth. The toothbrush enters their mouths and they let their arms jerk and spasm and hop berserk against their molars. I shake, but not that bad, and the dentist keeps upping the wattage on my electric toothbrush because I'm weak. I wondered now, as I lifted my tea to my lips, if the wobbling hot liquid would fall on my shirt. If maybe I was heading for Parkinson's level one day. But today, I shook for reasons beyond medical.

It was a day after KC confessed his feelings for me. A blender roared behind the counter as baristas in green aprons capped latte cups and called out names. The exotic musk of coffee beans clashed with the frigid weather outside. Behind my table, the glass door opened and a gust of cold air rushed in. Someone sighed and stamped their feet on the welcome mat. I looked up as the petite person walked around and pulled out the chair across from me. Mags.

"Hey," she said. Cheeks flushed from the cold and lips a little chapped. She wore a van Gogh printed scarf and pink, fingerless gloves. I'd asked her to meet me here after she clocked out of work the next day; Mom had to go to the bank again last minute anyway and dropped me off for a quick half hour. Tomorrow was Thanksgiving, and today was only a half day of school. I didn't see KC.

"Hi," I said. "I'm sorry."

Mags snorted. "You're already apologizing. What's going on?"

"Do you want coffee?" I said.

"Just tell me."

"KC has feelings for me." It burst from my throat.

"Ohhh . . ." Mags leaned back. Her eyes rested on the table. I was confused by her reaction. Why was she thoughtful, not shocked? Why didn't her mouth drop?

"Oh, what?" I said. "Wait, did you know?"

"I mean . . ." said Mags. Out the window next to us, flurries wisped through the air, but if you weren't looking right at them, you wouldn't see.

"You knew," I said.

"It was always obvious to me," said Mags. "I thought maybe you were dodging him."

"No." I shook my head.

"Okay, then, how do you feel about it? What did you say?"

"I didn't say anything, I didn't know what to say because I don't know what I feel. I mean, he's been my friend since kindergarten."

"I know," said Mags. "But you have to say something."

Silence stretched. The tea clutched in my hand was cooling. Why was it so easy to desire nearly every man I came across, but with KC, I couldn't figure out how I felt?

I'd been attracted to him. But I'd never thought of him romantically until now. We were just too close. For too long.

"You know . . . he's a nice guy, Maeve."

"I know," I said, but it was almost a snap.

And then there was Cole.

"Just text him back and ask him if he can meet up with you," said Mags. "If you need some time, he might understand."

Might.

"You have to make a decision between him and Cole for yourself, though. If Cole is even really in the running."

I ripped at the cup sleeve with my thumbnail. My heart sped.

"This sucks." Mags tried to validate the situation. We paused.

"On the bright side"—I swallowed and forced humor—"I have a taste of what's it's like to be you."

"Maeve." Mags groaned and tugged off her scarf. "That's not a bright side."

Al Roker interviewed a little kid in the bleachers on TV. The boy stared blankly at him in his fluffy black earmuffs and wouldn't answer any questions. Behind them flowed the Thanksgiving Day Parade. I watched on the miniature kitchen TV while Mom ran the sink.

"What's the next ingredient, Maeve?"

The turkey was already basted and roasting in the oven. Mom knew exactly what the next ingredient for the sweet potato casserole was, but she wanted me to learn. I glanced at the *Southern Living* recipe snippet and read out the next dosage of brown sugar. She ripped open the bag.

Seems like now would be the perfect time for my domestic fantasies to rage. Dad was in the next room watching ESPN after putting up some early Christmas lights in the front yard. "Smells good, Mom," he'd said after coming inside. So much material for domestic daydreams.

They were blank.

Per Mags' advice, I replied to KC and asked if we could meet up, nothing more. He kept his cool and said *sure* but that he was going to his aunt and uncle's for Thanksgiving and couldn't meet sooner than tomorrow. The holiday provided a convenient detour from this, a chance for me to collect my feelings.

Never in a million tire changes did I think I'd be in this position. It dawned on me that maybe I was hiding too much behind my default; maybe it was arrogant of me to blame the lack of interest from men on my disease so quickly, now that it was hitting. Mags could have been right all along. I was not immune to this mess.

The Admiral was supposed to join us for Thanksgiving, but he called this morning and said he was going to haul his tractor up to Middleburg tonight instead to get it fixed tomorrow. Mom rolled her eyes and Dad huffed and we three sat at the table and said grace. Mom expressed sincere thanks for the new BiPAP machine that had arrived this week to replace the one I claimed malfunctioned. Dad nudged my arm without any of us opening our eyes.

Then we began. Platters steamed. The food was aromatic, but I had a hard time tasting it.

Finally, late that afternoon, when Dad was clinking dishes into the washer and Mom was upstairs changing into her pajamas already, I got a text.

COLE STONE
Text Message

My heart fluttered. Today?

COLE STONE

Happy Thanksgiving :)

MAEVE

Hey :) You sick of family or something?

COLE STONE

Maybe.

MAEVE

You can always talk to me instead.

COLE STONE

Yeah, you're probably the only one I would :P

I blinked. Hmm.

I gave a start and sort of hid my phone when Dad set a plate of pumpkin pie in front of me.

MAEVE

Want to call me?

I could go outside.

COLE STONE

Idk. I kind of want to see you

MAEVE

Okay. Tomorrow?

That was the day I promised to meet KC. Why did I just offer it up to Cole?

COLE STONE

No, like tonight :P

I blinked.

MAEVE

It's Thanksgiving boy I can't get a ride anywhere today

COLE STONE

What if I just came to you?

MAEVE

I figured you do all the time

COLE STONE

Pfffffft :P

I was smiling. With my fork, I carved off a piece of pie and ate it. The taste was spicy and sweet and smooth.

COLE STONE

Maybe you could tell your parents you're just taking a walk with your friend.

MAEVE

There's a park walkable.

6:30.

I texted him the park address.
Shit. What was happening?

I managed to escape the house without too much interrogation. Being partially true, I said I was just going for a walk with "one of my film friends."

"Sounds fun," Mom had said, lying on the couch with the Hallmark Channel on. Dad glanced at me with a little sharper curiosity but didn't object. Tonight was only supposed to dip to about fifty degrees, otherwise I wouldn't have gotten out of Mom's grip unfussed.

Dusk drew down behind the tops of trees, and I waited by this little park bench, shivering. The dusting of snow had melted, but more would probably come this week. Before me was this little playground made up of four sturdy sycamores and tree houses accessed with ladders, but one had a staircase that wound around the trunk. I used to be jealous of the neighborhood kids who could play in them. The ground was bark pellets like the inside of a hamster cage.

Houses lit up the grass a few hundred yards ahead now. It was 6:48. Night almost lapped over the twilight.

A quiet motor thrummed from up the street and I looked over to it. Headlights beamed across the dark asphalt and a beat-up silver car jolted a few times before it parked at the curb. I watched as it shook there for a moment, and then the engine cut. The lights disappeared to blackness.

The car door popped open and an enormous silhouette swung out. I couldn't see any of his features from here, but I heard a lanyard jingle.

He strolled towards me, taking his damn time. His stride was as rocky and boastful as his driving. I felt like my blood had retreated and left only helium in my veins. I couldn't catch a breath and may have needed this three-hundred-pound shell of metal to keep me steady. Did I wave? Did I watch his approach silently?

Did I check my phone to pretend I almost didn't care?

Cole appeared in front of me. He wore a navy-blue camo jacket just like his dad in the photo. His brown-black hair was combed forward, and his beard was trimmed just enough to see some of his jaw through it. Perfect length.

"Hey," I said. Dammit, I sounded breathless.

My ears involuntarily switched frequencies to prepare to catch Cole's booming reply. Instead, he nodded and bent down to me. With one arm, he folded me against himself. I closed my eyes, and my head buried into just where his ribs were. The jacket was warm and smelled like a garage. I imagined old rusty tools leaning on the wall next to where it always hung.

When he pulled back, he wasn't looking at me. Just gazing at the sycamores and the tree houses.

I opened my mouth to speak. To say something like, "Are you okay?" but he beat me to it.

"You ever been in there?" With his hands stuffed in his pockets, he gestured to the staircase tree house with his elbow.

"No." I sort of laughed. "But I was always jealous of the kids who were. So I pretended to lay siege on them sometimes."

Cole turned to me. Those premature lines under his eyes were a flaw by any other standard, but to me they hooded him gently. They gave something more for me to love.

He didn't reply again. I wasn't used to Cole being quiet. His gaze held me in a way that was intimate but oddly impersonal, as if he were studying me and thinking about me like I wasn't there. I don't know if I was imagining it. But I think there was a little light in his gaze that wasn't there before. If he were thinking about me, I think they were good thoughts.

"Show me your favorite tree," he said.

My throat went dry as I tried to translate that. Cole stared at me. His eyes glimmered but, ever the actor, his mouth was in a neutral line. Waiting on me.

Show him my favorite tree. *Take me into cover with you.*

"Okay," I whispered. And my voice trembled.

I rolled onto the mixed terrain of dirt and bark pellets. I prayed the melted snow didn't soak it enough to make me sink, and in my stupidity, I even voiced this to Cole.

He walked close at my side. "I'll just push you out."

The side of my wheel hit the sycamore closest to us and the ladder rattled. I fumbled for breath as Cole walked around me. In front of me.

There he stood. Towering. Just a dark figure, but I knew every shadow and crevice, and I loved every shift of his body. He kept watching me, as if to make sure I was coherent and okay and with him in the present. The tree was at my back, close enough that he reached his arm over me and touched it. Its low braches sheltered us.

"This one, huh?" said Cole.

"Yeah," I breathed. Oh God, he was going to touch me.

"Not the one I can carry you up into?"

Please touch me. I don't know how, but please figure it out.

Cole smiled, seeing I was too scared and excited and inebriated by him to reply.

"Maybe next time," said Cole.

Without thinking, I flopped out an arm for him. It caught an inch of his sweatshirt but fell. He looked down at it then up at me, still wearing that smile.

"What were you reaching for?"

"You," I said.

"Is that all?"

"I don't know . . ." My voice trembled with anticipation.

He thought about it for a beat. "You don't need to reach for me." To prove his words, he moved closer. His arm still held the tree branch, but he brought my leaden hand up to his lips. For a moment, I thought he would put my fingers in his mouth. Instead, he kissed them and let my arm fall again like a piece of iron. Just like that.

We hung there, too long, too painfully. We didn't move.

His voice dropped an octave. "Do you want me to touch you?"

Yes.

"I need to know you want me to." What did he want? Consent, or more attention? When he came out here, I wanted to talk and understand him and forge a deeper bond with him. But now that he asked me this, it was all I wanted.

I nodded.

His colossal shadow moved down to me and absorbed the space between us. The heat from his body engulfed me, seemed to pulse against me. Slowly, he grazed the stiff fronds of his beard across the sensitive skin of my face. I shuddered and reached a weak hand for him. My fingers found his soft jacket sleeve and curled to hold it.

He breathed in jerks against my neck, but didn't kiss me yet.

"Cole," I whispered, in the sort of way that didn't need an answer. All of my fear disappeared. I felt safe with him. Completely.

His hand reached down to my seat belt. "How?" he breathed.

"Click it."

He did.

"Reach in," I said.

It took some maneuvering. With his beard still scratching my neck, he used an arm to dig under my knees and shuffle me out a little. "I don't know if I can," he said.

"You're almost there," I said. His hand was just inches away. With another shove under my waistband, he found me. I half-choked, half-gasped.

My skin was sandpaper, and his fingers, the match. His hand convulsed with just the right pressure, just the right rhythm, and I had just enough time to think, *Holy fucking god, this is happening,* before my head swam into nothing. It took me a few moments to realize his other hand was busy on himself too. We both grunted. He seemed to support me, pin me just right against my chair with his strength. I heard his hand jerk irregularly below his belt, and he stepped even closer. Occasionally he swung his head up to glance around and make sure we were alone with the night. When the pleasure came, I collapsed against his broad shoulder and heaved breath in and out. My eyes closed and I snuggled into his coat.

But we were both silent. He became very still.

"You okay?" he panted, pulling back at last.

"Yeah," I said. "I mean, I don't know." Elation shook my voice.

He chuckled. "You're not okay."

"Did you get anything on my chair?" I said.

He wiped a camo sleeve along the red bar of my chair fast. "Maybe."

I reached out a shaky hand for him. He caught it and rubbed my fingers.

"Do you need me to fix you?" he said. I was lopsided in my chair.

"Yeah."

He stepped around without hesitation and braced one arm at my back and the other under my knees, almost like he was going to carry me. With one yank, he righted me. "Good?" he said.

"Yeah," I said.

We stood there awkwardly. No other words to be passed.

"Well," said Cole. "Happy Thanksgiving."

He poked my nose with a finger. I looked up at him and we latched gazes. His still glowed.

I stayed outside long after his Lexus zigzagged out of sight, the headlights streaming. I heard it zoom half a mile down the neighborhood. When I finally returned home, I asked Dad to put me to bed.

He came into my bedroom, looked at my lap, and reached to click open my seat belt.

It was already undone.

I froze. Dad paused.

He lifted me without comment.

23

Dad braked for the red light, and I surged forward and grasped the side of the ramp. "Sorry, Trout," said Dad.

He didn't need to be. The more stop signs and assholes that cut him off, the more time I had to think about what I was going into. This was weird. I never was . . . *nervous* to see KC before now. But this secret he revealed, his feelings for me, it shook the Etch A Sketch version of him I had in my head and drew him with sharper lines, bolder blacks. I needed to figure out what those new lines meant. I needed to know if some of those lines could include me.

The light flipped green and Dad accelerated, faster than Mom ever did. But not faster than Cole. I almost dropped my phone onto my footplate. Habitually, I tapped the screen.

No replies from Cole or KC. To KC, I'd texted: On way. To Cole, a whopping six hours ago, I texted: Morning :)

My lips pursed and I lifted my eyes from the phone to the window.

The radio blasted Dad's favorite classic rock station: Springsteen, Queen, AC/DC, the singles he grew up on. I didn't recognize the current song, but it sounded like U2.

"What is this?" I asked.

Dad dialed down the volume. "What?"

I repeated.

"'Stuck in a Moment You Can't Get Out Of,'" said Dad.

I watched traffic glide by out the window as the lyrics hit me. Tough love, speaking right to my idiocy. Bono said he never thought I was foolish, but "darling, look at you."

Funny. I actually smiled with irony. Looked down once more at my empty phone.

Yeah. Look at me.

Bowling pins crashed and boomed in the alley. The fake wood floors glared back fluorescent ceiling lights. Pin decals danced on the walls, and grease cleaved to the knobs and levers of the ancient Pac-Man and Donkey Kong machines in the corner. It smelled faintly of french fries that I didn't think they served here anymore and bowling shoes.

KC and I agreed to meet here at 2:00 p.m., as it was one of the only cheap places besides the movie theater open the day after Thanksgiving. He slumped deep in a tan chair next to an empty aisle. A Shirley Temple on the table before him. The score display glowed above him on a boxy monitor. My wheels squeaked as I approached. I'd never been self-conscious of that kind of thing around KC until today. It must have been loud enough to draw his eyes, though.

He shifted and rose. For an awkward beat, he just stood there and said, "Hey." As if I wouldn't want to hug him like normal.

So I wobbled out my arm and clawed his shirt sleeve. My finger snagged a button on his sleeve, and I tugged. Reeled him into me. His lean arms enveloped me. I'd say they caged me, secured me, locked me to his warmth, but no amount of sweetness could remove the connotation of *cage*.

But he never quite squeezed me in. He held me like I was fragile, only close enough for my senses to pay attention to him rather than be engulfed by him. Sometimes, when I know someone's coming down to embrace me, I flip my joystick power off real subtly. Too much body and they might hit it and make me swerve. With KC . . . I never felt I had to.

KC's breath shook. I just closed my eyes and held him. His scent was familiar and soothing, mixed with cherries from his Shirley Temple. He said *hey* again, and his gentle voice was peace in my ears. The light blue plaid shirt he wore had been through the wash too many times, making it extra fuzzy.

"Want to play?" I said when he pulled back. KC nodded, almost as if relieved I'd asked.

The staff pushed out this strange, three-foot-high metal slide used to help me bowl. The ball had to be placed at the top, then, with absolutely zero skill, I'd nudge it down the slide and the ball would topple and roll uncomfortably slowly towards the pins while everyone watched. If I struck down a decent amount, I got high-fives I did nothing to earn. But it was fun.

"We need to rent you some shoes?" I said.

"Nah," said KC. "I brought some."

I raised an eyebrow as he pulled a beat-up pair of bowling shoes from his backpack.

"Bowl often?" I said. I remembered he'd brought a deteriorated pair of ice skates from home that one time too.

"Not . . . really," said KC. He didn't look up to meet my eyes as he put them on. I thought the skin of his neck reddened.

KC took the first turn. He exhaled through his lips and poised himself, holding up the ball with both hands facing him. I noticed his shoulders square, his muscles ripple. Then he skirted forward and swung it. The ball coursed down the aisle and hit a complete strike. *Boom!*

I glanced at KC. He continued to stare at the pins as they were swept away. He panted. I couldn't decide if that performance was anger or nerves, but I don't think he counted it down for skill.

"KC," I said.

He looked over. An urge to touch him prickled beneath my skin, but it was different than the urges I had for Cole. Did it matter? They were different people. I was looking at someone I'd loved for years.

Wasn't I?

My voice was a whisper. "Want to talk?"

His eyes clung to me. Above, the monitor flashed that it was my turn.

"No," said KC. "Not yet. It's your turn."

I glanced to the monitor as if to chastise it and moved forward. KC swiveled the metal slide in place. He crouched and eyeballed the angle. Helping me get the perfect shot. Something in my heart wriggled.

When he heaved the maroon bowling ball onto the slide, my hand fell in line with his. We touched fingertips and froze. The heat between our skin was sticky, not electric. My reaction was instinctual—I rubbed him with my thumb. KC swallowed. Together, we shoved the ball down the slide. The huge slide clacked and the ball rolled five miles-per-year towards the pins. KC rested his clasped hands atop his head and watched it.

With one more bowl, we earned a spare together.

"I never knew you liked me, KC," I said softly.

KC smirked and walked over to his seat. "I'm easy to miss."

"No," I said.

"You can just tell me," said KC. "It's cool."

"Tell you what?"

"That you don't like me back."

"If I didn't, I'd tell you." Ugh. This was confusing and not fair to him, but it was the truth.

"Maeve, it's a pretty easy question."

"It's not, KC. It's . . ."

He let me finish.

"It's a shock for me, because I've always loved you, and now I'm questioning what type that love ever was."

Hope sort of blended with the sheepishness in KC's eyes at the word *love,* and I prayed I wouldn't have to hurt him.

It was like a million feelings were knocking on a million doors inside me, and I was hiding under the couch with the shades drawn.

"If you'll give me some time, I'll figure out what this is I'm feeling," I said. "But you have to let me figure it out."

"Okay," said KC. Although I know this was emotional for him, he was ever practical, ever downbeat. For some reason, that comforted me. Normalcy spilled back into my chest.

"It's your turn."

We bowled the entire game and loosened up as it went on. The more KC smiled, the more I did too. Soon, I'm not sure I ever stopped.

After, a staff member refilled KC's drink and brought one for me too. We sipped.

"I love being out with you," said KC.

"I do too," I said.

"I like helping you."

I chuckled. "Thanks. Plenty more where that came from." I punched him with awkward weakness. ". . . Sport."

Like usual, he just watched my fist pathetically slip away.

"I don't know." KC's voice was low. "You make things a little better."

"The world still suck?" I said.

"Lots of people should probably just die." KC wasn't bantering. I shook my head and just sipped my drink.

"Want some food?" he said. "I brought snacks." He pulled out a little lunch pail from his backpack. An ice pack was inside—including a banana and some yogurt. I opted for the banana, he took the yogurt. KC peeled it for me before handing it over.

"Happy Thanksgiving," said KC.

I resisted recoiling. Cole poking my nose lovingly flashed back to me.

My teeth sank into the banana, and KC scooped some yogurt into his mouth.

He blanched. KC choked and dropped the spoon.

"KC," I piped. "K—"

He clutched his stomach and coughed so hard his eyes streamed. My heart raced. How do you choke on yogurt? "KC!" Some of the staff craned their heads to check it out.

"It's okay," he wheezed. "It's—" He glared at the yogurt. Before he could pull it away, I snatched it and turned it to read the expiration date.

My eyes bulged. It wasn't just a few weeks overdue, even a few months . . .

"KC, this is *two years past date.*"

"Yeah," he spat, "I didn't notice."

"KC," I said.

Something . . . something didn't feel right. The random film props. The old skates. The bowling shoes. This yogurt.

But mostly, the way he looked at me now: with defeated . . . shame?

"Don't worry about it," said KC.

"Why don't you want me to come to your house?" I said.

"Maeve, please." He swiped for the yogurt.

"KC, what's going on at home?"

"*Stop!* Okay?"

I tried to touch his hand. He jerked it back. "I—I gotta go."

"KC." My voice was sweet.

"I'm sorry," said KC. "I'll—I'll text you later." He rose and streaked for the exit before I could call him back.

I blinked and leaned back in my chair. The feelings knocking at the doors forced in the walls and broke the windows and love and fear and confusion flooded in, taking the form of tears swimming in my eyes.

Dad would be here soon to pick me up, but I couldn't move.

"Miss?" A staff member finally approached me. "Can I get you anything else?"

"No," I said. "Just . . . the bill please."

"You're good to go, miss," said the staffer. "Your friend already paid."

ELLIOT

Finished editing Cole's retakes.
FINALLY.

My heart skipped. As much as I loved Elliot, I was disappointed the text was from him. And no, I didn't want it to be from Cole either.

KC hadn't returned any of my messages. I even tried to call. Twice. I started thinking about where I'd draw the line before I'd need to alert another adult. It'd been three days since KC ran out of the bowling alley. Four since I'd seen Cole. He avoided replying too. Next week was the last week of film class, the day we premiered our final video. Then we'd all hibernate and plan our next projects and pray the principal allowed Billings to film the baseball team this season so we could enroll again in the spring.

ELLIOT

I'm gonna export it to the drive
and then get turnt

MAEVE

Make sure it's not the other way
around

ELLIOT

Lol. You've never seen me
smashed.

MAEVE

I'm sure you're epic

He was probably the affectionate drunk, not the aggressive one. That was probably why so many sophomores at the community college offered to buy for him.

ELLIOT

I make all the little basics take a
seat

MAEVE

I'm already sitting.

While I bantered, I didn't feel any humor. My mouth was set.

ELLIOT

How are things going with Cole?

The temperature in my body dropped a little. How could I answer that now?

MAEVE

I told him I want to cast him in a Michael Bay remake of Love Actually

ELLIOT

Pitch it to me

I hadn't reached out to Mags either. It's not that I thought it'd bother her or she wouldn't care. I just . . . felt like I needed to work this out myself. And by the silence on her end, she must have thought the same.

I sighed. François rumbled out snores beneath the kitchen table where I sat. His head rested against my front wheel: that was how much he trusted me. Opened on the surface before me was the *Beauty and the Beast* script I'd been reading and a dish of Flintstones vitamins and potassium supplements Mom wanted me to eat.

After a moment's thought, I grimaced and pushed off the table. François leapt up.

"Mom, I'm going for a walk," I said, passing by her office.

Mom was scrolling through a PowerPoint for her work presentation next week. "What?" she said.

"I'm. Going. For. A. Walk." I didn't mean to be grumpy to her, but . . .

"I don't think that's such a good idea," said Mom. "It's getting cold today."

"I'll be fine."

"Did you eat the vitamins?"

"Yeah." I didn't mean to lie either.

"Let me at least put a co—"

I rammed the door open with the side of my chair.

True, it was supposed to get colder, and next week they

forecasted more snow. But today was typical of bipolar Fredericksburg winters. It was wet and mild. I relished the gentle splash and ripples from my wheels slicing through puddles on the street.

I made it to the end of the block before realizing I'd left my phone on the kitchen table. Maybe that wasn't totally unintentional. I needed a . . . break. From its noise and its silence. From its vibration and its stillness.

KC needed more help than I could give. I didn't think his parents abused him. I thought something else was going on. And I believed him that he had feelings for me . . . I could even believe he loved me. But something had been bothering me besides my concern for him.

I like helping you, he'd said. *You make things a little better.*

When I was young, I dreaded asking for help. But then one day, in Wegmans, I pointed up and asked this woman to help me reach the Special K. She sprang to attention and said, *Absolutely!* and then asked if I needed anything else or if she could take it to the register for me. It seemed to make her happy. So I started asking more. I even got to the point where I'd ask strangers in the food court to cut my food. One guy said, "I'd be *honored.*"

It's almost like it gave them something to feel good about. Purpose, I guess. For a little.

KC was experiencing the same thing with me. And . . . I *did* believe he had feelings for me. I did. But could he be glorifying me too? Could he be drowning at home, and I was the pool noodle?

Was Cole *my* pool noodle?

And suddenly I realized that's basically all life was. Everyone a pool noodle, sinking and thrashing out for another's noodle to stay afloat. The rainbow of slapping and flailing filled my imagination.

After looping the neighborhood twice, I retreated home. My brain felt like it was carrying a piano inside it.

But on my way back, I made sure not to pass the sycamore tree. I took the other way.

Mom was right: not far into the week, frost aged the grass outside. When I showered now, steam clouded our windows.

Dad had been going to work early every day and Mom had her presentation, otherwise I think they'd have noticed my glumness. François did, at least. He rested his head on my lap and looked up at me with big brown eyes. I petted his smooth fur.

The only activity on my phone was a call from Quinten. It rang in my palm and for some reason, I just stared at it until voicemail snatched it away. I listened immediately after.

"Maeve, hey." Pause. "It's Quinten." Pause. My mouth twisted down. For some reason, it sounded like he knew I'd ignored his call. "I saw that article online about you . . . guess that woman didn't want to let it go. I told my nephew I was interested in *donating* and had him look up her schedule on the camp website. They've got a holiday dinner tomorrow night, Friday. Press will be there. I can't come because . . . you know. The shuttle doesn't . . ." His voice wheezed. "Anyway. Might be a chance to correct things with the media. And you still got that recording I gave you."

Another long pause.

"Miss you."

He hung up.

Crazy as it sounds, that whole situation had faded from my priorities. I was busier looking up *what to do if you think your friend is suicidal* and *how to produce beauty and the beast* when that got too depressing. I'd finished reading the script last night. I'd sated myself by envisioning how I'd direct it and strategizing my words to Mr. Billings to convince him to help me produce it.

I imagined the text I'd send Cole asking him to reprise his community-renowned role.

All an effort to work with him more. To elongate our guaranteed time together because I didn't trust him enough to give me that time without it.

Maybe I was drowning my pool noodle.

The project at least gave me nourishment enough to avoid texting him for real, to give him space, to act like I was not thinking about him every moment of every day.

I'm not stupid enough to have thought there wasn't a reason he was avoiding me. Yes, his pattern had always been . . . inconsistent at best. But after what happened beneath the sycamore, silence meant something. He didn't enjoy himself. He didn't realize how bad my handicap was. I said something. He regretted all of it.

And since there was nothing I could do to help KC, no more class video to edit, and nothing to plot against Wheelchair Charity Woman besides simply turning up at that dinner tomorrow, all I could work on was this idea.

Producing Together ✕

Roman Santiago

Producing Together

Roman,

Sorry to email you at your personal address. I wanted to thank you again for the sick stabilizer you gave me and for talking with me in your office.

I also want to ask you something.

Do you remember that *Beauty and the Beast* poster you showed me? From when you produced it on Broadway?

I paused.

Before I could finish and hit send, Dad appeared in front of me. I jumped. "Dad. Home early!" I hadn't even heard him come in. He still wore his ID tag and blue collared shirt.

"Yep, 'cause guess what?" said Dad.

"What?"

"We're going Christmas tree shopping."

"Right now?" I said.

"Yep."

"Do we have to?"

"Get in the car immediately."

I laughed. "Daaaaad . . ."

"Tough shit, it's Christmas. Let's go."

So we did. Dad, Mom, and I browsed through the garden section at Lowe's. Carols echoed from inside the store and gloved personnel hauled Douglas firs through orange netting. While all the other garland in our house had ma-triculated to artificial, the live tree was sort of our last hur-rah. I liked it, but every year here I imagined my future. I daydreamed of having my husband go to the farm with me and actually cut one down. When we had kids, I'd tell them, "Daddy will chop whatever one you choose." And then Mommy would try really hard not to blatantly *rrrmph* with lust while he did.

And damn me, it was easy to see Cole there. It was easy to see his strong hand grasp a tree while an axe hung in the other. It was easy to see him pleased that he knew I was watching. I could imagine his knowing, arrogant half smile. I bet his equally large and equally bearded dad did the same for his wife. I bet masculinity was a virtue in their family.

Picking a tree out at Lowe's was nice, but sadder since they all leaned together in a pile, no roots, already drip-ping needles. It was the screenwriter in me, but I'd always had this thing where I felt badly for inanimate objects. It was easy to imagine Christmas trees having feelings. It was easy to imagine they were sad when they weren't picked.

When Mom narrowed the choices down to two, Dad picked one, and I, before it was taken away, always snapped a twig off the discarded one. Sometimes I even whispered something to it.

I knew what it was like to not be picked.

The aroma of Christmas filled the van on the drive back, and Mom raved over the festive lights lining downtown Fredericksburg as the sun turned the sky the color of sweet potatoes. I suppose a little warmth filled me. Something *was* charming about Christmas in the almost-South.

The emotional shield of that warmth and the colors of the domestic fantasies in my head were enough to push my patience over the limit.

Mom and Dad argued in the next room about the straightness of the tree in its stand, Dad on his stomach on the floor trying to screw it upright. When I got to my bedroom, I texted Cole.

MAEVE

Hey.

Not five seconds later, he replied.

COLE STONE

Howdy

A zap of annoyance hit me. So he'd been glued to his phone as much as always, but just never replied to me before now.

MAEVE

Hey. Where've you been?

COLE STONE

Idk.

My heart stilled. Something cold slid through my veins.

MAEVE

Is everything okay

COLE STONE

Yeah

I blinked. If I let it go, he'd probably slip under and disappear again, until, maybe, he spontaneously craved sex.

MAEVE

Cole I want to talk to you

COLE STONE

Shoot.

Last chance. No turning back now. I hesitated. And
swallowed.

MAEVE

How do you really feel about
me?

25

The dry erase board squeaked as my honors English teacher
wrote homophones with a faded green marker the next day.
Everyone took notes. I stared at my phone under the desk.

As quickly as Cole had replied, he disappeared quicker
when I asked that last question. *How do you really feel about
me?* No matter how many times I scrolled up and down
with my thumb, it didn't make a message from him appear.

My shoulders felt too heavy to lift; my head too weak to
look up at the board.

One of the students scratching notes several desks to my
left was Nate. This was the only other class we had together. He never talked to me in it. But I tried harder not

to look upset in front of him. I clicked my phone to sleep and caught his glance from across the room.

"All right," said the teacher. "Take five and group up when you get back."

Chairs rumbled out and backpacks swung onto shoulders. Half of us stayed seated while the other half cut for the door for the break. Nate coursed right by me and into the hall.

I texted Mags.

MAEVE

Nate doesn't know about the KC/Cole situation, does he?

I must have been feeling pretty grammarly with the text punctuation since I was in English.

MAGS

Maybe a little. I mean I told him you were into Cole but that he wasn't being that steady with you. Why?

I sighed and almost shook my head. I didn't mind Mags telling someone, but it disappointed me that she thought Nate would care. It probably just reinforced his belief that my love life was artificial.

MAEVE

Just wondering.

MAGS

You in class rn?

MAEVE

English.

MAGS

I'm heading into psych

MAEVE

Last exam?

MAGS

Lol boy I'll die in here.

Half my mouth perked up.

MAEVE

Can't be worse than me last semester

MAGS

?

MAEVE

The teacher didn't even teach us about psychology. Like he taught us about how the tongue works and Zicam.

MAGS

That's weird

Students began pouring back in. Five minutes goes fast. The teacher passed out papers and asked us all to read and compare thoughts. It was two pages: a personal essay written by a college student ten years ago.

He wrote about how he fell in love with some girl in Colorado on his Mormon mission, and when he returned home, his best friend revealed her romantic feelings for him too. Irony! He rejected her and told her about this other girl (like, immediately), said that's why he just *had* to chase his heart. Then he waltzed into all these philosophical feelings like he was fucking Oprah narrating a documentary about space and how that year changed him and then how all of it didn't matter after his father died, and I didn't even feel bad for him. I just hated this guy.

"What did you all think?" said the teacher. A few students said it was heartfelt. Powerful. Well-written.

I raised my hand.

"Maeve." The teacher nodded.

"I think this guy was a dick."

The class laughed. My face was straight.

"Okay." The teacher chuckled. "Interesting. Tell us why."

"He rejected his best friend without giving a damn about her."

"Hold on a second . . ." I cringed at the sound of that drawn-out, placating voice. Nate leaned forward over his desk to look at me. "Just because someone rejects you doesn't make them a dick."

Heat flushed me. "Yeah, okay, but he immediately vomited all these feelings on her that he had for *the other woman*. Like he's telling *her* how amazing *the other woman* is."

Some of the female classmates made sounds of agreement.

"That's what adults should be able to do," said Nate.

"Or they could lie to you and leave out that you just never gave them a boner."

"Nate," the teacher warned.

Redder. My voice wobbled. I had to raise it as the class was getting louder. "Which is exactly why men have the reputation of caring more about that boner than their literal best friend standing right in front of them."

"Standing or sitting?" said Nate an octave lower.

My phone slipped in the sweat of my hand. Chatter supporting Nate and some supporting me crowded the room, and it seemed to have missed the significance of that last remark. The teacher hadn't heard either. His eyes lingered at the clock behind us. He looked a little tense.

"I think we'll end class there. Final essays due next week! Last day!"

The students were still talking, laughter interspersed, as they rose to leave. My breath was quick. I couldn't help sneaking one last look at Nate.

He was watching me, yes. But it wasn't with total malice. Just sharp focus. Almost like he really was trying to figure out what my situation was, and what made me tick—what got to me beneath the obvious.

Or maybe he was just being a dick.

"Hey," said Dad. "You sure you feel up to this? You look a little . . ." He tilted his head.

"I'm fine," I lied to Dad. But in a way, I never really lie to Dad. Dad always knows when I'm lying and I always know when he's lying and we let each other lie to each other sometimes.

He'd picked me up right after school, and I asked to be driven to this fundraising dinner Wheelchair Charity

Woman was putting on—unsurprisingly lamely early at 4:30 p.m.

Dad winced closing the wheelchair ramp into the van, as always. François was in the back seat, dressed for work, and sneezed upon seeing me. I stuffed my school papers into the back seat's pocket, and a moment later we took off.

After a few miles on the highway, we thundered down a gravel road and a large, cabinlike building appeared with green roofs and wooden verandahs all the way around. Ramps affixed to them, of course. Brown paper bags were alight with fake candles in the parking lot, and Dad raised one eyebrow in the rearview mirror. Handicapped children were being lowered from mechanical lifts, and with enormous grins, others wheeled their way to the ramps. Two white satellite vans were parked in the corner.

"Uh . . ." said Dad.

He knew this looked like the last place in the world I'd want to be.

"I told them I'd read to the kids this summer with François," I said. "This is like an orientation dinner."

"Oh," said Dad. "That's nice."

He veered into a parking space and let me outside. Handed me François' leash. "Text me when you're ready to come home." I saluted him.

The planks thudded like bongo drums as I rolled up the ramp and onto the verandah. I could see a pasture with horses behind it, the grass gold and copper like a riverbed. I admit the air was fresh and sweet.

Like traffic at the Holland Tunnel, I had to let a few other wheelchairs motor inside ahead of me. All of the children were under eighteen, and they practically squealed with delight to be going inside. A few others were quieter, shier maybe, rather than actually speech impaired. It was hard not to compare how healthy, unhealthy, thin, heavy, straight, twisted they were next to me. It was hard not to envy the ones who pushed large, manual wheels that might be temporary and looked just a little less cyborg, and cringe at the motorized ones who were in the club of permanence like me.

François wagged his tail equally for each of them.

Finally, I made it inside.

Vinyl tablecloths covered a dozen round tables. A buffet of Italian food with white plastic silverware was at the wall. Christmas, Hanukkah, and all the politically correct assortment of holiday decals hung from the ceiling like a giant mobile. A small empty stage was on the left side of the room, and two *really bored-looking* reporters played on their phones on the opposite side. My instinct was to go to them—the normal people. Maybe even a cute intern. But I had a mission here. I had to find Wheelchair Charity Woman.

How? I sighed. There were campers and helpers everywhere, getting food, talking. Unfortunately, I probably blended in.

Then someone tapped a microphone. The audio screeched and a few people *oophed*.

"Soooorry!" said an overenthusiastic New York accent. There she was. On the stage. I watched. Everyone chuckled politely.

"Welcome, everyone! My name is Patricia Weinhart, and I'm the CFO and head counselor here at Caring Hands Camp!"

Applause.

"I know we have the same food every year for our holiday dinner, but the kids just *love* pizza!" A few more laughs. I rolled my eyes. Jesus.

Then I glanced around and saw the kids nodding and

playing with the stringy mozzarella and realized she was kinda right. François was still wagging his tail at them. When one clump of cheese splatted onto the floor, François tugged for it.

"Hey," I said, pulling him back.

He looked at me with big eyes but obeyed.

"I'd like you all to please watch this short video put together by our PR team," Patricia continued.

The lights dimmed. *This oughta be good.* I just hoped she hadn't hired One Take Blake for it or something.

Then I cocked my head in alarm. Real tears, real emotion clouded Patricia's voice. "This is the story of my beautiful niece. My favorite little angel, Ginger T. Duke, who passed away three years ago this evening. I started this camp in honor of her." She stepped aside and clapped high in the air as others joined.

I shut up.

Ginger T. Duke. Why did that sound so familiar?

And suddenly the memorial sign with her name on it on a door in Dr. Clayton's office came back to me. A shiver ran down my back.

The short movie was just a slide of photographs of a sweet little girl with some form of muscular dystrophy. Coldplay music served a heart-tugging backdrop. Years passed in the slideshow, and the little girl got older to country music. She was deteriorating gradually, and soon shackled up in tubes.

The older she got, the more my blood slowed.

The older she got, the more—in an uncanny, doppelgänger-type way—she looked like me. Her wheelchair was even the same shade of dark red.

Was this why Patricia wanted my photo so badly on her website?

I watched as the tears streamed down her cheeks, but she smiled at the photos. Could I really have reminded her of someone she loved that deeply? It was a weird way of taking her grief out on me, but what if the grief was real?

When the video was over, the lights flickered back on. Tissues dabbed eyes. My heart beat a little quicker. I thought and stared for a long time.

Wheelchair Charity Woman retook the mic. "Thank you, everyone. So please, sit down, relax, and later we'll have some fun announcements for this year's camp and even a few special campers interviewed on Facebook Live!"

Patricia waved her hand and hopped off stage.

I snuck over to the Facebook Live wannabe-crew. It was, like, two dudes in their thirties with goatees and douchebag beanies. The name of their basement studio was printed on their black T-shirts.

"Hey. Buddy."

The cameraman pulled his brow together and glanced at me.

"Yeah," I said. "Sup?"

He didn't answer at first. Swept his eyes around at the other disabled kids, as if it was weird that I was talking to him and knew such casual lingo.

"Can you follow me to the camp owner? I'm supposed to be the first interviewee."

He paused and stared down at François, who kept wagging. François must have looked trustworthy enough for him to pick up his tripod and agree. The other dude followed.

I tracked my way through the minglers. François' nose wriggled at all the pizza crusts on plates.

"François," I chastised. "Keep it together."

He flapped his ears as if needing to dispel the temptation. Was it possible he really did just prance over for Patricia's burrito at the mall? He's no more perfect than I am, but a lot sweeter.

Soon, Patricia was in sight. She spoke to another adult, drinks in hand. She wore the dangliest earrings and high heels, and she beamed and glowed and waved at the kids who clearly knew her, and suddenly I wondered if maybe I was being a little mean. She looked so happy. The kids looked happy. The camp was happy . . .

I slowed down.

But it was too late.

I could hear the little snap of breath Patricia took. She saw me, and the Facebook Live bros assumed we'd reached our destination so they rounded forward. A little red light was already on the high-tech phone camera, and the adults around her backed up joyfully to let her *do her thing*, probably.

I swallowed. Something, even something minor, switched gears in my brain. The muscles at Patricia's collarbone tensed. She glared at the camera, and then looked at me with bitterness but mostly fear. My lips pursed.

"Patricia." I reached out my hand.

With the cameras rolling, she had no choice but to come forward and shake my hand. She couldn't diss a handicapped person onscreen.

Then we were side by side with the camera and mic for *News 6 Community Pulse with Rob and Timm* trained on us. Facebook viewers watching live. Patricia gasped in a breath and started to say something, but I cut her off.

"We have some things to set straight here in front of the media," I said. "First of a crapload of things, I am *not* and *never in my life* would be—"

"Puppy!"

A little girl with leg braces limped forward right into our interview. She couldn't have been more than eight. On her last step, she actually fell, and her arms looped around François. She cried at first with fear, but then François' tongue probed out. Her eyes closed tightly, and she hugged my dog. She started to laugh as his tongue brushed her, and her caretaker rushed forward and pulled her away. She giggled, and the caretaker carried her back to her metal walker.

I swallowed.

Maybe tears were in my eyes.

The camera still rolled.

"Hey, my name is Maeve Leeson," I said. "And this is my friend Patricia." I turned to Wheelchair Charity Woman. She cleared her throat warily but gave an unflattering, toothy smile into the camera. "For this interview, *I'd* actually like to ask my friend some questions."

In my lap, I flashed the hard drive Quinten had given me with our conversation recorded on it so Patricia could see, but I don't think she looked down.

"Patricia, am I or was I ever a camper here at Caring Hands Camp?"

Long pause. She blinked. The camera light shone. François continued to wag.

"No," said Patricia. "You aren't. W-weren't. Ever."

Right answer. I actually squeezed her hand—not aggressively—to let her know.

"Exactly," I said. Then I looked right at the lens. "I'm not a camper here, and it's not for me. But it's a pretty cool place for others with special needs. My photo was used mistakenly on the website, then shared to the *Huffington Post*, kinda funny how that works. So I'd like it taken down and not used again . . . but I'd like to replace it with new ones."

I turned to Patricia once more.

"I'll be coming in this summer with my service dog to read to the kids." Patricia gazed at me, some of that fear clearing away in her eyes. "I think that should take up a whole gallery on the site."

She was speechless for a moment. Then she too squeezed my shoulders with her arm. "The campers can't wait," she said. "Thank you, everyone on Facebook, for your generous support."

"Anything else you want to say?" the cameraman asked.

My eyes fell to François. The little girl in leg braces mowed her walker forward and giggled for him again. He rubbed his fur against her. I found it incredible that the little girl could laugh while tears of pain stained her cheeks.

"No," I said. "I'm done."

26

I guess a decent way to avoid checking my phone for Cole's reply was to illegally sneak into the Smithsonian and abduct footage of security guards with Elliot.

It was the last weekend before winter break, before our project was due, and Elliot and I made the hour-and-a-half trip to the Museum of Natural History in DC for our B-roll at last. I'd called Quinten the night before to report on Wheelchair Charity Woman right after the dinner, but made a pact that that was it. I had to focus now on finishing up this video for good.

We stuffed a Canon 7D behind my shoe on my footplate and a tripod across the back of my wheelchair. I waited in line at the museum entrance. Tourists held out their arms and guards waved batons over them. Bags were plopped onto tables and searched.

Skateboarders take pride in skating landmarks in DC and running off before police can chase them away. It is the same with filmmakers: DC has a strict no-tripod, no-filming law anywhere in the district. But a radical respect for stolen footage exists among the local film community. Elliot and I needed just a *few last shots* for our project due tomorrow. We wanted to snatch some *real* museum footage to make our little Fredericksburg location appear bigger than it really was. We needed an exterior of the whole Smithsonian, a few patrolling guards, and—at my insistence, not Elliot's—a shot of the guards' lockers.

"You—over there." A heavy, sassy female guard (acrylic nails three inches long) pointed Elliot into another line. She waved me forward.

With effort, she rose to inspect me. "Do you have any bags?"

"Just my oxygen bag, ma'am," I said, pointing at the empty bag we used to cover the tripod.

"Okay," she said. "You're good."

They let me through. God, I could make money as a cartel lord. One time I had a spiked mace and probably a kidnapped baby at the Air and Space Museum and they let me through too. I snuck a thumbs-up to Elliot as we wandered inside.

"Ooph," said Elliot, shaking himself after being wanded, "let's make it quick."

The getaway van—aka my handicapped car Elliot drove us here in—was just outside at a meter in case we needed it.

I left tire tracks across the tile corralled with WET FLOOR signs. The flow of tourists merged to the right, into a tunnel with screens and cast bronze sculptures of early humans. You know, humans with problems like, *Let's not get eaten by the tiger* or *It's really fucking cold* in comparison to my first-world romantic problems. We followed a pod of chattering fourth graders.

The blank, pupil-less bronze eyes of the first humans passed me. I couldn't help but lock gazes with them and try to see something there. It's never escaped me that, had I been born in any other century, I would not have survived. I would never have made it out of bed. But these busts looked just as human as the ones who keep me alive today are. They seemed to pierce right into me.

Would you have taken care of me? The statue continued to stare as I asked. *Would you have left me to die?*

"Hey," said Elliot, "your shoe is untied, hold up . . ."

It wasn't. But Elliot lowered in front of me and slipped the 7D from behind my foot. He glanced around to make sure no one saw and affixed it to the stabilizer that Roman had given me. Attached to the armrest of my chair, the stabilizer looked like just another appendage of the medical equipment. "I like the shot at my six," Elliot whispered, and when he moved, I saw the security guard he'd spotted. He was a gruff mustachioed officer with visible keys and walkie-talkie, but best of all, he was looking at his smartphone. The blasé attitude perfectly suited the downbeat comedic vibe of the short film. I turned on the 7D and tilted it on the stabilizer, a gust of thrill whizzing through my veins at my first time controlling a camera solo. I tried to hide its bulky, long lens with my forearm. Elliot sauntered around at the exhibits to appear natural, and I focused the lens just a little and hit record. My neck was scrunched down in order to see the feedback screen.

After three seconds of footage, the guard seemed to sense

an eye on him and looked up, right into the camera. I laughed-cursed under my breath and threw my arm over the camera, veering away with my other hand. Elliot jumped with me and a flock of Czech tourists submerged us in their foreign-language-speaking, fanny-pack-wearing cover.

"I think I got enough," I said. We bounded for the elevator.

"How many seconds?" said Elliot.

"Like, three? It'll be quick, but it's enough."

Elliot punched the elevator button. "Shit." He laughed. "Let's just get our exterior shot and get out of here."

"No!" I said. "This is my holy grail!"

"A damn locker room?"

"Yes. It'll push it from student film to profesh." The elevator dinged. Elliot laid an arm across the seam to hold it open.

"You know they're gonna let you off and give me the time, right?" said Elliot. We both chuckled.

Inside the lift, Elliot sighed. We were alone. "So what's going on with you lately?"

I shifted in my seat. The elevator smelled like lemon Pledge. No music played.

"Nothing much," I said. I didn't look at him, though.

"What's new with Cole?"

My stomach twisted. I once again noticed the weight of my phone silent on my lap.

"He's . . . dodging me, I guess."

"Really?" said Elliot. "Why?" I loved how real the concern in his voice was. So real that I told him everything that'd been going on with Cole as we moseyed out of the elevator and past the Hope Diamond wing of the second floor. I ended with how Cole left me on the ledge, not replying to my question about his true feelings for me.

"Maybe something happened to him," said Elliot. "Something personal going on."

"Maybe," I said. "But that's more likely the case with KC." So I told him that too.

"Damn," was all Elliot said. We were silent for a few moments as we searched for an employee room. "One day," Elliot said at last, "you're going to be a famous director. You're gonna write a script about all of this shit and get rich, and I'm going to be a bouncer at your rooftop parties."

"I'll be the bouncer at *your* rooftop parties," I said.

"We'll both be so rich our bouncers will have bouncers."

I smiled sadly. "I don't know about that."

"Come on," Elliot encouraged sweetly.

"I think life is learning how to live without what you want," I said.

Elliot didn't answer. He grasped a bar of my wheelchair and kept walking at my side. For a second, I worried that I'd convinced him.

When my phone buzzed, my heart didn't even race. It was resigned to whatever it would face.

MAGS

Are you back in Fxbg yet?

MAEVE

We're still in DC. Why?

MAGS

Idk, I just tried to call KC again. I feel like we should go over there. Does Elliot know his address?

"Mags wants to know if you know where KC lives."

"I don't . . ." said Elliot regretfully.

MAEVE

He doesn't. I feel responsible for this a little.

MAGS

Why?

Ugh, Mags. Don't make me explain.

MAEVE

He's upset about me partially. And I'm upset about Cole. And both of them like my attention for the wrong reasons. Clearly I just shouldn't be with men. I wish I were a lesbian.

MAGS

Same

I ran out of things to reply when Mags sent me screen-shots of KC's latest Facebook posts getting darker and darker. What started with Rammstein lyrics and more ink skulls spiraled into three-word sentences about meaning-lessness. There had to have been times before when KC refused to have us over to edit or storyboard or just hang out. We should have pressed it harder. We should have asked him why. I frowned and stroked his profile picture with my thumb before closing the app.

Next, Elliot and I passed the fossil wing. Used to be one of my favorites. I remembered last time I was here, a middle-aged woman in an almost-identical wheelchair wheeled up to where I studied this enormous fossil mounted to the wall.

"Cool, isn't it?" I'd said. She didn't answer for a beat. Then her voice grumbled out a few words.

"You ever feel like just another exhibit here?"

I'd turned to her then. In the following pause, I'd tried to think of something ironic or uplifting to say. Nothing came. She left a moment later.

I suppose I understood her point. Little kids liked to look at me too. They asked how this happened to me. Usually, I said, "*Cigarettes!*" That day, however, I was quiet until the kids' parents took them away.

Elliot shoved my shoulder at that moment. "Look. There." He nodded to a security officer walking into a dark hall that had a NO ENTRY sign.

"You go," I said, "you'll be quieter."

Elliot guffawed. "Are you kidding? This is *your shot*. Get in there."

"Fine," I huffed. "I'll just act mentally disabled if they apprehend me."

"Quit stalling."

I cruised forward. Right past the NO ENTRY sign.

My confidence was almost giddy. Controlling that camera on the stabilizer all alone made me a new woman.

The chatter and light of the main hall faded away as I delved into the narrow employee passageway. It started to smell less of lemon Pledge and more of rubber and cold metal. Because time would be precious, I rolled the camera on my knee. Ahead was an ajar door I'd heard footsteps disappear into . . .

The pressure I gave my joystick was soft. I tried to turn my wheels without the slightest sound, and soon the nose of my camera was poking into the doorway.

Perfect. A few guards talked and attached guns to their belts. Their heads were turned away, so I wouldn't have any trouble with film festivals if they asked for release forms. As for the guard who looked into the camera, well—that's what Adobe Premiere Pro cuts are for. Lockers lined the wall, and a large MUSEUM POLICY poster could be read at the far end. My camera ate it up. Four seconds, six . . . that should be enough . . .

I jumped when my phone not only buzzed, but *rang.*

Fuck!

"Hey!" said a guard.

I skidded against the floor and bolted out of the hall.

"Go, go, go!" I yelled at Elliot, and we fishtailed for the elevators, making a few tourists leap aside. Luckily, one elevator was already open, people filing in, and Elliot and I dove inside just as the doors closed and shoes squeaked in our direction. My heart pounded so hard I gasped, clutching my chest.

We played it cool until we hit the ground floor and, before anyone could be notified, poured out of the museum and onto the bright sunlit sidewalk of Constitution Avenue. Cars honked, sirens wailed for bigger criminals than us, and we beamed and high-fived.

"Fucking savage!" said Elliot.

"I know," I breathed. Proud as hell.

"I'll get the exterior of the museum," said Elliot, taking the camera off the stabilizer. "You get in the van. You earned it."

An hour later, every damn shot perfectly accomplished, Elliot and I unwrapped the paper from these famous Georgetown bakery cupcakes because I had a moment of girliness and wanted to see it before we headed home.

Elliot agreed, only if we drove by the steps where the priest tumbled down and died in *The Exorcist*. Seemed a fair trade.

Orange sun kneeled over the Key Bridge and painted the Potomac. It would be a long drive back to the Rappahannock, but I'd already told the parental units I wouldn't be home before nine. Adrenaline and giddiness still shook my hands.

"That was awesome," I repeated.

"Bruh." Elliot laughed. "You were hardcore."

"I was," I said.

"I'll patch it together and render it for tomorrow," said Elliot. "Can't believe we're all done."

I shook my head and sank my teeth into the cream cheese icing.

"So who called you? Someone working for the fuzz?" said Elliot.

My eyebrows shot up and I made an alarmed sound. "I forgot to look!"

So I did.

When I saw, the giddiness drained and glacier water slid through me.

COLE STONE
Missed Call

He *called* me?

A text accompanied it.

COLE STONE

Sorry. Pocket dial. And I'm so sorry I haven't replied, there's been a lot going on :(I'll text you after work.

I blinked. That was the most communicative he'd been in . . . ever. But in the time he took to write that text, he could have also answered my question. That wasn't good.

And he *pocket-dialed me*. Okay. But that only happens when you pull up someone's text thread . . . to read it again . . . and accidentally hit the call button. Was Cole pulling up our thread and reading it over and over? I don't think he really had a lot going on. I think he had a lot he didn't want to deal with.

"Who was it?" said Elliot.

"Cole."

"Damn. What did he say?"

"He said he'll text me later. And that a lot has been going on."

Elliot smiled. "See? I told you. It'll be fine."

The set of my mouth exposed my doubt. You can bet the only reason Cole texted me was because he knew I'd see his accidental call. Otherwise he would have kept avoiding.

"He's a decent guy," said Elliot. "I'm sure he didn't mean to ghost."

"How do you know he's a decent guy?"

"I mean, I don't know him that well, but we had Latin together. And I saw that *Beauty and the Beast* play when it was going."

I wanted Elliot to convince me that Cole was a nice guy. I wanted to believe him. Right this second more than ever.

"Did you ever hang out together?"

Elliot shrugged. "One time." His voice was thick around his carrot-cake cupcake. "I hung out with the cast after that performance to recruit them for our audition."

More proof that Elliot would always be the superior director.

"We were just chillin' behind the school after they locked it up."

"What did you guys talk about?" I sounded like Mags whenever someone mentioned Nate.

"I dunno," said Elliot. "I told him about our audition, and then I think we just talked about how he doesn't understand the abstract art on display next to the theater."

My heart softened. Of course he wouldn't get art.

"Mmm," said Elliot. "It's on his Instagram." Elliot passed me his phone with Cole's Instagram pulled up.

There was a short video of Elliot standing under the lamplight with Cole near the school parking lot, the brick of the building and the backdoor entrance to the theater behind them. The caption read: *Last hangout with the cast as the Beast!*

I pressed play. Instantly, Cole's massive silhouette covered the grainy footage and he jerked and roared into it like the Beast does. I almost jumped. A few people laughed, including Elliot, and then Cole swung on his heel and walked towards the wall, shoving his hands in his pockets. He wore only a white undershirt, and his hair and beard were more unkempt for the role. Sweat still clung to his temple. He moved so familiarly, rocking side to side. "But yeah, I really don't get art." My ears tickled at his loud, throaty voice. "Picasso. You ever see somebody with an arm coming out of their rib cage? No? Okay." He laughed.

"Bruh," Elliot started to say in the video, "you should—"

The video cut off.

On the ride home, I found the video again and saved it to my phone. Elliot was talking on his own phone to his girlfriend as he drove us south, so I put my earbuds in and flicked through Cole's Instagram in silence. There was a photo of him with a yellow boa constrictor on his shoulder at the zoo. Save. A selfie of him lying in bed with a huge script and a comically overwhelmed expression. Save. A video of him taken on some punk friend's camera-phone at an Imagine Dragons concert; it was outdoors, at night, with pulsing stage lights. The audio blasted and was choppy, but I think it was of Cole pushing his buddy away and cussing as his friend tried to film him taking a leak in the mud behind the port-a-johns. Definite save.

Then I stopped scrolling. He'd posted a selfie on set of . . . *my* film. He smiled and had his arm around one of the tripods. Only one other person was in the photo, unaware, consulting a shot list.

Me.

Elliot hit a patch of rough road, and I bobbled. I squeezed the phone in my hand, swallowed, and stared.

The caption read:

Love this set.

27

Clear wrap crinkled as I held out the bouquet of roses in my hands. Elliot's expression popped when he saw them. "Whaaaat?" he said.

I smiled. "Every director needs roses on premiere day."

Elliot took them and shook his head. "Damn, girl. Good thing black don't blush."

"You'd be hot if I touched you," I said.

"Eyyyy . . ." said Elliot.

It was that Friday, and our last day of Video II. Mags smiled at us from her seat in the classroom, and Nate swiveled in his chair a few spots away, arms crossed. I rolled over to my desk and snapped my joystick into park. François darted under the table and *kaplumped* onto the floor. He yawned.

Usually I'd be yawning by the time I got to class as well, but today was the last day until break, and since next semester was uncertain, we treated it even more like the last day, period. Premiere day for all of our projects, including Cole's. I drummed the table.

The door burst open, and Mr. Billings cut to the front of the classroom. He pushed air on me as he passed. "All right, all right, the big day. No excuses, no explanations, just whatever work you put on the screen." He sighed and turned to face us. "I'm excited."

Elliot set the bouquet on his desk and fumbled to take out the hard drive with all our video files on it.

"Wait," said Billings. His expression furrowed. "Where's KC?"

I checked my phone clock. It was ten past—KC was never ten minutes late. Mags glanced at me as if to measure whether we were telling Billings about our concern or not. After KC's increasingly dark vague-booking posts online, I wondered if maybe we should.

"Did he text any of you?" said Billings. "I've told you guys since day one an unexcused absence means zero."

"He's been MIA for like a week," said Nate. Still swiveling.

"MIA?" said Billings.

"Missing in—"

Billings scowled and held up a hand. "I know what it means, but where is he?"

"In his house," said Mags. "Probably. He won't return messages."

I stayed still. And quiet. Billings hesitated.

"Let's hope he shows," Billings finally said. He waved to us. "Elliot, Maeve, come on up and present."

By the time the lights were off and the thumbnails of our projects were on the big screen, it was twenty past. No KC. I returned to my desk in the back and turned my head to the door on the left. Even as I heard Mr. Billings click play, I didn't look over. My hand curled tight around a bar of my wheelchair.

The music video played first. Annoyingly saturated colors flashed over us and the young pop star twirled with quick cuts into newer and sparklier outfits. Decent editing, I guess. The song was a cross between chipmunks and Shakira. Mags rested her elbow on the desk and her fingertips pressed against her temple like this was giving her pain. She was tethered to the screen.

Nate just continued to swivel in his chair. He even stretched his neck and stared at the ceiling a few times. It reminded me of how Cole rocks side to side on his feet. How he swings around weight with his hands in his pockets. Nate does it because he wants the world to know he doesn't care. I think Cole has other reasons.

Billings nodded a lot and made aggressively loud pen strokes on his clipboard, probably because he practically directed this entire video. When it ended, he stood and clapped. Mags brought a second hand to her temple.

"Nice, guys. I like it. Thoughts? What were your reactions?"

Only the sound of Nate's chair squeaking.

"Come on," Billings prompted.

"It was aight," said Elliot at last. Billings nodded.

"Exactly," said Billings. "Not the best budget or ideal location, but it turned out pretty solid."

He definitely wasn't looking for criticism.

I shifted in my seat and inhaled as Billings prepared to play the next project. Ours.

We opened with the stolen establishing shot of the Smithsonian and my trophy shot of the lockers. Then cut into the little Spotsylvania County Museum interior. Cole swaggered onto screen and joined his two costars next to the cannonball. The dialogue began.

Immediately I spotted my own imperfections. The costar's face was a little slow to react to Cole's first line. I should have coached that and massaged them all into a looser place before shooting. The camera shook for a hundredth of a second when I must have nudged the tripod. Cole was standing a step too far apart from the others. It gave him a powerful, untouchable appearance. Maybe that sort of worked.

But all the while I watched the film, everyone else was watching me.

Elliot kept glancing at me, and Mags, I'm pretty sure, didn't take her eyes off me. I sensed their gazes in my periphery but kept watching. They knew I had a lot in this film.

So many times I imagined calling cut. I imagined Cole straightening and his eyes grabbing mine. His gaze would calculate and at the same time dismiss and I'd be distracted by those unusual dark lines under his eyes and the way his mouth always seemed a moment away from curving into a half smile but never did. In the back of my head I heard the sycamore leaves shake.

Billings had a set face as he watched the screen, and when it ended, we all laughed at the final joke and applauded. Even Nate, demurely. Billings rose and had more critique to pass out this time, but I didn't pay attention. I saw my flaws perfectly. I always do.

When class ended, everyone rose and stretched, and I turned to the door again and frowned. Billings glanced at it too and made a mark on the attendance sheet. He pursed his lips in what seemed like genuine regret.

KC never showed.

DAD

> Mom wants to know if you're wearing your coat

I took a bite of my sandwich at lunch.

MAEVE

> You can tell her I am

DAD

> Okay. But are you?

MAEVE

> No.

There was a pause.

DAD

> She said thanks

About four pounds worth of coats piled over the back of my wheelchair because Mom said it was "the coldest day of the year" and that maybe I shouldn't come to school at all. Tonight, it would be seventeen degrees, but at least tomorrow they said it would rocket up to nineteen. Since it was premiere day, though, Elliot, Mags, and I were going to celebrate later tonight with an evening premiere of the next Harry Potter movie and Slurpees from 7-Eleven. Elliot offered to pitch in for my handicapped cab ride home instead of making Mom or Dad drive out that late to pick me up when it was over.

Students filled the cafeteria hall with blank chatter, but their faces were red and they wore boots and gloves. It was overcast beyond the tall windows and ice ticked against the glass as sleet fell. Even the school's industrial heat vents struggled to ward back the chill.

François lapped up water from a plastic takeout container on the ground. I shook his leash because he was drinking *a lot,* and I wasn't interested in taking him outside three times during the movie tonight. He kept slurping. After class, Mags and Nate had left together, probably to make out in the closed-off stairwell next to the math department. Elliot was still talking to Mr. Billings about opportunities for film in the spring semester and vying for a late recommendation letter for UCLA. When he was finished, I wanted to talk to Billings myself. I wanted to ask him who I needed to charm in order to use the black box theater. Hopefully someone who liked *Beauty and the Beast* and would agree to let me produce it for the community again—but this time with the modern spin I was thinking about giving it.

"All right, François," I repeated. Tugged his leash. François stepped away and licked his lips. He looked up at me and wagged as water dribbled down his muzzle. "Let's go see if Elliot's done."

I made my way back to class. Elliot was still standing outside the room with Billings, talking with his hands, enthusiastic. The bouquet of roses was under his arm. I slowed to give them space.

Today must have been test day for several classes, because foot traffic was heavy in the hallway—I never wanted to miss the final either. François shuffled to avoid oncoming students, and I veered to the right next to the black box theater entrance to be out of the way. Right now the only flier over the theater door was a holiday comedy skit ending this weekend. Then it'd be free . . .

Maybe I could head to the principal's office now. Maybe I could ask to produce the—

Bzzt.

Bzzt.

Bzzt.

Bzzt.

I froze. When Mom texted me over at Mags' house years ago that doctors decided there was no choice but to operate on my scoliosis, that came in four texts. When my cousin texted me that my grandmother was very ill, that came in four texts. Anytime anyone ever canceled a date or a meeting or said they couldn't come to my party, that was never less than three.

My blood was coolant, but I checked my phone.

COLE STONE

I'm really sorry I haven't talked to you. I'm not good at these things. I need to learn to just say what I want and stop worrying about what other people will think. The truth is that I don't think I feel the same way about you. I enjoy our walks and hey, I love talking to you, it's just right now I really need a friend more than anything. I'm just (1/4)

I stopped reading because the words wouldn't focus with just a blink of my eyes anymore. Tears gushed from me and burned down my face. My heart felt like it was a jackhammer against my throat and I jerked in breath and shoved it out too hard. People were all around, students, and I couldn't let them see this. They'd think I was in physical pain; they'd think the nurse had to be called; they'd never for a second understand. I had to go. I had to go.

With the front of my chair, I pounded open the door to the black box theater and dove inside. The room's empty, smooth, featureless black mouth and jagged camera-light teeth up above swallowed me. I doubled over my phone to stop the buzzing that kept coming in and clawed a hand over my eyes and cried. Not loudly. Just freely.

Why? Why did the odds land on me? Nate was right: Cole was not a jerk. He just saw absolutely everything that I saw. I know what I am. He cannot hate it any more than I do. But I'm open to learning.

The door opened behind me. I sniffled and straightened, punching my arm over my eyes to dry it, but it was like an open wound spurting blood, and no emotional will could act as my tourniquet. *Please, don't be Billings, don't be Mags, don't be Nate, don't be—*

"Hey. *Hey.*"

Elliot rushed to me. I swallowed, tried to blubber out words.

"Shh, hey." He wrapped me in his warm arms.

"Cole," was all I choked.

"No," Elliot whispered. "Just hold on to me."

So I did. I pressed my forehead against Elliot. I sobbed and mumbled. He bent over my chair and seemed not to let any open air touch me, only him. I shuddered into him and wept.

Elliot rubbed me and just shook his head. I don't know why.

28

Out in the hall, rapid footsteps squeaked. Elliot straightened, and I lifted my arm and let the running mucus from my face soak into my sleeve.

"Maeve?" That was Mags' muffled voice. "Has anyone seen Maeve?"

"The wheelchair girl?" said someone.

"Oh, fuck you," said Mags, still frantic.

"Wow," the person replied. "Yet another minority cause I'm socially unaware of."

"Yeah, you're really woke, homeboy."

Damn, she sounded mad.

"Maeve?!"

At that point I realized the buzzing coming in after Cole's initial texts may not have been him again. I pulled out my phone and saw three messages from Mags. Before I could read them, Elliot dove for the door and opened it.

"Mags?" Elliot called.

"El!" Mags doubled back from down the hall to us. "Where's Maeve?"

"She's in here. What's up?"

I rolled forward.

"It's KC," Mags gasped. "It's KC."

"What's going on?" I pushed alongside Elliot, and then Mags met my eyes and shook her head.

"Didn't you see my messages?" Her voice was higher than normal. "Look. Right now."

I whipped open my phone's lock again and pulled up her messages.

MAGS

We need to go

MAGS

Right now

Followed by a screenshot of KC's Facebook post.

It was a suicide note.

For forty bucks I bought a membership to a Whitepages website and unlocked Hector and Beth Douglas' address. The site reported they had one child over eighteen living there as well: KC.

He lived near school. Only a ten-minute walk past some town houses and into a wooded neighborhood. I followed Elliot and Mags behind Elliot's blue pickup truck. He was going five miles per hour, and I was going full speed in my chair. François struggled to trot fast enough. Frigid wind bit the fresh tearstains on my face, and by this time, I was using my wrist to push the joystick; my fingers had become brittle in the cold.

Elliot had already called the police. But God, I hoped we wouldn't be too late.

My heartbreak had to be put on hold. I collapsed it and shoved it into a little PO Box in my head and shifted adrenaline into gear. Without hesitation, I skipped my last class, Western civ, for this, although I probably would have anyway. And our Harry Potter movie was forgotten.

I bumped over the seams of the sidewalk and watched the taillights of Elliot's car. At last, he flipped on his blinker and turned left onto a long driveway. The mailbox at the driveway was tilted and its wooden post rotted.

Ahead, finally, was KC's house, isolated at the end of the long path in the trees. No police cars were parked in front yet. I cursed.

The closer I got, the tighter the cramp in my chest. The house was a plain white, two-story ranch. Green mold stained its front. A screen door hung open over the front steps and cardboard pressed against the windows. But that's not what made Elliot gently brake in alarm.

Garbage littered the lawn, everything from takeout boxes to old vacuum cleaners. Next to the garage were beat-up sheds and spare tires. Piles of garden tools and tarp and dirt rose like giant anthills. A musty scent ground against the fresh wet smell of trees. Somewhere in their neighbor's wire-fenced backyard, a mastiff was chained to a post and barking like mad at François.

Only one window on the house was clear and clean—the top left. A decal of our school logo was in the corner. That must have been KC's room.

Elliot parked, and a second later the car doors popped open. Elliot slammed his shut and spun to take this in. Mags cursed and didn't even bother to shut her door all the way, drifting forward with an open mouth. I commanded François to jump into the flatbed part of the pickup, and he lay down on the tarp in the corner, staring at me with pointed concern. I didn't want him near the front door in case another mastiff like that was inside.

Slowly, I wheeled onto the spongy grass lawn and joined Mags as we walked up to the front door. We said nothing. We only gazed at this jungle of waste.

I stopped at KC's front step. My breath puffed in the freezing air as I watched Elliot scale the stair and knock on the door. Mags was staring at the cockroach that scurried along the welcome mat.

Several moments passed. I glanced at the sun sagging low on the horizon, pulling the heavy clouds down with it like a stage curtain. Soon it would be gone.

The front latch creaked, and Elliot stepped back as the door opened.

A woman with thick, round glasses that enlarged her eyes and short, flyaway brown hair opened the door. She wore a pink cooking apron with ducks on it. Her makeup was normal, her fingernails evenly trimmed. Her black pants were from Anne Taylor.

No matter how long she looked at us, she did not speak.

"Are you . . . Mrs. Douglas?" said Elliot.

"Where's KC?" Mags blurted.

KC's mom, I assumed, blinked. There was a pause. "You're Maeve, aren't you?" she said, looking at me. "KC talks about you all the time."

My stomach bunched over itself.

KC's mom pursed her lips and touched her forehead, distressed. "I'm sorry I can't get you in here, but you're not missing much. It's . . ." She looked over her shoulder and into the house. ". . . Crowded."

I craned to see inside, but I couldn't even find the stairs

to the second floor. A huge felt kitty playground was stuffed upside down over the staircase rail. I knew for a fact KC didn't have a cat—he was allergic to Mags'.

"Ma'am," said Elliot calmly. "We called the police because your son left a suicide note online. Can I come in? We're from his film class."

"It was you who called the police?" She reddened.

"You mean you know?" I said. My voice was shrill, and in an attempt to get closer, I bumped a wheel into the concrete front step.

"They were here just a little bit ago, but I . . . I turned them away."

"He's trying to kill himself, dude!" I cried. "Call them back!"

"He's just upstairs, though," said Mrs. Douglas. "How about I ask him to come out? I'll be right back."

She closed the door before I could reply, and I heard trash tumble over and shuffle aside as, I assumed, she climbed the staircase.

"Yo." Elliot jogged over to KC's window and looked up. "KC! Open up, bro!"

Nothing.

"KC!" Elliot yelled.

A minute later, KC's mom opened the door again. That pungent musty odor wafted out.

"I'm sorry," she said. "He said he can't come out right now."

"You need to get him out of that room," I said. "Please. I'll call the police again."

"Police can't come here no more." A deep, croaky voice startled us, and KC's father—or maybe it was his uncle or grandfather, I couldn't tell—appeared at the doorway. He was thin and lanky. Loose skin, colorless hair. His accent was deeper South than Fredericksburg could foster. "Can't even come for a break-in. It's right poison for their boys tryin' get in here."

"This is life and death for your son," I said.

"The boy's fine. I already sent the police on home. How would they even get in?" said Mr. Douglas, peering around at the clutter at the stairway. "Look, it's good of yeh kids to come on by. I'll go up and talk to my boy. But he ain't gotta come out if he don't wanna. Yeh hear?"

"You'll talk to him?" said Elliot.

"Yessir, I'll give him a talkin' to."

"I don't care if they need to bring a crane and lift your roof," I said. "I'm calling the police again for KC."

"Do that, and he'll get a real talkin' to," spat Mr. Douglas. "An' more'n that." He flexed a fist at his side. I quieted. Elliot and I shared a dark look.

If we called the police again and made them enter, there'd be a lot of trouble for Mr. Douglas. They'd pick up on this hellish living condition, and probably myriad other abuses. But what KC was hesitating on doing, this man might do to him for real if we called his bluff.

Heat flared into my cheeks. "Fine," I said. "But we're staying right here until he comes out."

"You're what now?"

"I'm staying here," I amended, excluding Mags and Elliot. "Tell him Maeve is staying right here, outside, for as long as it takes for him to come out. If I need to wait for his body to come out in a stretcher, I will, and be dead myself, then."

"Gon' be cold tonight," said Mr. Douglas.

Elliot grasped a handle of my chair. "Tell him we came," he said.

"All of us," said Mags.

Mr. Douglas' jaw went a little slack. He scanned all three of us. Then he shrugged. "I'll tell 'im."

"Will you be all right?" said KC's mom. "I'm sorry you can't come in. I just—"

"C'mon, Beth." Mr. Douglas tried to close the door.

"We know you care about him, we just—"

"Let's go." Mr. Douglas closed the door.

Almost at the same time, the automatic streetlights on the driveway illuminated. I realized that my eyes had begun to see spots and shadows. Dusk covered us.

Mags fired a text to KC, relaying the message we all didn't trust his father to give.

When she lowered the phone, the blue light of the screen illuminating her face, we all looked at one another. Snow began to fall.

"We need to get you home." Elliot's frozen hand touched my shoulder. François whined in the pickup. I fluttered my eyes open. It had been two hours of my sit-out, and every blanket Mom had given me piled over my lap. Still, I could not curl my fingers. They atrophied with the cold; they stuck at the joints.

"She's an adult," said Mags. "She can stay if she wants to, Elliot."

"No." Elliot's hands balled into fists. "It's time. I'm not letting her get sick on my watch."

Mags sobered at that comment. She sat on the ground with her knees drawn up. Her breath puffed clouds. Occasionally, she checked her phone for KC's reply to her pleading messages.

We knew he was alive, because he did respond to Mags'

texts occasionally. He responded, I need to die. And, Go away. And, I'm sorry.

I tried texting him too. I told him I knew now. I understood now. I knew why he was the sad boy, the angry boy. I'm sorry. Please talk to me.

He would only reply to Mags, but for some reason, in my head, I imagined him staring longer at my messages and crying at them harder. Maybe I was self-absorbed. Or maybe I just loved him and knew that he knew that. I loved him so much.

We'd done everything we could think of in those two hours.

We tried climbing up to KC's window. I'd parked my chair against the side of the house and Elliot scaled onto the back of me. Even with Mags on Elliot's shoulders on attempt number three, we fell at least two feet short of making it.

Once we'd found ground again and sighed, Elliot insisted I at least huddle in his car for warmth. Before I could say no, before I could tell him that KC needed to be able to see me right here, through his window, Elliot cursed.

We'd found his car battery dead. The interior lights had been left on when Mags neglected to close the passenger door.

That was Elliot's last straw. Now, the wind picked up. "I just called you a handicapped cab, Maeve, and he's going to give my truck a jump," said Elliot.

"I'm not leaving," I said, but fifteen minutes later, the red-and-white-checkered van popped gravel as it rolled up in the driveway. A lift was installed at its rear. "Mags," I said, "tell Elliot I'm not leaving."

But Mags looked at me with pursed lips as she held her torso. "I think he's right, Maeve. I'm sorry."

"Mags," I said.

"I'm sorry," she repeated.

"No." No what?

The taxi driver pressed a button on the car door and unfolded the mechanical lift, which was more high-tech than my manual ramp. I looked back up at KC's window as Elliot passed the cabbie some money and indicated his truck with jumper cables. Snow dusted his windshield.

Within minutes, both engines were vrooming. Elliot twisted the key and his truck roared to life. Mags hopped in the passenger side to get a lift back to her car at the school, and Elliot rolled down the window.

"You know I don't live too far, Maeve. I'll check on KC in the morning. I promise," he said. "There's nothing we can do for him out here."

His face saddened when I didn't reply. I only prodded my joystick and entered the back of the cab.

Slowly Elliot and Mags drove off as the cabbie cranked metal hooks and locks to my wheels. Heat blew into the van and a tip calculator screen faced me from the back of the chair ahead. The cabbie reeled out more buckles to drape over me every which way, and I felt like a prisoner, like someone no one trusted with her own life. Tonight, though, I was grateful for its delay. It gave enough time for Elliot and Mags to leave.

After ten minutes of securing me, the cabbie finally leapt into the driver's seat and shut the door.

"Where to?" she said.

I paused.

"Ma'am?" said the cabbie.

"Let me out," I said.

She blinked in the rearview mirror. "Excuse me?"

"You heard me."

The cabbie scoffed. "Seriously? I just finished securing you."

"Let me out," I said.

I didn't need to be secured.

So I sat on the lawn outside KC's front window alone. I texted him that I would not leave until he came out.

The hours went on. The cold seeped into my lungs with every breath. My body fought back. My body offended the chill with a heat of its own.

François whined at my wheels. Soon, no cars could be heard driving down the street. The night pushed past 11:00 p.m., and the temperature dipped further. I dozed in and out. But the heat of my body spiked. It felt like chalk was in my throat.

By midnight, my phone rang an endless vibration. I let it. It stabbed me a little inside, but this was something I had to do. Mom and Dad had to know this.

I'd texted Dad.

MAEVE

I know this is crazy, and I'm sorry, but KC needs me right now. I'm safe, with Elliot and Mags, and warm. François is okay too. I'll text you when I can come home. I'm sorry.

I lied, and Dad knew I was lying, but this time he didn't let me.

DAD

> Please. Mom is worried, I'm worried. Tell me where you are.

And ten minutes later:

DAD

> Tell me right now where you are.

I closed my eyes when I hit ignore on Dad's fifth phone call. Dad didn't know where KC lived. He didn't know where to find me, but I'm sure he was downloading every GPS tracker app he could now.

When next the phone rang, its light blurred my vision, but I realized with a little tinge of fear that I could no longer feel its buzz.

I hitched in breath and lost consciousness.

The next time a sudden hand shook me, I must not have woken up.

"Oh my God." That was Elliot's voice. How did he get back here? "*Maeve.*"

François was barking. It was an odd, clumpy warble I didn't often hear. He's supposed to be quiet. I opened my eyes. Chills rolled down me. When I took in breath, it was garbled with mucus.

"What's going on?" said Mags. It sort of echoed.

"She's burning up," Elliot breathed. "Her dad called me and said she didn't come home."

"Same," said Mags. Her voice was swollen as if her hands were over her mouth in fear.

"No," I said. And then I jerked in a reflex inhale because for some reason it felt like I was breathing through a brown paper bag. "No," I repeated, but my throat was swollen in phlegm. KC needed me. I was strong enough for this. I'd been careful; I'd trained my lungs.

"What did she say?" said Mags.

"I can't understand her," said Elliot. "I'm calling nine-one-one." He swung my phone up to his ear. How did he get it? How did I let it slip away?

"No," I tried to repeat, but the streetlights started to swirl. I couldn't push the air into my lungs. They felt chunky and stuffed. Hot mucus strangled me.

That was when I realized I couldn't breathe.

"I can't breathe," I said matter-of-factly. But I didn't think they heard. "I can't—"

"She can't breathe," Elliot translated.

"Dammit, Maeve!" Mags finally broke down.

"Fuck." Elliot wiped a hand down his mouth as he called the paramedics. François buried his fur into me. "I should have watched her go. I should have . . ." Did Elliot actually sob? "What did we do?"

I took short, dizzying breaths, but my lungs ached like they were punching bags.

Even when Dad arrived. Even when he was cursing and his headlights were blinding my eyes and the ambulance following him was twirling lights in my head, I was saying the same thing.

"No."

29

I will hurt you.

I know I will hurt you. And I will be taken from you. But I love you. I hope that counted for something.

When I was fourteen, after reading an article about my disease and its usual progression, I left this note, followed by a handwritten will, under a loose tile behind the never-used cappuccino maker in our house. I didn't tell anyone. I thought I had more time to decide who to trust with that information. But it could be too late.

They might need it now. They might.

I heard beeping.

I can't breathe.

I felt tubes.

It hurts.

I didn't have time to be afraid: isn't that always how everyone wants to die? Some people jump into death and others sink. I always wanted to jump. Now I was sinking.

You can fantasize your death. You picture worlds stopping and helicopters circling and all the people who'd never get over it. When Mags' brother died a few years ago, people posted on Facebook and had tournaments in his name. I thought he was the coolest person in the world, but after a while, people stopped remembering the day, and laughter and music happened again as if he were never here at all.

I'm not the first person who would ever die or the last who ever will.

But I was being eaten by my own phlegm, and my lungs were not strong enough to punch out a cough or suck in a breath. The steroids and oxygen tubes in my mouth held me by fingertips.

Mom was crying.

Dr. Clayton's voice spoke low.

Everything went dark.

When I woke next, and I did, I could not move, but I felt someone take my hand. A strong, male hand. Familiar.

"Maeve." It was hushed. Injured. Everything else was slow and quiet; it must have been night, and it must have been only us. "Maeve," said Dad.

I'm listening. Sort of.

"This is not how it ends." His voice broke. "*You can't go like this.* Listen to me."

I am.

"You're not going to die like this. Okay?" He choked but was almost angry. "You're going to live. You're going to make your films. You're going to graduate. You're going to move out and you're going to do *stupid things* with that boy from Thanksgiving."

Now his voice flooded with tears. I'd never head Dad like this. Whatever was left of my heart broke.

"You can't leave me."

Days later, the beeping grew a little louder. Days later still, the mucus began to rattle when I inhaled. Slowly, it loosened. I could open my eyes. I could function.

Mom bent over the hospital bed and kissed my forehead. Chasms were under her eyes. Dad sat on the guest chair next to the divider curtain and watched me with a resigned gaze, exhausted, head lolling. His glasses were crooked.

"I'll tell Dr. Clayton you're up," Mom whispered. She left the room, and her footsteps disappeared down the hall.

I shifted. My hospital gown was cool and fresh; someone must have changed it. But my hair stuck to my shoulders. The oxygen was no longer stuffed into my nostrils. I read the medicine they were giving me on the dry erase board across the room. Next to my bed on the table were three GET WELL balloons floating halfway up their twine and bumping into each other. The card at the base read: *Love, Fred.*

"You okay?" said Dad.

"Yeah," I croaked. Then sighed. Every breath bruised my ribs.

"You should go back to sleep," he said.

"No," I replied. And that word brought me back. "KC," I breathed. "Is he okay?"

Dad straightened slowly and blinked. He rested his elbows on his knees. Some anger was in his voice. "He came out when he saw me arrive and rush for you. His arms were bleeding with knife cuts. Self-inflicted. You could say that if you didn't get so sick, he wouldn't have ever come out and would have finished himself off in his room."

"Where is he now?"

"He's here. They took him to the hospital too." Dad sighed. "Don't try to talk to him yet, Maeve. He needs help right now."

"I'm sorry, Dad," I whispered. Dad remained stiff. Then he covered his mouth with his hand, breathed evenly, and looked at me for a long time. It seemed as if he were playing Tetris with the words in his head, trying to make them all fit right before he spoke. He finally did.

"You know, Maeve, KC almost did something to you."

A shiver hushed me and told me not to speak. Told me to only listen. Something rare and powerful was in Dad's voice.

"He almost destroyed you. With loss. Grief. Years of regret."

He waited for me to nod. To agree. Then he leaned forward.

"And you almost did that to us."

My throat closed. Dad continued. "You almost condemned Mom and me to years of heartbreak and emptiness."

I inhaled, not to speak, just to inhale, but Dad held up a hand.

"Please." A pause. "You're an adult, Maeve. And your intentions were noble. But all of us . . . *all* of us . . . give so much to help you choose life."

Tears trickled into my eyes. I couldn't be sure, but I think Dad's filled too. I shouldn't have closed him off that night. He would have helped us. My need to be independent made me more dependent than ever in this hospital bed. I knew that now. But Dad deserved to reprimand me. He deserved to tell me all the things I already knew.

"I don't have lacrosse wounds, Maeve," he whispered.

Now the tears fell from my cheeks like rain down a gutter. He didn't ache and groan from old sports injuries. He ached and groaned for me.

"But you're like me," said Dad.

"What do you mean?" I said. My voice was choked.

Dad rubbed his shoulder. His false "lacrosse wound." The one he pulls every time he lifts me, or closes up the wheelchair ramp, and gets worse by the day.

"Your love kills you."

He gazed at me, and I didn't look away.

"Excuse me?" A nurse appeared at the door.

Dad and I both turned.

"Maeve, you have a visitor, but I know the doctor is on his way. Should I tell your guest to come back later?"

"No," I said. "Let her come in."

"Him," said the nurse. "And one second."

I rested my head back and stared at the ceiling. This would be KC. Guilt-ridden. I didn't want this to happen now, but at the same time, I could get it out of the way. I still loved him.

As soon as the figure appeared at the doorframe in the corner of my eye, I knew I was wrong. My heart smacked into my chest and stopped.

He was too big. Too tall. Too awkward. To be KC.

I turned my head to meet his eyes.

Cole Stone stood at the door.

30

Dad rose and immediately made for the doorway. He didn't say anything, only nodded and offered his hand. Cole shook it.

Then Dad left.

Dad left.

Heat swelled inside me. I wasn't looking too good. This wasn't my best outfit. Not my best hair day. Not really killing it at being alive right now. But Cole just looked at me and seemed to gather breath the way one gathers marbles into a bag.

We were alone.

"Cole," I whispered. Tried to shake my head. "What— what are you doing here?"

He stepped into the room, and I realized then that he wore his nametag from set, completely crooked, completely upside down.

"Are you all right?" I'd never heard his voice without volume. I never realized just how throaty it was when it didn't boom.

"I'm . . ." I looked at myself. "I probably don't smell good."

"That's not what I asked." Cole laughed nervously.

"Why did you come here? I thought you . . ." I didn't know what to say.

"I don't know," said Cole. He scratched his neck fast.

"You don't know why you're here?" I said.

"Maybe."

I pursed my lips. "Just tell me. I'm not scary. I don't bite."

Cole glanced over his shoulder. Then he made a face like *fuck it* and lunged for the side of my bed and kneeled down. He was my level now. His arms folded over the metal rail. "You are scary," he said. "And you do bite."

Carefully, his hand reached into the bed and took mine.

I squeezed it. His fingers were strong. They were rough. They were everything I wanted them to be.

"What does this mean?" I said.

Cole didn't answer, but he kept rubbing my hand. "I don't know." A pause. It lasted forever. Finally, he murmured, "But my nametag is lopsided."

"I can fix that," I said. We both smiled.

I tried to roll my body towards him. I reached weakly

for his nametag. He shifted closer. He pushed against the
bed to hover nearer, still kneeling. His scent engulfed me,
his heat. I strained to touch him, and then he abruptly laid
his hand on the side of my face and lowered his mouth to
mine. His whiskers almost grazed my lips and blood rushed
in my body to meet him.

I pushed my fist against his firm chest. He stopped,
hanging over me.

"What?" he whispered.

I stroked his beard with my fingertips. They shook.

"Not here. Not like this."

31

A few months go by fast.

With the click of a laser pointer, I struck the black floor
of the stage with a beam of light and moved forward. My
chair echoed in the auditorium as it moved in an *S* shape
like a remote control vacuum cleaner for all the empty rows
of seats to see. Dust floated in the shine of the spotlight.

My first ever stage production was in just a few weeks—
and it was a good way to prove to everyone still sending
me cards and fruit arrangements since the hospital that I
was alive and okay.

The boards creaked below me, and my wheel covered a
stage marker—a white, taped *X*. I spun under the spotlight
and faced my actor.

Cole Stone stood there with his arms crossed and his feet kind of spread, wearing a smug, frustratingly handsome smile. I clicked off the laser pointer.

"So that's the blocking," I said. "For the dance."

"And when I return to the table?"

I moved about five feet to stage left. He followed me with his eyes.

"Sort of here."

"Is that where you want me?"

I looked at him. "I think so."

Weeks ago, we'd met below the sycamore when I'd returned home and I was healthy and it was warmer. He'd swayed next to the trunk, eyes on the dead branch he was absently tugging like a caveman, and I rubbed my hand along his belt (suggestive, I know, but really all I could reach) and told him what I wanted for real. A relationship. A future. And for him to carry me up that staircase on the last sycamore and into the tree-house so we could make out and someday make love.

He never met my eyes as he pulled on the branch, but I could see the thoughts working on his face. He was silent the whole time.

And when I said the words *make love,* Cole stopped tugging. His fingers traced the seam of my blouse and I gripped the fuzziest part of his forearm in anticipation. Then he stopped and exhaled a long, low breath. It didn't go further.

He wanted to avoid decisions altogether.

Now I was his director again. There were decisions I had to make for him.

Cole hummed. He walked forward into the spotlight, and it was amazing to see how his presence dominated the stage.

"Show me again," he said. "This time with me."

I swallowed. Dance?

"Uh." My throat dried up. "Okay." When I rolled forward, he stepped back in pace. "You start here."

He stepped in front of me.

"Turn."

He did, so he always faced me.

"And then back up with her," I said, reversing my chair. It drew him forward, but this time, he pressed his strong arm hard against the armrest of my wheelchair as he did. He lowered a bit too. I slowed. So did Cole.

His scent filled me, and the pocket of space between us seemed minuscule.

"And then what?" His voice was low.

I kept reversing slowly, and he kept stepping forward one small pace at a time.

My heart sped, and finally there was a click. I stopped.

"Then you stop," I whispered.

"Do I?"

"Yeah," I said.

"I don't have to," he said. Cole continued to drape over me, holding the wheelchair. He leaned down farther.

"You're not the boss," I whispered.

He was so close to me that I only knew he smiled by the shifting of his beard.

He nodded. "I know."

And he crushed his lips against mine.

The lights in the theater flashed, and the flow of audience members streamed for their burgundy seats. The room filled with eager chatter.

I inhaled, looking around. The playbill was in my hand. In a moment I would go backstage and report the packed room. Ten minutes to showtime.

In Aisle F was KC. He sat next to his mom, and his arm was looped in hers. I couldn't hear them over the crowd, but she said something to him and pushed hair from his forehead. He gave a small smile. I did too. KC was in therapy, and the state had finally intervened after the emergency vehicles they sent me had noticed how bad the site had gotten. They separated his dad and ordered the place cleaned up. KC was okay. We were talking and taking things slowly.

"Are you mad at me?" he'd said after a long breath the first time we spoke since leaving the hospital. "I know I— you have every right to—"

In the middle of his sentence, I'd dropped my forehead onto his arm and closed my eyes. He stopped talking. We just existed.

We promised each other to continue just existing.

In Aisle G were Mom, Dad, and Mr. Billings. Dad was in his suit with François' white body draped over his lap, wagging. Dad petted him subconsciously and studied the stage. Mom pecked her BlackBerry, but she had a box of Sno-Caps under her arm and a bouquet of flowers in her lap she'd bought for me for later. Lilies. On the other side, on the balcony, were Mags and Elliot. I arranged those tickets. They laughed at some joke, and Elliot wiped tears of mirth with his thumb and forefinger. Elliot's girlfriend's mauve coat hung on the back of the seat next to him, and I had held my nose and secured a seat for Nate next to Mags too. But he wasn't there. So I logged that little detail away for later. It'd been awhile since I'd seen them together—since the hospital, four months ago, actually.

An hour earlier, just after she'd applied some mascara on me at home and made her way to the theater, Mags had texted me.

298 S. C. MEGALE

> I'm lowkey really proud of you.
> Break a leg cuz it isn't like you
> actually need it

I'd huffed.

My friends are awesome. And thanks to some even more awesome reels and recommendation letters from Billings . . .

We'd all be going to UCLA this fall.

This close to curtain, I headed down the carpeted ramp for backstage. A tall, olive-skinned usher in a grey uniform stopped me.

"Can I see your ticket, ma'am?"

"I'm—"

"Our handicapped section is full tonight."

I looked over to the front row—devoid of seats—to see a parking lot of wheelchairs. I knew it well. When I go to rock concerts, the staff like to sandwich me in the back between ten or so wheelchairs staring lifelessly at the stage lights like FDR statues. But tonight's row was anything but lifeless. At least seven campers from Caring Hands Camp were there. They grinned, waved playbills, and wiggled their shoeless feet. My initial reaction of annoyance was rejected like a crumpled dollar from a soda machine. I waved to them warmly. Patricia Weinhart sat next to a severely disabled camper and gracefully wiped saliva from his mouth. She didn't see me.

"I'm the director," I said to the usher.

"Oh." The usher stepped aside. When he did, I noticed another man behind him in the handicapped section as well. My eyebrows rose as I approached.

"Quinten?" My hand squeezed his forearm. He jumped.

"H-hey." He smiled through his wheezing. Then he might have blushed. It was hard to tell in the dim light.

"I'm so happy you're here!" I said. I looked him over. He wore a bright yellow polo and his hair was combed, but he looked frailer and thinner. He stooped a little farther towards the floor. "Did your nephew drive you?"

Quinten nodded. The effort it took forced his playbill to slip from his grasp. Its pages shuffled to the ground. We both stared at it ironically.

"I'd help you if I could," I said. Only after it echoed in my ears did I realize the maybe double meaning behind that sentence.

Quinten struggled to lift his gaze to me. I met it, and, after a pause, a small, melancholy smile creased my lips.

"Enjoy the show," I said to Quinten. Then lifted my hand to place it on his cheek lovingly before moving away.

Through a few cramped doorways, I burrowed my way into the catacombs of the stage. Tape marked random areas of the floor and ropes hung above. It smelled like old wool and sawdust. There were black sheep costumes and glittery gold Elvis jumpsuits hanging from bulwarks. I rounded a bend and plowed up the makeshift wooden ramp pushed against the stage. When I scaled it, I could see the illuminated stage ahead of me only a few yards away.

"Five minutes!" called a voice that tried hard to suppress excitement and sound professional. I caught Roman, my showbiz buddy, pressing a hand to the earpiece and speaking into it. Then he caught sight of me.

"Maeve!" He lumbered over. "Where have you *been*? Let's go!"

"It's a full house out there." I beamed.

"Get back there," said Roman. "One of the actors asked

for you." He pointed in the back. I glanced in the direction he indicated, where the costumes and mirrors were, and pulled my brow together. I rolled over, nerves and possibly a smile developing. Suddenly I was aware of the loud squeak of an ungreased wheel—probably my front left, maybe a loose bearing. I tried to sit up straighter.

And when I arrived, I realized I had nothing left to be self-conscious of. Cole Stone was sitting there on the seat backwards, feet around either side of the chair. He was dressed in his lapelled blue jacket for the prologue. Because we put a punk spin on the production, the blue jacket was leather; it had zippers and a patch on its shoulder. His beard was as well groomed as I'd ever seen, and the natural lines beneath his eyes were beastly. His dark gaze shone. I wasn't nervous around him anymore. Not since the hospital.

Since the hospital, he replied to texts within hours. He was down to meet up and watch people or eat food. He'd poke my temple. Through months of rehearsal after that kiss, we'd danced the same dance of flirting and pulling back when we got too close because I refused to ask him twice for what I wanted. When I'd near him, his hand would run down my back, but when I shot him a responsive look, he'd pivot aside like nothing happened.

One night, I just texted him flat out:

MAEVE

What are we?

COLE STONE

I don't know

MAEVE

What don't you know?

COLE STONE

> I don't know how to like you.

I gazed at that text for a little.

All I knew was that he didn't treat me as more fragile or closer to that hospital bed. He didn't change the way he viewed me. I loved Cole Stone, and I could only control that much. I couldn't control if he noticed my crookedness or my metal or anything else. The thing was, to notice something, you needed to at least look at it.

Right now, minutes before opening night at last, he laid his arms over the backrest of the backwards chair and his eyes were hooked on only mine.

"Ready, Cole?" I said.

"Just about."

"Roman said you need me."

Cole retrieved an object between his feet. It was hair dye called Amber Blaze. He rattled it. The dye was a warmer brown than his dark hue, and more recognizable as the Beast's color. I swallowed and glanced at it then back to his steady gaze.

"Just—in your beard?" I said, coming closer and holding a hand out for the dye.

"Enough for the back row to see."

My fingers shook as he squeezed the cool dye onto them.

Silence fell between us. I was not sure he even breathed.

Slowly, Cole lowered his head so that my weak hands could reach his beard. He waited.

With an uncertain shudder, I reached out and touched him. I brushed the highlights into his beard. My heart pounded. His hair running through my hand was rough. Stroking it was the only sound in the room. His body was taut in the chair, and the tension between us nearly made me hitch for breath.

I drew back my hand, the dye smeared across the lines of my fingerprints. He was ready. Cole rose and kicked out the chair. He towered over me just as the theater lights extinguished and Roman waved everyone forward frantically. Maybe that was supposed to be my responsibility, but I'd done everything before—rehearsals, props, advertising— that I deserved this moment in Cole's dressing room, just for tonight . . .

Moments later, Cole stormed onto stage and boomed his first lines without hesitation. The spotlight made the Amber Blaze shimmer in his beard. I sat behind in the shadows of the curtain and watched, script in hand, next to Roman. Pride swelled within.

About halfway through the performance, the first violin notes weaved over one another to produce *Beauty and the Beast*'s classic theme. A beautiful young actress in a yellow dress rose to offer Cole her hand as she had in my envying fantasies.

Cole stood as he was supposed to, using his hands to push from the table surface. But then he did something he was not supposed to.

He paused.

He paused and stared at me offstage. I tried to see if he needed something, forgot a line, anything. Concern flickered past the actress' countenance next to him as she glanced for the "ballroom" he was supposed to accompany her to.

But Cole just stared at me. Absorbed me. He looked so close to smiling that his eyes burned.

I stared back. The moment lasted so long that I did something I'd never done: looked away first.

———

Cole clicked a button hanging from his lanyard and his silver Lexus sedan chirped, unlocking, in the parking lot. I wheeled alongside him. The March night air was mild, and by this time, all the cars making up our audience had driven off. The final night of *Beauty and the Beast* had ended an hour ago. It neared 11:00 p.m.

Dressed back in his regular clothes, a white button-down shirt and dark jeans, Cole wiped his sleeve across his jaw to free any last drops of sweat from his beard. I carried the play's poster rolled up at the back of my chair.

Cole had been waitlisted to UCLA. He might be going in the fall. He might not. I tried to keep my voice hopeful.

"You were amazing," I said.

"I'm used to it," Cole replied. "Not far from real life."

"More like good directing."

I reached for his hand. It skimmed over my skin for a second, but he pulled it away. Poked my temple instead.

He approached his car and opened the door. Bent into the front seat and stuffed his costume beneath the cup holders. I waited to say goodbye.

He straightened and turned to me. The sky above him was black. His eyes searched me for a moment. Then the moment passed.

"Well," he said. "This was fun."

I tried to smile. I didn't want to say goodbye.

And then his voice dropped to a breathy murmur. "See you, kid." He looped his great arm around me and pulled me into him. My forehead pressed against his ribs and I closed my eyes.

I felt his body fill and release with air and heard the hushed rushing of his heart. The quiet burble of his stomach. I loved being held by him still, but heat and moisture prickled my lashes.

When Cole pulled back, he must have caught the shine in my eyes. He tensed and froze right there, looking down at me. I didn't have the courage to look up.

Cole's thumb hovered at my eyelash. It shook as he tried to brush away the tear. Without a word, he pulled me hard to him again, this time with both arms. He turned his head and rested the side of his face over my head. Squeezing me. I don't know how long it lasted. It felt like forever. But I had never felt him hold me that way.

Cole released me once more. He tossed his head to free some hair from his face and then gripped the rim of the Lexus and swung inside. He slammed closed the door and started the engine. I rolled back a foot. Still trying hard, and failing, to smile.

Cole cruised a few yards away, eating two or three parking spots, but never really hit the accelerator hard. Then his red taillights glowed. The car stopped. It thrummed there for a minute. Chugging out exhaust.

He cut the engine. I blinked.

Cole opened the door just as I rolled up to him. Still sitting in the front seat, he turned outward and rested his feet on the pavement. His hands were crossed loosely in front of him, and he looked up at me.

"What?" I laughed.

"Do you want something else?" said Cole. His eyes glimmered with hesitant mischief.

I shivered into silence.

"Well?" said Cole.

"Yes," I said.

"You don't ask, you don't get."

"I want you," I said.

"All right," said Cole. Then lower. "I want you too." He looked around. Over his shoulder. Past the car mirrors. Then with expert hands he undid his belt. I swallowed and froze. Heart hammering thrill into my blood.

"Come here," said Cole.

I did.

"Go ahead."

"I've never—" I began.

"I figured." Cole waved me forward. "Go ahead."

So I wrapped my small fingers around him. His flesh was hot.

Cole moved forward and kissed my neck with a low grumble. Then my shoulder. His familiar hand ran across me with the backs of his knuckles. I might have made some undignified sound of pleasure and then lost strength; my head fell back and I couldn't pull myself back up with no headrest. Cole's large hand slipped behind me and held me up. He shifted to support my weight while we kissed.

He pulled back into the car again.

"We have some unfinished business."

"Yeah," I breathed.

"How are we gonna do this?" said Cole.

"I don't care," I said. "Let's do it right here." I continued to just hold and stare.

"Not out in the open like this." He laughed.

"I don't care," I repeated. Already pleasure tried to pound across me.

"Let go for a second," he said. I did, reluctantly. He sighed, redid his belt, and stood. He stepped around and did a full radius search of the parking lot with his eyes.

"Your car," I said. "Carry me into your car."

"Yeah?" said Cole.

"Yeah," I said.

Cole used his hand to conduct a circular motion at me. "Park there."

I parallel parked beside his car. My thumb fumbled to click off my seat belt while he popped open the back door. Then Cole shuffled to my side. He slid one arm beneath my knees and readied the other around my back.

"Tell me when." He was poised, but would not lift until I consented.

"Now," I said.

He swung me into his arms. I'd never seen the world from so high; I could touch the black sky over the treetops surrounding the parking lot. Strength and energy buzzed through his muscles; more than Dad ever had, more than Dr. Clayton. I had never let a man so young, my peer, carry me before. I felt safe. He forged us both into the back seat of his sedan.

The world became quiet inside the car, and there was only the smell of leather and the creases of his crisp shirt in my face. He laid me down on my back in the back seat while he pulled a condom out of his wallet. The parking lot outside became shaded over in brown from the window tints.

Cole shut the door and climbed in after. Being such a big man in a small car, he grabbed onto whatever he could find to keep his weight off me.

"How do we do this now?" he said.

"I'm not very flexible," I warned.

"Okay," he said, and he tried to negotiate his body between my legs. They didn't extend far. "Let me know if I'm hurting you."

He did, a little, but I didn't say.

In one smooth motion he returned himself to my hand, and I was happy.

"Help me undress," I said. Still playing with my new toy.

He undid one button, two, until my blouse was falling off my shoulders. And then he did something strange. He burrowed his face into my shoulder, exhaled, and dug his arm under my back. For a long pause, he just held me. I closed my eyes and rubbed his cold ear with my thumb because it was all I could reach. Joy filled me.

Slowly, he pushed down my pants and we managed to find a position. I'd fantasized this moment a million times, but nothing could describe the real thing. My body lit up and loosened under Cole. And I liked it. I closed my eyes and whispered his name.

As my lips moved, they caught a brush of his beard. He'd swooped down and folded his mouth against mine. Fuck. I was kissing him. I didn't know what the hell to do, so I just moved my lips in a way that I hoped might convince him to continue. He wrestled with breath, shifting his weight. There wasn't enough room in this car.

I thought he was getting closer, because the grunting got louder as I pulled on him. I pulled on him the way I always pulled on men's silk ties at weddings because they hung at just my height. I was probably about as good at this as I was at kissing. But it seemed to work for him.

"What do you want?" he gasped. He was there.

"All of you," I said.

"Are you sure?" he said.

"Yes." Hurry up.

"I don't know if I can be there always, Maeve," he said.

"I know," I said. "It's okay."

"But what about everything you want?" said Cole. "What if I can't?"

I pawed my free hand for his face. "Cole," I ordered. "I

want this." He shoved himself inside me in one downward stroke, as if his strength broke. He rocked against me the way he rocks on his feet. Pleasure and a little pain throbbed up my body. Cole was building me up, and all I felt, saw, smelled was him.

I don't know about the future. I don't know how I will figure out so many things. I don't know. I'll be there one day—I'll jump or sink. All I can know is what I want right now.

That's okay.

And right now, I just want to fuck Cole Stone.

ACKNOWLEDGMENTS

My parents, Larry and Megan, are my everything. Mom, you're my best friend. Daddy, I'll always belong to you. I never want to be apart from either of you. When your arms are open to catch me when I'm sick or your hands are pulling my covers up to my ear, I close my eyes, glad that you made me as I am so that I can be your daughter. Thank you both for making me feel like I can stand on my own two feet. Thank you also to Kelley, my older sister and greatest role model, for cheering me on everywhere, and for being my first phone call whenever I succeed. I love you each with everything I am. This accomplishment is for and because of you.

Thank you to my exceptional "Agent 007," Jessica Sinsheimer, for being the kindest, strongest, and way-smarter-than-me representative I don't deserve. You are a gift, Jessica, with a keen taste for alfredo. I look forward to a lifetime of knowing you.

Everyone at St. Martin's Press and Wednesday Books deserves my profound gratitude for being such a powerful team behind this green-as-grass debut writer. Lauren Jablonski, my editor, is a woman of insight and grace. I am amazed I get to be your author, Lauren. Thank you, Sara Goodman, Kerri Resnick, Meghan Harrington, Eva Diaz, Christa Desir, Melanie Sanders, Karen Masnica, Anna Gorovoy, Brant Janeway, DJ DeSmyter, and everyone whose sheer hard work, spirit, and brilliance is the reason I am here. Your press is a dream come true, and my book—and myself—are better for it.

Additionally I wish to thank the many exemplary professionals who believed in me throughout my writing journey: Matthew Baldacci, Linda Parks, Patrick Kennedy, Joanna Volpe, Rosemary Stimola, Nina Jacobson, Kiffin Steurer, Richard O'Sullivan, Avi Gvili, Bob Solon, and Tricia Skinner.

Thank you to my dear, dear friends and fellow authors (I cannot believe I can say that now) John Flanagan and Suzanne Collins for your endless mentoring. I love you both with all my heart. Deep thanks also to David Baldacci for your selfless support.

My three writing groups hammered this book into shape before anyone else, and they are: The Hourlings, The Writers of Chantilly, and a mysterious closed group known only as "Varsity." I love and thank *all* of you. Of the members, Nick Bruner, John H. Matthews, Denice Jobe, John F. Dwight, Jason Winn, Erica Rue Gravely, David Keener, Liz Hayes, Mary Ellen Gavin, Ruth Hersh Perry, Martin Wilsey, Steve Moriarty, Terry Williams, Pat Kallman, Loretta Phelps de Córdova, and Angela D. Glascock are due particular debt for their help. Nick, does your wife know I have a crush on you yet?

Every young writer and human needs teachers, and Little Shea had the best. I want to thank all my teachers, but especially Caren Williams for being my sixth-grade teacher and first editor, and Catherine Conley for being my second. Thank you to Kelsey Nieves Martinez, Betty Kelly, Regina O'Shaughnessy, Cat Caldwell, and Lizzy Kemp, and the secret agents lying dormant out there (you know who you are) who were my first fans and readers receiving Word attachments in their email inboxes, or spiral-bound print-outs. Which reminds me; I want to thank FedEx Office Print & Ship Center and Office Depot for all the copies. Office Depot, I've been using a sketchy discount card printed off the Internet for six years now and you are always super cool about it.

There are literally, like, a thousand (okay, twenty-two) cousins in my family, but we are all so badass. Thank you to them and to the family that supports me: my grandparents, Ed and Judy O'Shea and Joe and Pat Megale, and my aunts and uncles.

I almost-finally wish to thank Professor Chris Stallings for teaching me so much about film, and to thank, especially, Room 142. You select few reading this know what that means. No one can be a part of 142 but us. Thanks for all the action, and here's to a lot more.

So it is clear that many have carried me here—literally and figuratively. I'm sorry to anyone I forgot. This short section thanks my personal guardians: Mercer, God, and C. S. Lewis.

And this last addresses my hero:

Matt. Oh, Matt. I wish you were here to see this. I am forever your little Bird. And this very last sentence of my first ever published novel is for you.

I love you, big brother.